DESERVING HENLEY

The Refuge, Book 2

SUSAN STOKER

CHAPTER ONE

Henley McClure had just finished a particularly emotional group session at The Refuge, and while she was tired, she was also filled with satisfaction. That always happened when one of her clients had a breakthrough in a session.

Being a psychologist was her calling, and she loved it. She worked for a thriving practice in Los Alamos, but in recent years, she'd actually reduced her hours at the office in town in order to spend more time at The Refuge. Working with the men and women who visited the nationally renowned retreat in the mountains of New Mexico was more satisfying than she'd ever dreamed. Even though she didn't get to know her patients very well, since she usually only saw them for a few sessions, knowing she was helping them come to terms with the traumatic events they'd been through—events that had led them to The Refuge in the first place—filled her heart with gratification.

She also had the highest respect for the seven men who owned and ran the retreat. They were all former military, each having gone through their own traumas, which had led them to want to help others dealing with PTSD.

Of course, there was one owner she was drawn to more than the others.

Finn "Tonka" Matlick had caught her eye from the first moment they'd met. Not because he was extremely handsome—which he was. In fact, all of the owners were.

No...it was because of the hurt she saw deep in his eyes. One that matched her own when she looked in the mirror some mornings. Where she'd had the benefit of many more years and excellent therapy to help manage her anguish, Finn's was still raw and visceral. He did his best to hide his pain from the world, but it was there. Lurking in the depths of his soul.

In the couple years that she'd known him, Henley had never tried to talk to Finn about what had put that agony in his gaze, despite being qualified to do so. He was extremely standoffish, preferring to tend to the animals at The Refuge rather than talk to the guests, or even hang out with his friends.

He'd attended many of the group sessions Henley offered to the guests, but he never contributed, never spoke about his past. Still, just having him there when she shared her own traumatic past with her patients made it a little easier to tell the tale. Seeing sorrow and empathy in his eyes made her anger and grief over what she'd endured feel just a little less sharp. But that was as deep as their relationship went.

She'd actually thought maybe things between them would change after the horrible incident from two weeks ago, when a man came onto the retreat's property with the intent of kidnapping Alaska, the girlfriend of owner Drake

Vandine. During that scary event, Henley and Finn had connected on a level they hadn't before...or at least Henley had thought so.

But since that night—the night he'd cried in her arms in the barn as they protected the animals from the intruder—he hadn't treated her any differently, which was a huge disappointment. Her only consolation was that she would swear Finn was now hanging around the lodge more often. At least when she was there.

She wanted to think it was because maybe he wanted to talk to her, but whenever their eyes met, he'd inevitably turn away.

She was frustrated with the man. Even more so with herself. She was a competent psychologist and an independent woman. Despite that, she couldn't find the courage to make the first move toward seeing if they could maybe have more than an acquaintance.

In addition, years of single motherhood were beginning to take a bit of a toll. Stress was a constant companion, what with two jobs and Jasna fast approaching an age when she wouldn't want Henley's relentless protection much longer. And last but not least, since the night in the barn with Finn, Henley's growing loneliness was also thrown into sharp focus. She hadn't been in a relationship in years.

She was growing more and more exasperated with herself, and with Finn. Every day, she swore she'd talk to him. See if maybe he was interested in developing something more...or if she should turn her attention elsewhere.

Doing her best to push away thoughts of Finn, Henley reached into her purse and grabbed her phone to make sure her daughter hadn't texted while she'd been in her session. As soon as she grabbed the cell, it began to vibrate, scaring the crap out of her. Huffing out a laugh at her jumpiness, Henley brought the phone up to her ear. She didn't recognize the number, only that it was local.

"Hello?"

"Is this Henley McClure?"

"Yes."

"This is Betty Turner, the nurse at Mountain Elementary School."

Henley's heart rate sped up. It was only eleven in the morning. Her daughter, Jasna, had seemed a little off this morning, but they'd been running late and her daughter wasn't a morning person, so she hadn't thought too much about it. "What's wrong? Is Jasna all right?" she asked the nurse.

"She has a fever. She threw up as well and says her stomach hurts. It's probably the bug that's going around, but because of the fever, we're going to need you to come pick her up."

Henley frowned. Jasna was a fairly quiet kid. She had a couple friends in the apartment complex where they lived, though for the most part, she was content to play by herself or read. But she was rarely sick. And she *never* complained. She was tough and easygoing, so if she was saying her stomach hurt, it had to *really* hurt.

Looking at her watch, Henley thought she had just enough time to pick up her daughter, drop her off with a neighbor, then get back to The Refuge for the afternoon session she'd scheduled with a guest. From what she understood, while in the Army, the woman had been captured and held for a month before being rescued. Understandably, she was having a hard time with everything she'd been through, and Henley didn't want to let her down or postpone the session. With a trip to town and back, she'd be cutting it close.

"I'll be there in about twenty minutes."

"Don't rush. Jasna's safe here. She's napping on the cot in my office."

"Thank you. See you soon."

Jasna was Henley's entire world. She was an old soul. Twelve going on forty-five. She'd been conceived while Henley was slogging through a decade of schooling. Not when she would have chosen to have a child, but...between her class schedules, work, and the demons from her past, she'd used men in a bid to ease her stress. Instead, she'd added to it with motherhood. But she wouldn't change it for the world.

Getting pregnant had been the wake-up call Henley needed to get her shit together. It hadn't been easy to be a single mother—and it still wasn't—but she'd done it. Henley was extremely proud of how she and Jasna had managed to overcome every obstacle thrown in their path —so far.

Still, what she wouldn't give for a shoulder to lean on. A companion. A partner. Especially at times like this.

She couldn't help but think about the fact her daughter was only slightly older than Henley had been when she'd lost her own mother. She didn't want Jasna to ever go through something so traumatic. She'd do whatever it took to protect her. *Anything.*

With that thought in mind, she gripped her phone and grabbed her purse as she headed out of the room she usually used to meet with clients at The Refuge. She needed to call Mrs. Singleton, her neighbor, and see if she'd be willing to watch over Jasna for a while until she could get home later.

Looking around, she didn't see any of the guys, but Alaska was sitting behind the reception desk.

"How'd the session go?" she asked as Henley approached.

"Good. I need to head out for an hour or so," she told her.

Alaska stood up, her brow furrowing slightly. "Is everything all right?"

"I think so. My daughter's sick. The school nurse called and I need to go pick her up."

"Oh, no. Is there anything I can do?"

Henley smiled warmly at the other woman. Many people might consider Alaska Stein plain, but she had a heart of gold, which was way more important than looks in Henley's eyes. She and Drake were made for each other. They'd been friends nearly their entire lives, and only recently realized that friendship was an amazing foundation for love.

Something Henley couldn't help but wish for herself... with Finn.

Shaking the thought aside, because she and Finn were *nothing* like Alaska and Drake, Henley shook her head. "Thank you, but no. I'm just going to run to Los Alamos, get her settled at my neighbor's place, then come back for my afternoon session."

"I'm sure we could reschedule," Alaska told her.

"I know, but I don't want to. I really want to meet with Christina."

"All right, but if you need anything, just yell. I'm working for another hour or so. We're interviewing a few potential housekeepers to replace Alexis. I mean, I'm happy for her that she got that inheritance from her great-uncle or whoever he was, but she left us in a bit of a bind. We're hoping to hire someone today. Anyway, you have my cell number, right?"

Henley nodded. She actually had the numbers of all the guys in her contacts, as well as Alaska's. They'd insisted she have a way to get a hold of any of them in case of an emergency. "I do, thanks," Henley confirmed.

"Okay. Drive safe and tell Jasna we all hope she feels better soon."

It was a sweet sentiment...and a very recent development. Henley had kind of kept her daughter a secret from everyone at The Refuge since her employment. Not intentionally, or because she didn't trust them. Beyond idle chitchat or talk about work, her conversations with the owners usually weren't personal, so Jasna simply hadn't come up. But the night of Alaska's attempted abduction, Henley had been stuck at The Refuge late into the evening, and when it was suggested that she just spend the night, she'd explained her need to get home to her daughter.

Now that everyone had found out about Jasna, they frequently asked about her, and Alaska always scheduled Henley's sessions so they were over before dinnertime, so she could get home to her daughter.

"Thanks, I will." Henley waved at Alaska before hurrying for the front door of the lodge.

As she walked to her car, she went to her contact list and clicked on Mrs. Singleton's name. Her neighbor had been a godsend over the years. Babysitting at a moment's notice and generally being there for both Jasna and Henley when they needed her. She was in her sixties, and her children were all grown and had moved away from Los Alamos. Her husband, Gerald, had passed about a decade before, and she seemed to love having Jasna to fuss over.

But when the phone rang and rang in her ear, Henley frowned. She left a message—and wasn't sure what to do next. Mrs. Singleton was always available.

Taking a deep breath, she prayed Mrs. Singleton called back before she picked up Jasna. She had no other babysitting options. It wouldn't be the first time she'd had to postpone a session with a Refuge client, but she hated to do it all the same.

Henley passed the entrance to the barn as she walked toward the small parking space for employees. There was a separate parking area for guests, and the guys who owned The Refuge parked near their cabins. So at the moment, her and Jess, one of the housekeepers, were the only ones with vehicles in the lot. She stopped at her Honda CRV. It wasn't new, but it did well on the mountain roads, especially in the winter.

Climbing into the driver's seat, she quickly put her key in the ignition and turned it.

To her surprise, nothing happened. Not even a click.

She blinked and tried to start the car again, with the same result.

Then again.

She hit the steering wheel and let out a frustrated shout—mortified when she felt the telltale sting of tears.

Her dead car was apparently the last straw today. Her frequent stress, loneliness, Jasna being sick, her inability to get a hold of Mrs. Singleton, worrying about missing a session—it all decided to hit her at once.

Henley gripped the steering wheel and lowered her forehead to rest on her hands as she tried to keep tears of frustration at bay...without luck.

Her pity party lasted only about a minute before a knock on her window startled her so badly, her hands flew to her chest as she lurched sideways, away from the sound.

Looking out the window, she saw it was Finn. And he wasn't happy. He took a large step away from her door and held up his hands, doing his best to prove he wasn't there to hurt her.

Taking a deep breath and trying to compose herself, Henley opened the door and got out of her vehicle.

"What's wrong?" Finn immediately asked.

Henley sighed.

"Are you hurt? Is it your daughter? Why are you just sitting in your car? It's too warm out here for you to be in there with the windows up. And you've been crying. Talk to me, Henley."

She wiped her cheeks with her hands and almost laughed. This was the most she'd gotten out of the man at one time...well...*ever*.

With another sigh, she looked up at him. The man was *so* tall. She'd always been a little afraid of tall men, because when her mom was killed, the guys who'd done it seemed huge to her tiny ten-year-old self. Though she'd never, not once, been afraid of Finn.

She knew he was two years younger than her thirty-six, but despite whatever hell he'd been through, he looked even younger. He had thick dark hair that was usually mussed, as if he ran his hands through it constantly. Today was no exception. His beard and mustache were closely trimmed to his face, and his chis-

9

eled cheekbones made him look outdoorsy and rugged. He had on his usual faded and well-worn denim shirt over a khaki T-shirt and jeans. His boots were dusty and dirty, and his brown eyes were, at the moment, focused intently on her.

She'd caught him staring at her more than once in the past, but as soon as she made eye contact, he always looked away. Not today. In fact, he was staring at her so closely, it was almost disconcerting. She wondered what he saw in her features at the moment.

Stress and exhaustion, she assumed.

She forced herself to smile, even though it was an effort. "I'm fine. And it's not that warm out here. I think you're just hot-blooded," she joked. But when Finn didn't even crack a smile or relax a fraction, she shook her head. "Jasna's sick. I doubt it's anything too serious, as the school nurse said it seems to be going around right now. I need to go pick her up and my car won't start. And I can't get a hold of my neighbor, who usually looks after her when I need a sitter. Without someone to stay with Jasna, I'll have to cancel my session this afternoon with Christina, and I really don't want to do that to her."

Henley was aware she was speaking too fast and the tone of her voice was rising just slightly, right along with her stress, but because she was on the verge of tears again, she didn't even care.

To her utter shock, Finn reached behind her into her car and grabbed her purse. Then he shut the door and put his hand at her elbow, steering her away from her CRV toward the barn.

"Finn?" she asked uncertainly. This was the first time he'd touched her since that night in the barn, when he'd held onto her so tightly, almost desperately, while dealing with whatever demons were swimming in his head.

He didn't answer, just walked around the barn to where his F-250 pickup truck was parked. It was a beast of a machine, an older model, had dents all over and the bed was full of dirt, hay, and who knew what else. It was a working truck, and for some reason that appealed to Henley. He didn't care if it got banged up, as long as it was reliable and did its job. And as he was constantly hauling things for the animals at The Refuge, it got a lot of use.

"Finn?" she asked again when he walked to the passenger side and held open the door. "What are you doing?"

"Taking you to town to get Jasna," he said simply.

Henley frowned. "But—"

He didn't let her continue. "We can swing by your place, and if your neighbor isn't there, we'll bring her back here. I'll take a look at your car and see if it's something simple that I can fix while you're in your session with Christina."

Henley could only stare at him with her mouth open. "What?" she asked, utterly flabbergasted.

Finn ran a hand through his hair and shrugged. "Your daughter's sick, your car won't start, and you need to get to her. So I'm making that happen."

Henley swallowed hard, tears threatening once again. She'd been on her own a very long time. She wasn't used to people doing things for her, outside of Mrs. Singleton's willingness to babysit. "Thank you," she whispered.

"Climb up," Finn said in response.

She was grateful for his hand on her elbow as she hopped—literally hopped—into the huge truck. The height was no big deal for Finn because he was over six feet, but at her five-four, it wasn't quite as easy. She clicked her seat belt on as Finn walked around to the driver's side. He started the truck without a word and pulled away from the barn, heading for the main road that led to town.

He didn't say anything else, but Henley was used to silence, so it didn't bother her. She dialed Mrs. Singleton again, but when it went to voice mail, she hung up without leaving another message.

"When you get to town, turn on Diamond Drive," she said quietly after a while.

Finn nodded.

He pulled into the parking lot of Mountain Elementary School a short time later, and Henley glanced at him. "I'll be right back."

"Take your time," he said in his rumbly voice.

"I...I appreciate this."

Finn merely nodded.

She stared at him for a beat, wanting to ask so many questions. But instead, she gave him a small smile and reached for the door handle. She jumped out of the truck and walked toward the front door of the school. It was hard to believe her baby would be in middle school next year. Jasna had always been a quiet, introspective child, and Henley wasn't ready for the possibility of teenage angst. But if it was going to happen, it would do so whether she was ready or not.

Taking a deep breath, she pushed open the door and headed for the main office. Something occurred to her as she traversed the halls. Finn had said they'd bring Jasna back to The Refuge if she couldn't find Mrs. Singleton. She'd never brought her daughter to work before. Not for any particular reason; there just hadn't been a need or an opportunity.

She wasn't sure about bringing her there now. Where would she hang out while Henley was with her patient? She was sick; the last thing Henley wanted was for her daughter to spread her germs to the guests, or any of the guys or Alaska. And Jasna herself might not want to go either. If she felt like crap, she'd probably want to go straight home, to her own bed.

It was probably best if she just had Finn take them both to her apartment, and he could head back to The Refuge on his own. Of course, that would leave her without a car, but Henley would figure that out later. Her car wasn't working at the moment anyway.

One thing at a time. And first up was getting to her sick daughter.

CHAPTER TWO

Finn "Tonka" Matlick sat in his truck and drummed his fingers on the steering wheel, waiting patiently. He wasn't sure why he'd volunteered to take Henley to pick up her daughter.

No—that was a lie. He knew. Ever since that evening when shit had hit the fan with the man who'd tried to kidnap Alaska, and he and Henley'd had their...*moment* in the barn, Tonka had been trying to figure out a way to talk to her. To get a little...closer.

Of course, being the emotionally stunted wreck that he was, he hadn't been successful so far. Not since that night, and not in the years since Henley had started at The Refuge.

But seeing her crying in her car had hit him hard. She was normally a very calm, positive person—or at least, that was the image she projected. Seeing her so upset had felt wrong. He hadn't meant to scare her by knocking on the window and could kick his own ass for not thinking before acting. The fear on her face wasn't something he ever wanted to see again, especially not because of something *he'd* done.

When she'd told him what was wrong, he'd responded automatically. To him, it was an easy fix—take her to town to pick up her daughter. But now, as he sat in the truck and waited for Henley to come out of the school with Jasna, he regretted yet again not thinking more carefully.

He'd never been around kids. Didn't know what to say to them, didn't know how to act. Though he supposed in many ways, they were like the dogs he used to work with... dependent upon others for nearly everything.

Tonka quickly forced himself to think about *anything* else. He couldn't think about his former canine partner, Steel, for longer than a few seconds without having a breakdown.

He turned his thoughts back to the situation at hand. It was a shock when he'd learned Henley had a daughter, and not just for him, but everyone at The Refuge. He wondered what she looked like. Would she be petite like her mom? Have the same beautiful long brown hair and hazel eyes? Would she be talkative, a tomboy? Into makeup and fashion? He had no idea...and for some reason, that irked him.

Of course, him not knowing anything about Jasna was no one's fault but his own. He'd wanted to ask about her since learning of the girl's existence, but he didn't know how to talk to Henley without looking like a total idiot.

It was ridiculous. He used to be quite the ladies' man, actually. Had no problem hitting on women in bars or on the base in Virginia. But now? He got completely tongue-tied. And honestly, he didn't have the interest anymore.

His life had been gray for years. Only recently had a little bit of color started to come back.

His attention had been glued to the front doors as his thoughts whirled, so he immediately spotted the woman and girl who exited and began to walk toward his truck. Tonka quickly got out and went around to open the back door. His lips twitched when he saw that Henley's daughter, at twelve, was almost as tall as her mom. Jasna was slender. Reminded him of a colt who was still growing into its legs. Her hair was more dark blonde than brown, but there was no doubt that she and Henley were related.

The pre-teen stared at the ground as they walked, and Henley kept glancing at her worriedly.

"Hey," Henley said somewhat shyly as they approached. "I hope we didn't take too long."

"Not at all," Tonka said.

"Jasna, this is Finn. Finn, this is my daughter Jasna."

"It's nice to meet you," Tonka said quietly. "I'm sorry you don't feel well."

The girl looked at him, and Tonka sucked in a quiet breath. The color of her amber eyes was very unique—and almost the exact shade Steel's eyes had been.

"Thanks for coming to get me. Mom told me that her car wouldn't start."

Tonka forced himself to stand still and not back away from the girl. It wasn't that he was afraid, exactly. Or that he didn't like the color of her eyes—quite the opposite. It was just such a shock.

Memories of the last time he'd seen eyes that color, how they'd pleaded for help, were almost overwhelming.

Tonka swallowed hard and did his best to regain his equilibrium. He turned to look at Henley for his own sanity. But of course, she saw more than he wanted her to, like always. Had already noted his strange reaction to her daughter.

He caught a glimpse of disappointment and sorrow on her face before she managed to mask it.

Shit. This wasn't going well. Some impression he was making. He'd never manage any headway with Henley if she thought he didn't like her daughter.

"I thought maybe we should head right back to The Refuge, without worrying about your neighbor." Tonka returned his gaze to Jasna, and this time he was ready for the impact of her eyes. "Jasna, you can hang out with me in the barn with my animals, if you want, while your mom does her thing at the lodge. There's an office in there with a sofa bed, so you can nap if you're tired. Or if you feel up to it, you can watch me feed everybody."

"Really?" Jasna asked, sounding excited.

He nodded.

"I'm not sure that's a good idea—" Henley started, but her daughter interrupted.

"*Please*, Mom? You've talked about Melba so much, I can't wait to meet her! And see the horses. And the goats who're always trying to eat people's clothes. And didn't you say there are new kittens? Pleeeeease?"

Tonka couldn't stop the rush of pleasure that swamped him at hearing Jasna's words. He liked that Henley had talked about the animals with her daughter. They were his pride and joy.

"I don't know, Jas. You've got a hundred-point-three fever. And when's the last time you puked?"

"Can we not talk about me puking in front of your friend?" Jasna muttered.

"Sorry," Henley said with a small grin. "I just think you might be more comfortable in your own bed."

"But you have that session you wanted to do today. And you were the one who said that Mrs. Singleton isn't home. I could totally stay home by myself, but I know you won't let me."

Tonka frowned at that. Leave this young girl home alone? No way in hell. But Henley's next words reassured him.

"You aren't staying home alone. Not until you're at least sixteen—and maybe not even then." She looked up at him, and her teeth sank into her bottom lip. "Are you sure you don't mind? I mean, I'm guessing I could put her in one of the unused rooms in the lodge, if you'd prefer."

"I'm sure," Tonka said. And to his surprise, he found that he meant it. He still wasn't confident in his abilities to entertain a kid, but maybe she'd fall asleep and it would be a non-issue.

"Yay!" Jasna said. Then she winced and put a shaky hand on her belly.

"Come on, let's get you settled," Tonka said firmly, gesturing to the back seat. He wanted to help her inside, but didn't want to touch her without her approval, or that of her mom. Before he shut the door, he walked to the bed of the truck and grabbed a steel bucket that he kept there. He placed it on the floor at Jasna's feet and gave her a small smile. "Just in case," he said before shutting the door.

He didn't want to embarrass the girl, but if she had to puke again while they were on their way to The Refuge, he didn't want it all over his truck. He didn't care about cleaning it up; he'd had worse things than vomit back there from transporting animals. He just had a feeling she'd be humiliated if she barfed all over the place.

"Thanks," Henley said quietly as he reached for the handle of her door next.

Tonka nodded and once again put a hand under her elbow to help her up into the passenger seat. Once she was settled, he shut the door and walked around to the driver's side.

He had no idea what he was doing. He just prayed inviting Jasna to hang out with him in the barn wouldn't backfire. He was terribly curious about the girl. He hadn't managed the nerve to ask about her, and Henley didn't really mention her at all—clearly, since he hadn't known she'd existed before a couple weeks ago. But he wanted to know pretty much everything about the psychologist who spent so much time at The Refuge, so that included getting to know her daughter.

Tonka *wanted* to care about the things most normal people did. He also wanted to act on the interest he frequently saw in Henley's eyes, because he'd felt the same interest since meeting her. To do that, he knew he'd have to talk about things he'd avoided for years.

The thought of sharing what had happened to make him the shell of a man he was today was repugnant. But he had a feeling if there was anyone he could talk to about that incident, it would be Henley.

He'd acted impulsively today—something he *never* did —but was surprisingly okay about it. He'd wanted to do something to show Henley how much he appreciated her support when he'd almost lost it in the barn a couple weeks ago. But he'd been a chicken since then. Hadn't been able to approach her at all.

Tonka might not be the man he used to be, but he'd never been a coward. And he wished he could say his offer of assistance today was a breakthrough. Instead, it was more of a deep necessity.

The decision to help her, and Jasna, hadn't even been a conscious thought. She needed help, and he'd instinctively needed to provide it.

If things went well with Jasna, this could be the start of a new kind of relationship between him and Henley. If it didn't, it could be the end of anything before it even started.

"Ready?" he asked after he'd started his truck. He glanced over at Henley, who nodded at him with a small smile on her face. Then he looked over his right shoulder to the girl sitting in his back seat. She looked a little pale, but she nodded at him too. Taking a deep breath and hoping this was the start of a good thing, Tonka pulled out of the school parking lot and headed back to The Refuge.

Thirty short minutes later, Tonka was alone with Jasna in the barn. Henley had given her a hundred different instructions before getting her settled on the small couch in the barn's office. Tonka had to admit, he found it endearing how much Henley fussed over her daughter. The girl seemed to enjoy the attention, yet was embarrassed about it at the same time.

After Henley had left to go to the lodge for her session with Christina, Jasna immediately wandered into the main area of the barn. Tonka took great pride in keeping the space clean and uncluttered. The horses were out in the paddock, the goats were also wandering around, probably eating something they shouldn't, but Melba was currently in the barn.

The little girl's eyes were glued on the huge beast. "Can I pet her?" Jasna asked shyly.

Tonka supposed he should probably tell her she should be in the office sleeping, but he didn't have the heart. She was so excited to meet the gentle giant, he couldn't deny her.

"Of course. She'd love that. Come here," Tonka said, holding out his hand. He'd only meant to guide the girl to the front of the stall, but to his surprise, Jasna took hold of his hand and smiled up at him with total trust.

And just that easily, Tonka was a goner.

She reminded him so much of Steel—her eyes, her friendliness, the trust she was showing him—although he supposed she wouldn't appreciate being compared to a dog. But Steel wasn't *just* a dog. He'd been his best friend. His partner. The trust they'd had in each other was absolute...which made what happened all the more horrific.

Steel used to look at him the same way Jasna was at that moment. And *that* was how he wanted to remember his old friend. How he'd gaze at him with trust and excitement, knowing they were going to do something fun, whether they were at work or going to the park to throw a ball around.

Tonka wasn't sure he deserved that trust. Knew it came with a huge responsibility that he hadn't thought he'd ever want again. Or that he could *shoulder* again. But somehow, with Jasna's hand in his, her amber eyes staring up at him, he felt a protectiveness so intense, it was almost painful.

Her brow furrowed. "Are we gonna go see Melba?" she asked.

"Sorry, yes," he told her, as he turned and headed toward the large cow.

Her brown eyes were fixed on them as they came near. Tonka grabbed a large carrot from a bin he kept well out of reach of the animals who might decide to help themselves, and handed it to Jasna. "There are two things Melba likes more than anything in the world...being scratched under her chin, and carrots. If you give her this, she'll love you forever."

The smile the girl gave him was radiant, and with a jolt, Tonka realized exactly how pretty she was. Henley was going to have her hands full when Jasna got older.

"Awesome!" she breathed. She gripped the carrot tightly as they neared the stall.

Melba mooed, and Tonka felt Jasna jerk in his grip.

"Easy, it's okay. She's totally friendly. She's just excited about that carrot you have in your hand," he told her.

"What do I do?" she asked, her voice trembling.

"Here, climb up on the slats of the gate," Tonka told her. He put his hand on her back, still stunned by how protective he felt of the girl. "Step up one more. I won't let you fall."

When she was high enough that she could easily reach over the top into the stall, he said, "Now hold the carrot out and Melba will do the rest."

"Will she bite me?"

Tonka couldn't help but laugh. "No, sweetie. She's much more interested in that carrot than your fingers."

Jasna nodded and held out the treat to the massive animal.

Melba, as if understanding that the girl was nervous,

very delicately took the vegetable from her, and he could've sworn she was smiling as she chewed.

"Can I pet her?" Jasna whispered.

Tonka's smile grew. "Of course."

"Will you hold me steady?" Jasna asked.

That warm feeling filled Tonka once more at the innocent trust she was showing him. He put his hands on either side of her waist and held her firmly as she leaned over the top rail to get closer to the cow.

Melba, not being stupid, stepped closer to the gate, making it easier for Jasna to reach her. Jasna's giggle was carefree and joyous as she pet the spoiled cow.

There were lots of things Tonka needed to do. Clean stalls, make sure everyone had fresh water, rub down the horses...but nothing seemed more important at that moment than witnessing this girl's happiness.

"She's awesome!" Jasna breathed.

"Yeah."

"Mom said you guys adopted her after a fire?" she asked without taking her gaze from the cow.

Again, a little thrill went through Tonka at hearing proof that Henley had shared information about The Refuge with her daughter. "Yeah. The barn she was in caught fire and she was traumatized because of it. Her owner didn't have the patience to work with her on her fear of being in a barn after that, and he gave her up."

"That's not fair. I mean, if I'd been inside my home minding my own business, and all of a sudden I couldn't breathe very well and it was hot and I thought I was going to die, I wouldn't be all that thrilled about voluntarily walking inside again either."

Tonka swallowed hard. "Exactly," he whispered.

"And the goats like to eat anything they can get their mouths on, including people's shirts, because they were left behind when their owners moved and they almost starved to death, right?" Jasna asked.

"Yup."

"And you guys have rescued the horses and cats too."

It wasn't a question, but Tonka nodded anyway.

"I think that's so cool. Everyone should have a home where they're loved and protected. Some of the kids at school make fun of me because I don't know my dad, and they say mean things about my mom, but I don't care. My mom loves me, and even though she's overprotective, it makes me feel good inside that she cares so much."

Tonka's first reaction was to ask the names of the kids who were bullying this precious girl, but he swallowed the words down. It wasn't as if he could go and threaten a bunch of sixth-graders. "I'm thinking you're the most important thing in her world," he said instead.

"I am," Jasna said without guile. Then she turned her head and said, "Mom says you and your friends all went through bad things and that's why you opened this place. Because you want to help people."

Having her amber eyes staring at him was getting less startling the longer Tonka was around her. "She's right."

Then Jasna shocked the shit out of Tonka by lifting a hand and placing it on the side of his face. In a serious tone, she said, "I'm sorry about whatever happened to you. But I'm glad you're here to help animals like Melba. They can't talk and they don't have thumbs, so they can't take care of themselves. They need you to do it for them."

He wanted to laugh at the thumbs comment, but her words struck a chord so deep within him, he couldn't speak. He was thrown back into another time, when another animal, his beloved dog, needed him and he hadn't been able to do a damn thing to stop his pain.

It wasn't until he felt the little girl's hair brush against his face that Tonka realized Jasna had shifted off the gate to Melba's stall and was hugging him. She had her legs around his waist and her arms around his neck. She was light in his arms, and he was gripping her too tightly. The last thing he wanted to do was hurt this child who was too damn perceptive for his peace of mind.

Tonka stepped away from Melba's stall and headed back toward the office, holding Jasna carefully. He needed some space. He felt too raw.

Leaning over, he placed Jasna back on the couch she'd left earlier. She let go of his neck and stared up at him with a gaze that seemed to be able to spot all his secrets. "I'm sorry if I said something I wasn't supposed to."

"You didn't," Tonka reassured her without hesitation.

"Mom's so proud of all of you. She likes you and your friends a lot. She says that life isn't fair, and it hurts sometimes, but it's also beautiful. And when bad things happen, it can be harder to see that beauty, but it's there if you look hard enough."

Tonka studied Jasna for a long moment, not sure how to respond.

"Mom went through bad stuff when she was little. But she says I was her saving grace. My name is Slavic...that means it comes from Europe. It's popular in places like Croatia, Bosnia, Serbia, and Montenegro."

It sounded like the little girl was reciting something she'd been told many times before.

"It means clear or sharp. Mom says she named me that

because until I came along, her life was blurry. But when she had me, her focus sharpened. She said it was also the name of a woman who came to see her when she was a girl in the hospital, after the bad thing happened when she was little. She never forgot how nice that woman was. So she gave me her name to honor her."

Tonka sat on the edge of the couch, suddenly not so anxious to leave. "Yeah? I didn't know that," he said.

"What does your name mean?" Jasna asked.

"Which one?"

She looked confused. "You have more than one?"

"Well, my given name is Finn, that's what your mom calls me."

She nodded.

"It means white or fair-haired."

"But your hair is brown."

Tonka grinned. "I know. But apparently when I was born, it was super blond. When I was about your age, I researched my name and found out one of the great heroes of Irish mythology, Finn MacCool, was a warrior with supernatural powers. He was also extremely smart and generous. I prefer to think I was named after him."

"Ooooh, like being able to fly?"

Tonka chuckled. "I suppose so."

"I'd love to be able to fly. It would be so cool," Jasna enthused. Then she seemed to remember what they were talking about. "What about your other name?"

"Tonka," he told her with a nod. "That's what all my friends call me."

"Like the toy?" she asked with a frown.

"Yup. More specifically, a toy truck. When I was training to be in the military, I was bigger than I am now.

I had a lot of muscles. So people started calling me Tonka."

Jasna looked confused for a moment before she shook her head. "I like Finn better."

"You can call me whatever you want," he reassured her.

"Finn?"

"Yeah?"

"Thanks for letting me hang out with you in the barn."

"Of course."

"It's just...I'm weird."

Tonka blinked in confusion. "What?"

"I'm weird," she repeated in a matter-of-fact tone of voice without any hint of sadness or angst. "I like to read. A lot. And I don't like boys, and that's all most of the girls in my class want to talk about. I don't like makeup because it makes my face itchy, and I'd rather wear sneakers and comfy sweats than dresses and shoes with heels on them. I'm weird," she said again with a shrug.

"Does it bother you?" Tonka asked.

Jasna shook her head. "Not really. Mom says that I should be myself and if other people don't like it, don't like me, that's their problem, not mine."

"Your mom's smart."

"I know."

It was hard to believe a few minutes ago, Tonka felt as if he was on the verge of a depressive episode, and now he was smiling. This girl might think she was strange, but to him, she was a minor miracle.

As he stared at her, the color seemed to drain from her face.

On instinct, Tonka moved and grabbed the bucket he'd brought in from his truck to put near the sofa. He got it under her just in time as she vomited up the rest of whatever had been in her belly.

Jasna moaned a little and wiped a hand over her mouth. "Gross," she muttered.

At any other time, Tonka would've smiled at that, but he was too worried about her to do so. "Lie down," he said firmly. "I'll go get you some water to rinse your mouth and clean out the bucket."

"Okay," Jasna said as she practically fell sideways onto the cushion. "I think I'll just take a little nap."

Tonka grabbed a throw blanket that was on the back of the sofa and covered up her slender frame. She was tall, yes, but she didn't weigh much. She looked tiny lying on the couch with her hands under her cheek.

Forcing himself to move, Tonka got up and took care of the bucket, then reentered the office with the water he'd promised. Jasna was sleeping, and he didn't have the heart to wake her. He put the water on the small table next to the couch and placed the bucket on the floor where she'd be sure to see it if she needed it.

It took several minutes before he could force himself to leave her side. He was drawn to the little girl, which was extremely out of character for him.

Jasna clearly had him wrapped around her little finger. He hadn't been in her presence for longer than an hour or so, and he was already as drawn to her as he was her mom.

Tonka didn't understand it. Was a little unsettled by the realization. But at the same time, there was a rightness in his chest that made him want to do whatever it took to make sure mother and daughter were safe and happy.

Looking at his watch, he saw that if he was going to get all his chores done before Henley finished with Christina, he needed to get moving. He also needed to look at her car and see if he could figure out what was wrong. Hopefully it was just a bad battery or an equally easy fix.

Taking one last look at the sleeping girl, Tonka headed for the door. He only closed it partway so if she woke up and needed him, he'd be able to hear her.

Melba mooed pathetically, as if asking where the sweet little girl who gave her treats had gone, and Tonka found himself grinning at the animal. He spared a minute to reassure the bovine that Jasna would be up later and would probably give her another carrot before he went over to the wall and grabbed a shovel. The stalls weren't going to clean themselves...and for the first time in a long time, he looked forward to the end of the day. Because it meant he'd get to see Henley again.

CHAPTER THREE

Henley kept taking subtle peeks at Finn as he drove her and Jasna back to their apartment. Her appointment with the former POW had gone long, and afterward, Drake and the other Refuge owners had encouraged her to stay for dinner. Robert, their resident chef, had outdone himself by making several different casseroles—vegetarian, taco, gluten free, low fat, and a potato, bacon, and noodle one, as well.

She'd checked on Jasna, who was sleeping hard at the time. As deeply asleep as she was, nothing short of a bomb would wake her. Henley had assured Finn that it was okay to leave her where she was while they grabbed something to eat, but he'd refused to leave her alone in the barn.

His insistence on making sure he was nearby "just in case" was...

She didn't know *what* it was. Surprising, at the very least, since he'd just met her daughter today. Heart-warming for sure. Henley had always had the responsibility of looking after Jasna by herself. Even if it was only for today, it felt good that someone else seemed to be just as worried for her daughter.

So she'd gone back up to the lodge, loaded up two plates, and took them to the barn. There was no way she was going to leave Finn out there alone, looking after her daughter, while she sat inside and ate.

They had dinner together in the loft, where Melba and the goats couldn't get to them and beg for food. And it had been...nice. Finn didn't talk a lot, but he did tell her that Jasna had loved meeting Melba. He also broke the news that it looked like the battery in her CRV was shot and she'd need a new one. He volunteered to take her and Jasna home, stop and get a battery, install it, then get her car back to her apartment, so she could get to work in the morning.

She usually spent the mornings at her office in town, where she worked with three other psychologists, before going to The Refuge in the afternoons. At first, the job with the guests at the retreat had simply been for extra money. But a couple of years in, she found she enjoyed it much more than her other job. It wasn't that she didn't like helping the residents of Los Alamos, but...she'd actually had a couple clients who'd scared her a bit and were beyond her abilities to help. That sucked to admit, but it was true. And unlike at The Refuge, her Los Alamos practice didn't have several burly men who could assist if a patient got out of hand.

Now Finn was doing her yet another favor before spending who knew how much time working on her car to make sure she had transportation. She'd gotten better over the years at accepting help, but this seemed like...more. Most people wouldn't go this far out of their way to help her. They might call a tow truck or an Uber, but they wouldn't go to the lengths Finn was.

Did she dare wonder if it meant he might be loosening up around her? That maybe, just maybe, he saw her as more than simply a Refuge employee? She didn't know, but she could hope.

"Are you sure Jasna's okay?" he asked as they neared her apartment complex.

"Yeah. She's always been like this. When she gets sick —which is rare—she sleeps hard at first, and then wakes up almost as good as new. It's kind of annoying really." She grinned as she said that last bit. But when Finn didn't seem to relax even a little, she got serious. "I'll check in on her a few times throughout the night and take her temperature. If it goes up, or if she keeps throwing up, I'll bring her to the urgent care clinic in town. But I'm fairly sure this is just that twenty-four-hour bug that's going around her school."

Finn nodded, still looking concerned.

"Thank you," Henley told him.

"For what?" he asked.

For what? Was this man for real? "Well, for looking after her today. And not wanting to leave her alone even though she would've been fine. For figuring out what was wrong with my car, for driving us home, and for fixing my CRV and bringing it into town. But most of all, for caring about Jasna. I can't remember a time when anyone other than me, and maybe my neighbor, truly cared."

"She's a good kid," Finn said with a shrug, ignoring all the other things she'd thanked him for.

"She is," Henley agreed.

"What do you do in the summers with her?"

Henley frowned. "Meaning?"

"When you're working...you said you wouldn't leave her alone, so I'm assuming when she's not in school, she's not hanging out at your apartment by herself, waiting for you to get home."

"Oh! Of course not. For the last few years, she's either been going to a daily kind of camp for kids, or Mrs. Singleton has watched her. Now she's too old for the day camps she's gone to in the past. There are a few others for older kids that I'm considering."

"What does *she* think of the camp idea?" Finn asked.

Henley was thrilled he was voluntarily conversing so much, and she vaguely wondered at the sudden change as she wrinkled her nose at the question. "She's not a big fan, since she's more of a loner. But she's also a good kid and knows it's worrying me, so she hasn't complained too much."

"Hmm."

Henley didn't know what that noncommittal noise meant, but she didn't have time to ask as they were pulling into the parking area of her apartment complex.

"I really do appreciate you driving us around," Henley said again.

Finn nodded and climbed out of the truck.

Henley wasn't really surprised he wasn't a big fan of being thanked, but that didn't mean she wasn't going to do it. She got out on her side and went to open the back door, but found that Finn was already there. He was reaching in for Jasna and somehow managed to pick her up without waking her.

"She really is out, isn't she?" Finn asked with a small smile on his face.

"Yup. She's always been like that, even as a baby. But it can take her a while to go down, especially if she's hyped-up about something."

His lips twitched as they walked toward the building. "Like when she gets to meet Melba for the first time?"

Henley chuckled. "Yup. Like that."

Her apartment was on the second floor, and Henley was impressed by how easily Finn carried her daughter up the stairs. She unlocked her door and held it open. "Her room is the last one on the left down the hall," she told him.

She followed behind him as he carried Jasna to her bedroom. He placed her carefully down on the bed and ran a hand through his hair as he straightened. Then he nodded at her and left her to put her daughter to bed.

It didn't take long. Henley managed to get Jasna's clothes off and get her into her nightgown. She left to find a bowl to put next to her bed, just in case...and found Finn pacing her apartment.

"Oh, I thought you'd left," she blurted.

"I wouldn't leave without making sure you're good," he told her with a frown.

Henley's heart lurched at his consideration. "We're good," she assured him.

"Your daughter's room is the master," he said next.

Frowning, Henley said, "It is."

"Why? Why didn't you take the bigger bedroom for yourself?"

Henley shrugged. "I don't need a lot of space. I'm fine in the smaller room. I'm only in there to sleep. I'd rather Jasna have more space for her toys and books."

Finn stared at her for so long, Henley felt uncom-fortable.

"What?" she asked a little harsher than she'd meant to.

"Nothing. I think it's...nice."

Henley managed not to wince. Nice. Ugh. That wasn't the adjective she wanted this man to use when he thought about her. She forced herself to smile. She was tired. It had been a long day, and if Finn was going to stop at the store to get a battery for her car, install it, and bring her car back to town, he probably needed to get going. "When you get here with my car, let me know and I'll come down and get the keys," she told him.

But Finn shook his head. "No. It's going to be late. You need your sleep."

"Then how will I get my key? Will you leave it in the car? Under the mat or something?"

"No way. That's a good way for it to get stolen. Text me when you're up in the morning, and I'll swing by and drop it off."

Henley frowned. "No, Finn. I can't ask you to do that. I know barn work starts early. It's bad enough you'll have to come back tonight. Just let me know when you're here later and I can come down."

"It's not a big deal. I have to come into town and pick up some feed and hay in the morning anyway."

Henley couldn't read him. She had no idea if he'd just made up that errand or not.

"Besides," he added belatedly. "I wouldn't mind seeing Jasna and making sure she's okay."

This man was *such* a good person. "Okay," she said quietly.

"Okay," he agreed. "You have my number. If anything

comes up, give me a yell. And if she's not well enough to go to school tomorrow, you can bring her to The Refuge again if you want."

She was going to cry again. But she managed to keep the tears at bay. Barely. "Thanks."

Finn nodded and turned for the door. For a second, Henley had a fantasy that he'd step toward her, put his finger under her chin, tip her head up and kiss her. But this was real life. And while Finn definitely hadn't been his usual closed-off self since coming to her rescue, it was a bit early for him to be declaring his undying love and kissing her silly.

"Lock this behind me," he said firmly.

Henley wanted to roll her eyes and tell him of course she was going to lock her door once he left, but instead she merely nodded.

Finn paused in her doorway for a long moment, then turned and walked out.

Taking a deep breath, Henley locked the deadbolt, put the chain on, and made sure the doohickey on the knob was turned before heading toward the bathroom in the hallway. She was dead tired, but wired at the same time.

Things between her and Finn had changed today, but she wasn't sure if it was in a way that would lead to something more than friendship or not. Either way, she'd take it. She respected and liked Finn Matlick. And the fact that he didn't merely tolerate her daughter, but genuinely seemed to like and care about her, was a huge bonus.

* * *

Tonka took a deep breath before he started his truck and headed for the automotive shop. It had taken everything in him not to pull Henley into his arms before he'd left. He probably would've freaked her out if he'd tried. He'd kept his attraction to her under wraps for years. But one day in her company, seeing the love she and her daughter had for each other, and he already knew he could no longer keep his distance.

All the reasons why he should stay away tried to creep in. She was a psychologist and would eventually try to psychoanalyze him. She'd want to "fix" him, and he wasn't sure he *could* be fixed. She was basically an employee. She had a kid.

But no matter how hard he tried to tell himself things between them wouldn't work out, he couldn't stop thinking about her.

Henley was a damn good psychologist. He'd seen her in action with the guests. She was able to make even the most reluctant guest relax and open up. She seemed to like animals, something that was important to Tonka. She was protective, which he approved of, and she'd done a hell of a job raising Jasna by herself. She was considerate, hard-working, and on top of all that...the woman was sexy as hell.

Her long brown hair was always slightly mussed by the end of the day, and Tonka constantly wanted to smooth it back from her face. She was petite, almost a foot shorter than he was, but with her friendly, outgoing personality, she seemed larger than life. Her hazel eyes sparkled with humor and affection, but he also saw pain there.

Just thinking about what had happened when she was around Jasna's age made his muscles tighten.

He'd heard the story a few times while sitting in on her group sessions at the lodge. Her parents were Native American, and she was alone at home with her mom on the reservation one evening when two men had broken in and attacked her mother. Henley had hidden under her bed right before the men burst into the room, dragging her mom with them. They'd raped and stabbed her, all while Henley had hidden under the bed, terrified out of her mind that she'd be next. They'd left without finding her, but Henley had been so traumatized, she hadn't spoken for five years.

Her dad had never gotten over what happened, and the day after she'd turned eighteen, he'd been killed in a knife fight—that he started—at the casino where he worked.

Henley had experienced severe trauma, and he suspected that was a large part of what made her such a good psychologist. She could empathize with her clients on a level many doctors couldn't, and they probably felt as if she truly understood what they were going through, especially when she shared her past traumas.

Tonka couldn't deny a part of him felt the same way.

He'd actually looked up her case, wanting to find the men who'd killed her mom and make sure they paid for what they'd done. They'd both been arrested and had died while behind bars. They wouldn't ever be a problem for Henley or Jasna, which was a huge relief to Tonka.

He didn't know what the future held, but he knew he could no longer stay away from Henley. He had no idea if he'd be able to work through the shit in his head to have a healthy relationship...but he wanted to try.

Feeling lighter than he had in years, now that he'd finally made that admission to himself, Tonka pulled into the parking lot of the auto store. Pipe had already said he'd help change the battery out in Henley's car and drive him back to town to drop it off.

There was no need to leave the car in her parking lot tonight, since Henley would be asleep and he wasn't leaving the keys. But he had a feeling most people—beyond her neighbor—didn't offer to help the single mother very often. This was something he could do to show her that he didn't mind going out of his way for her.

He appreciated even more that his friend didn't pry into what was going on between him and Henley. For all Pipe knew, he was simply helping out one of their employees.

Then again, Pipe wasn't stupid. Tonka had never gone out of his way to help *any* of their employees. He couldn't keep his interest in Henley a secret for long. But he didn't really want to.

Like everything else in his life, once he put his mind to something, he was one hundred percent committed. It had been the same with the Coast Guard and becoming a dog handler. And investing in The Refuge, making it a safe place for abused, neglected, and unwanted animals as well as people.

Feeling better than he had in a very long time, Tonka entered the store and made a beeline for the batteries. Henley had seemed surprised he was as concerned about her and Jasna as he was—but she hadn't seen anything yet. She'd had a tough life, and he wanted to do everything in his power to make the struggles she'd been through seem like nothing but a bad memory.

* * *

Christian Dekker crouched in the fort in the woods behind his house and watched with cold detachment as a squirrel slowly bled to death in the trap he'd set. He'd found the creature as he'd approached the crude wooden shelter he'd built when he was twelve, dragging it inside so he could watch it die.

All his life, he'd been fascinated with death. He couldn't remember how old he was the first time he'd seen a dead animal in the road...maybe six or so. He'd snuck out of the house later to examine the carcass.

He was different. He knew it. His parents knew it. His sister knew it. But Christian didn't care. About anything, really. He didn't care about his family, or making friends. School was stupid. The boys in his class were pussies. The girls were sluts. The teachers didn't give a shit about teaching, all they cared about was a paycheck and doing as little as possible for it.

When he was just eight, he realized how much pleasure he got from scaring people. It satisfied some need deep within him. He'd hidden in his little sister's room and jumped out of her closet. Her scream had sent goose bumps down his spine...in a good way.

He craved that exciting thrill, and ever since, he'd done everything he could to feel it again and again. Each time, his antics getting darker.

Killing the neighbor's cat and putting it on their doorstep.

Lighting the field behind the school on fire and watching the kids freak, thinking the school was going to burn down.

Sneaking into his parents' room and standing next to their bed, stark naked, not moving an inch, until they woke up and saw him there, staring at them.

He took the knives in the kitchen to scare his parents, leaving them to wonder what he might do with them. Sat precariously on the roof of the house...locked his sister outside at night.

The fear of others filled a gaping hole inside him.

When he was twelve, his parents had brought him to a therapist. At first he opened up to her willingly, sharing his darkest thoughts. But he quickly began to feel she was just like all the other adults he'd met in his life...simply pretending to listen. Being nice to him to get a paycheck. So he'd changed tactics and started fucking with the woman. In one session, he'd tell her everything she wanted to know, no matter how disturbing, and the next time, he'd pretend he hadn't told her anything at all. As if he had no idea what she was talking about.

It was the day he realized he'd gotten under his therapist's skin that helped Christian understand the amount of power he had over others. Scaring them was one thing... but making them alter their behavior, change their habits and routines just to avoid being around him, was a unique thrill all on its own.

He was disappointed when he'd shown up for a session one day, only to find out he had a new therapist. A guy. The woman had given up on him, just like his parents had. It pissed him off then, and he was still angry about it now.

Christian *hated* not having control over his own life— and she was just one more person in a long line who'd taken some of his control away. And before dumping him, the bitch even suggested he be locked away "for his own safety"! It wasn't a betrayal he'd ever forget.

He lived to manipulate people. Loved scaring them so

much they'd do anything to avoid him. But a therapist was different. She was *paid* to put up with his shit. She should've had no choice but to continue their sessions. Just like his parents had no choice...

He was well aware that his parents were scared of him. Of what he might do. They locked their bedroom door now, and had long since moved his room to the basement so he wasn't near his sister. Which suited Christian just fine. He snuck out of the house every night and did whatever he wanted.

As the years passed, Christian found that his need to scare people only got more pervasive. The fear and helplessness in an animal's eyes when it knew it was dying was thrilling, like a drug. The control Christian felt in those moments was overwhelming and exciting.

Although killing squirrels wasn't as fun anymore, he wouldn't pass up the chance to see this one die. The creature in his trap struggled, desperate to get away, to live. But neither of those things was going to happen. Christian was in control.

The thing died way too quickly for his liking, and he threw the carcass out of his fort impatiently. He wanted more. He'd recently found a stray dog that he'd befriended then tortured for a week before slitting its throat. Finding new ways to kill cats was getting boring.

No. Christian's next target was the donkey that lived in a field down from the high school. He wanted to know if killing something so big was more satisfying than the animals he'd tortured in the past.

He had a feeling it would be.

And he wouldn't stop there.

Couldn't.

A plan had been forming in his mind for a couple years now. Everyone he knew in Los Alamos was scared of him and smart enough to stay away. He was going to leave this shitty town and head down to Albuquerque. Make a fresh start.

But before he left, he wanted to make a statement.

He could kill his parents and sister, but that would be too predictable and everyone would suspect him. He wanted a challenge. He needed to strike where it was least expected.

And Christian knew just where that was. He had a score to settle.

In order to make sure his plan went off without a hitch, he needed to study his target. Decide exactly where and how to strike. What would make the most impact.

Doctor McClure had been the first person he'd ever wanted to impress. When she asked about his thoughts and deeds, delving into his mind, he'd stupidly thought she cared about him. Understood him. But she'd betrayed him just like everyone else. She'd pawned him off on one of her co-workers. A mealymouthed asshole who flinched every time Christian so much as shifted in the chair opposite him.

It had been a couple of years since he'd refused to go to any more therapy sessions, but he'd never forgotten the woman who'd given up on him without hesitation. She'd pay for that.

She was his target.

Christian could almost taste the fear she'd feel while he toyed with her. But he needed to be smart. Not let her know she was being followed or watched. He'd figure out her routine, wait for the perfect moment, then strike hard and fast.

A chuckle left his lips, and Christian felt a rush of anticipation he hadn't experienced in a long time. First the donkey. Then the doctor. Then he'd head to the city and go down in history as the most fearsome serial killer the country had ever seen.

He couldn't wait.

CHAPTER FOUR

The next morning, Tonka was feeling more eager than normal to get up and start the day. He knew it was because he was going to see Henley and Jasna soon. It was a little odd that he included the little girl in his excitement. He hadn't been around that many children in his life, had always assumed he'd find them irritating and underfoot all the time.

Although he had to admit, his interaction with Jasna yesterday probably wasn't normal. She'd been sick and had slept for most of the time she was at the barn. But he hadn't minded her questions when she was awake, loved seeing the excitement in her eyes when she'd met Melba.

Time would tell, once she was back to feeling like her normal self, if she'd annoy him or not. He had a feeling she wouldn't. There was something about her that made Tonka feel comfortable. Protective.

When he pulled into the parking lot of Henley's apart-ment complex, he realized he was smiling. He couldn't remember the last time he'd spontaneously smiled so easily.

Henley's CRV was parked in the same place he'd left it the night before, not that he thought it would be anywhere else, since he had the key. He'd made up the excuse that he needed to do errands for The Refuge this morning, but he didn't regret it. Henley looked exhausted last night, and he didn't want her staying up 'til God knows when, waiting on him. Which was a good thing, because it had been after midnight by the time he and Pipe had finished switching out the battery and gotten the vehicle back to her apartment.

Tonka got out of his truck and headed up to Henley's apartment. He was glad she wasn't on the first floor. Even in a small town, it was safer not being quite so accessible to anyone walking around looking for trouble.

He knocked on her door and was still smiling when it opened. But his smile immediately died at seeing Henley. Her face was blotchy and her eyes were red.

"What's wrong?" he asked quickly. "Is Jasna all right?"

"She's fine. She feels much better today. It's Mrs. Singleton."

"Your neighbor?"

Henley nodded. "I just found out the reason I couldn't get a hold of her yesterday was because she's in the hospital. She had a stroke."

Tonka gently urged Henley backward and stepped inside her apartment. He closed the door, then pulled her into his arms without thought.

She didn't resist, instead seemed to burrow into him as he held her. Her arms went around his back, and he could feel her fingers digging into his skin. "I feel *so* awful! I guess she couldn't get to her phone, and she lay on her floor for a while before she was eventually able to crawl to the kitchen where she'd left her cell, so she could call for help."

Tonka rested his cheek on top of Henley's head and held her even tighter. It took a few minutes, but eventually she composed herself and pulled away. Tonka loosened his arms, realizing it was an extremely difficult task. Henley wiped her cheeks with her hands but didn't step out of his hold completely.

"Is she going to be all right?" he asked gently.

Henley shrugged. "I think so, but when she's released from the hospital, her daughter's taking her down to Albuquerque to recover. She'll have to spend some time in a rehab center, I think, then she'll move in with her daughter. I doubt she'll be back here."

Henley sounded so sad, it was all Tonka could do not to give her another long hug. "You want to go see her today?"

She nodded. "Yeah. I thought I'd stop by the hospital after my morning sessions, before I headed out to The Refuge."

Tonka nodded. "You need me to talk to Drake or Alaska and see about canceling your appointments?"

Henley gave him a grateful smile. "No, I think it'll be good for me to head out there."

"What about Jasna? Is she going back to school today?"

Henley nodded. "I took her temperature this morning and it's back to normal. She says she feels fine. She's super sad about Mrs. Singleton though."

"Of course she is," Tonka said. "It sounds like the woman's been a huge help to you both over the years."

"She has," Henley said with a nod. Then sighed. "School's out soon, and without her help, I'll have to decide what to do. There aren't enough camps to keep Jasna busy all summer, and I won't leave her alone in the apartment."

"Can you find someone else to look after her?" Tonka asked with a frown. Honestly, he hadn't considered how difficult childcare was for a single parent. It just wasn't something he'd ever had to worry about.

Henley shrugged then took a deep breath. "I'm sure I will," she said. But he could tell she was trying to downplay her worries about the situation.

"What if she came to The Refuge when she wasn't at camp?" Tonka blurted. Once again with this woman, he didn't give a thought to what he was going to say. It just came out.

Henley looked shocked at the suggestion. "What?"

"You could bring her to The Refuge. I'm sure I could find things for her to do in the barn with me, and I bet Alaska could also help keep her busy. There's always plenty to do around the place. We could even pay her. She could earn some spending money."

"I...I don't know what to say. I didn't think kids were allowed on the premises."

Tonka shrugged. "Technically, they aren't. Some of our guests are triggered by babies crying, or the screaming some kids do while they're playing. But if someone comes who's triggered by children, we'll simply make sure she keeps her distance."

"Have you talked about this with the others?" she asked, though he was aware she already knew the answer.

"No," he told her honestly. "But I know without a

doubt no one will have a problem with it. *Especially* if the alternative is you taking the summer off from working at The Refuge because of childcare issues."

To Tonka's alarm, tears welled in her eyes once more.

"Henley?"

She tilted her head forward and rested it on his chest. "I don't know what to say," she mumbled.

"Say yes," he told her. It was almost scary how good this woman felt in his arms. Tonka literally couldn't remember a time in his life when he'd felt this content while holding another human being. It was as if she filled up all the holes in his soul with her goodness.

How he'd managed to go so long without letting her know how much he admired and liked her, he had no idea.

Henley lifted her head once more and stared at him. "It's just...Mrs. Singleton was always there for me. She never had a problem looking after Jasna, and now that she's gone—not *gone* gone, but unable to help out anymore —I'm realizing how much I took advantage of her. I don't want to do that to anyone at The Refuge."

"You didn't take advantage of her," Tonka said with a small shake of his head. "I'm sure she loved spending time with your daughter. You said she was alone here in Los Alamos, right?"

Henley nodded.

"I bet she cherished every moment she got to spend with Jasna."

"I hope so," Henley said. Then she sighed. "How about this—you talk to your friends today, see what they think. If anyone has any reservations, even minor ones, I'll find another solution for the summer. The last thing I want is to press any buttons for your guests and to cause anyone

49

extra work. Jasna's a good kid, but she's also extremely curious. And she's getting a little more moody as teenage hormones begin to creep in."

"It'll be fine," Tonka reassured her.

Henley opened her mouth to say something, but was interrupted by her daughter.

"Finn!" she exclaimed as she came running down the hallway.

Since Tonka still had his arms around Henley, he was knocked back a step when Jasna barreled into him, but he recovered quickly, raising an arm and wrapping it around the girl, who was now hugging him from the side.

"Hey," he said, a little surprised at her exuberant greeting.

She looked up at him with those amazing amber eyes, and Tonka could see that she'd also been crying. "Did Mom tell you about Mrs. Singleton?"

"Yeah. I'm sorry."

Jasna sniffed and nodded, but didn't let him go. Goose bumps rose on his arms as Tonka realized both McClures were clinging to him now.

A wave of sudden fear washed over him. The last time anyone had relied on him, he'd let them down in a huge way.

He cleared his throat. "Well...I came by to bring the keys to your car, so you guys can get to where you need to be today."

The feeling of loss when both Jasna and Henley stepped away from him was almost overwhelming. He'd fucked up—and he knew it. He'd let his past influence his present, *again*.

For a moment, Tonka wondered if he'd ever be able to

overcome the feelings of inadequacy and guilt that plagued him every moment of every day.

"I appreciate you fixing my car. How much was the battery?"

Tonka shrugged. "Not a lot. It's the least I can do for someone who's so valuable to The Refuge."

He saw the shutters fall over her eyes then, and for the second time in as many minutes, Tonka was kicking himself for saying the wrong thing. He wanted to take his words back, explain that he wasn't helping her because she was an employee. That he personally wanted to make sure she was safe on the roads...but the moment was lost when she turned to Jasna.

"Go grab your stuff and I'll drive you to school this morning. We've already missed the bus."

Jasna turned without argument and headed down the hall toward her room.

"I'd offer you breakfast, but we're going to stop and grab something on the way to school," Henley told him.

"It's okay," Tonka told her. "Let me know if anything seems off with the car."

"I will. Again, thank you so much for everything, Finn."

He nodded at her and stuck his hands in his pockets, feeling awkward all of a sudden. He mentally kicked his own ass for screwing up their intimate moment. "I'll see you when you get to The Refuge later."

She nodded, and there was nothing left to do but leave. Tonka nodded back and stepped toward the door.

"Finn?"

He turned back, his heart skipping a beat. "Yeah?"

"My key?"

Shit. He'd forgotten to even give it to her. He gave her a sheepish look and pulled it out of his pocket. His fingers brushed her palm as he placed the key in her hand, and it was all he could do not to grab hold of her and pull her close again. But he managed not to embarrass himself and once more turned to leave. This time, she didn't stop him.

Tonka wasn't sure why he'd offered to have Jasna hang out at The Refuge that summer. He definitely needed to talk to the guys about it, but he was relatively sure they wouldn't protest, not after hearing that Henley might not be able to have sessions with their guests if she didn't have reliable childcare.

As he drove back home, he was more sure than ever that he wanted both Henley and Jasna in his life. By some miracle, being around them drove out some of the demons in his head. It felt good to worry about something other than his past mistakes. To concentrate on solving Henley's problems. Was that a good basis for a relationship? He wasn't so sure.

All he knew for certain was what he felt when he was around them. He was *smiling* this morning...for absolutely no reason other than having seen them both. If that wasn't a sign, he didn't know what was.

It wouldn't be easy to break out of the melancholy that had taken over his life after he'd gotten out of the Coast Guard, but for the first time since Steel died, Tonka felt something other than guilt and sorrow weighing him down. Anticipation swam in his veins. An excitement that maybe, just maybe, he'd be able to put the past behind him eventually.

He'd never forget his partner, how Steel always had his back, but Tonka knew the way he was living his life wasn't any kind of testament to how brave and strong Steel had been.

He wanted to be a better person. Wanted to snap out of the funk he'd been in for years. Maybe Henley wasn't the woman he was meant to be with. Maybe she was just the push he needed to get out of his head and get on with living. Regardless, he had a feeling the McClures were put in his path for a reason.

He'd ignored the pull he'd had toward Henley for long enough. Once upon a time he hadn't been a coward, and he wanted to be that man again. *Henley* made him want to be that man.

* * *

Henley did her best to concentrate on her sessions that morning. She felt as if her brain was going to explode with all that she had going on. Stress about her childcare situation, worry for Mrs. Singleton, gratitude for her boss's understanding about being late that morning...and of course, confusion over Finn's sudden interest in her life.

It was a lot. And Henley wanted nothing more than to go home and sleep. But she couldn't. She had a ton on her plate, and she had no time to sit and take a moment for herself.

After her last session, she stuck her head into her boss's office. Mike Mackey was in his early fifties, had lived in Los Alamos all his life and never married. He'd started his practice twenty-five years ago, and Henley was so grateful to him for hiring her on when he did. She'd been new in town, with a five-year-old in tow and desperately in need of a job. It had been stupid to move to the mountain town without securing work first, but she'd needed to get out of the city. She didn't want Jasna to grow up surrounded by a concrete jungle. She wanted her to have an appreciation for Mother Nature.

"Henley!" Mike said when he saw her. "Come in, come in."

"Is everything okay?" Henley asked immediately. Mike had asked her to come talk to him before she left to head to The Refuge. The last thing she needed was more stress piled on top of her shoulders.

"Yes. Well, mostly yes. Sit and let's talk."

Mentally shoring up her shields, Henley gingerly sat on the edge of the chair in front of his desk.

"You doing okay?" he asked.

Henley smiled and shrugged. "Yeah. Sorry again about this morning. My neighbor had a stroke and went into the hospital."

"Cheri?"

It sounded weird to hear Mrs. Singleton being called by her first name. For as long as Henley had known her, she'd called her by her surname. "Yeah."

"Darn. Will she be all right?" Mike asked.

"From what I understand, yes. But she'll be moving to Albuquerque to be closer to her daughter."

"Ah...and there goes your childcare," Mike said sympathetically.

"Yup."

"Well, I'm sure you'll find something."

Henley simply smiled. She didn't blame her boss for being a little unconcerned. He'd never had to worry about childcare, since he wasn't married and didn't have kids.

"Anyway, I wanted to talk to you about Christian Dekker."

Henley immediately frowned. It wasn't as if she didn't know who Mike was talking about. Of course she did. She was just confused about why he was bringing him up to *her*. Yes, she'd been the boy's therapist a few years ago, but it hadn't gone well.

Well, that wasn't exactly true. She'd thought things were going well at first, but eventually she realized the boy was purposely manipulating her—and trying to scare her.

Henley firmly believed in the innate goodness of people. But the twelve-year-old boy she'd known had seriously dented those beliefs for a time. His parents had been beside themselves and didn't know what to do with him. Nothing they'd done on their own had been able to curb his destructive and dangerous behavior. They'd been at the end of their rope, and had even admitted to being scared of their own son.

Henley had thought she'd be able to help. That she could get to the root of what was driving the boy and help him work through it. But as it turned out, she hadn't been able to discover anything traumatic in his past. No difficulties with anyone at school—students or staff. No particular triggers that caused him to lash out. She'd even had a session with his younger sister, who swore their parents had always been loving and fair.

In the end, after many months, her professional opinion was that Christian Dekker was a danger to society, his family...basically to anyone he met.

It wasn't a decision she'd come to lightly. No one wanted to believe a child was too far gone for help. But after sitting across from the boy week after week, and seeing little beyond cold calculation in his gaze, Henley had finally gone to Mike and admitted she was making no headway. Told him she thought it would be worth it to see if Christian fared any better with a male therapist.

And while that was true…the additional truth of the matter was, Henley had been extremely uncomfortable with some of the things the boy had said. How he fantasized about hurting and violating his teacher, his sister… even his mom. He calmly and without emotion told her how he'd tried to burn down the shed behind his house, how he'd scraped the remains of a coyote off the road to examine it, and that one of his favorite things was finding the mice that had gotten stuck to the glue traps in their garage and bashing their heads in.

Pulling herself out of her thoughts, she realized Mike was staring at her, waiting patiently. She belatedly asked, "What about him?"

"You know that he stopped being a client here a couple of years ago." He waited for Henley to nod before he continued. "Well, his mother called. Said he's now even worse than he used to be. She begged me to come to the house to talk to him, but I told her that I honestly didn't think it would do any good."

Henley pressed her lips together and nodded again. "They're stuck between a rock and a hard place. Since he's a minor, they don't want to kick him out of the house, but they're also scared to death of what he might do. There aren't any private schools they can send him to, not with his grades and his records, and for some reason, they were reluctant to send him to an inpatient facility. So far, he hasn't been caught doing anything illegal that would send him to juvie," Henley mused.

"Exactly. All I could do was sympathize with her and wish her the best. But, Henley...that's not why I'm talking to you this morning."

She looked across the desk at Mike, nodding for him to continue.

"I wanted to warn you."

"Warn me? About what?"

Mike sighed heavily. "His mom found a notebook in Christian's room. She told me she goes in there when she's sure he's out of the house. She doesn't even know what she's looking for, or what she'd do if she found anything alarming, like weapons or something, but she said she couldn't live with herself if she didn't call me after she'd found the notebook."

Henley steeled herself.

"There was a list of names inside, under the heading 'People Who Have to Die.' There were twenty names—hers, her daughter's, her husband's, teachers, and neighbors. Even the girl who used to babysit him when he was five, who moved to New York a decade ago." Mike paused before adding, "And our names were on the list too."

Henley stiffened, although if she was honest with herself, she wasn't exactly surprised. The boy she'd counseled had been manipulative, angry, and downright mean. And when he'd been shifted to Mike's caseload, he glared daggers at her every time he'd seen her in the hall at work.

The sheer...*evilness* Henley had seen in his gaze unsettled her. She hadn't been upset the day Mike told her that he'd quit coming to his therapy sessions.

That had been over two years ago. It was a little hard to believe he'd been holding a grudge against them all this time. Then again, it really wasn't. There was something seriously wrong with the young man. It devastated her that she and Mike hadn't been able to help him...but she honestly wasn't sure *anyone* could.

She'd never believed some people were just born evil, but after meeting Christian, she'd changed her mind.

"I just wanted to make sure you were aware," Mike went on.

"When did he write the list?" Henley asked.

"His mom's not sure, but she guesses it was a while ago. All the pages after that were also filled in...with random ramblings, drawings, poems about death."

"What are you thinking?" Henley asked. She'd always respected Mike's levelheaded approach to life. He didn't get riled up about much. Tended to take one day at a time. He always said that he did his best not to stress about anything he couldn't do something about. It seemed like a good life motto.

"I'm planning on being a little more aware of my surroundings, but I'm not too worried. Teenagers are always a little hotheaded. They get riled up easily, but most of the time it fizzles out."

It was the "most of the time" part that Henley worried about. And Christian Dekker wasn't like most teenagers. Mike knew that, but she nodded anyway.

"Just watch yourself," he told her. "If anything seems off, take note and do what you need to do in order to protect yourself. And Jasna."

"Wait—was my daughter's name on the list?" Henley asked, her spine going rigid.

"No."

She sighed in relief.

"But you should be aware, just in case."

Henley nodded. "I appreciate you telling me."

"Of course. You've always been like a daughter to me."

She rolled her eyes. "I'm a little old to be your kid," she teased.

"Not really. Sixteen-year-olds have children all the time," he said with a wink.

Henley chuckled.

"Anyway, you headed to The Refuge this afternoon?"

"Yeah. I'm going to go see Mrs. Singleton at the hospital first, then I'll head up there and run a group session before coming back and meeting Jasna at home."

"All right, I'll let you get going then. Take care of yourself, Henley. You're too important to me, as an employee and a friend, for anything to happen to you."

"I will. And same goes to you."

Mike stood and Henley followed suit. To her surprise, he walked around the desk and gave her a quick hug. In all the time she'd known him, he'd never spontaneously hugged her. He was obviously a little more worried about Christian than he'd let on, but she did her best to push her concerns aside.

"See you tomorrow."

Henley nodded and headed back to her office to grab her stuff. As she walked out to her car, she took the time to study her surroundings. Everything was quiet. No one seemed to be lurking in the shadows, and since the parking lot was right next to the building and next to one of the main roads going through Los Alamos, there weren't any trees for anyone to hide behind while waiting to jump out and grab unsuspecting women.

Feeling better once she was in her car with the doors locked, Henley headed for the hospital. She needed to see

Mrs. Singleton for herself to make sure she really was going to be all right.

Then she shivered a bit as she thought about heading back out to The Refuge. She'd been going out there for years now, but for some reason, today she felt a little more excited. Things between her and Finn were changing... hopefully for the better. Even though he'd seemed a little standoffish when he'd left her apartment that morning, her mind replayed over and over how tightly he'd held her in his arms...and she hadn't missed the way he'd looked at her.

She'd seen something in that gaze. Something that hadn't been there even a week ago. A certain determination...and keen awareness of her as a woman.

Yes, something had definitely changed. She wasn't sure what, but she was thrilled. Now she just prayed she wouldn't do anything to mess it up.

CHAPTER FIVE

Tonka had been watching for Henley for at least an hour now. He'd wanted to text her and ask if she was all right. If her car was giving her any issues. To find out when she'd arrive. But he also didn't want to be a creeper. He had to play things cool. He couldn't go from basically ignoring her to wanting to know where she was every minute of the day.

After his morning chores, Tonka found himself doing something he rarely did...going up to the lodge for lunch.

"Tonka! Hi," Alaska said when he entered.

His lips twitched over the surprise she'd tried to hide when she saw him. "Hey."

"Is anything wrong? Is it Melba? Have the goats eaten someone's shoes they left outside their cabin again?"

"No, everything's fine. I just thought I'd come up and grab some lunch...and maybe have a word with Brick and the others, if they're around."

She stared at him in surprise for a moment before recovering and gesturing toward the other side of the huge open space. "Drake and Owl are already at a table, eating and chatting with some guests. I think Stone and Tiny will be up later, and Spike and Pipe are on a hike with a few other guests. They went out to Table Rock and, if everyone's up to it, they're planning on continuing to Sitting Rock."

Since Henley hadn't arrived yet, it was a perfect time to talk to Brick about her daughter spending some time at The Refuge that summer.

"Cool. You good? Need anything?" Tonka asked.

Now Alaska stared at him with an incredulous expression.

"What?" he asked.

"I just...nothing."

Tonka sighed. He knew he barely spent any time in the lodge, but still, he hated that his being here was such an anomaly that it rendered Alaska nearly speechless. He made a mental note to try to be a little more social. He smiled at Brick's woman before heading for the dining area.

There were four guests seated at the table, eating with Brick and Owl. Robert, their chef, followed behind Tonka, holding another tray of candied bacon, which was one of the favorites of the guests.

He snagged a piece as the man walked by and chuckled at the scowl Robert shot him.

"Sorry," Tonka said, not sorry at all. "One of the best things we've ever done is hire your daughter as your assistant. She put this on the menu, right?" he asked, holding up the piece of bacon.

At the mention of Luna, Robert grinned. "If I'd known how easy it was to make you boys and the guests happy, I would've put these on the menu way before now."

Luna hadn't been working at The Refuge for long, just a couple weeks, but she was already proving to be a great addition. She worked mostly part time in the mornings with her dad, before heading back to town to attend classes at the University of New Mexico-Los Alamos. She was earning her Associates Degree, and had already decided she'd continue her schooling to get her four-year degree. When her schedule allowed, she sometimes came back out to help Robert prepare dinner.

She was a beautiful young woman. In fact, with her long brown hair, prominent cheekbones, and long natural lashes framing dark brown eyes, she could easily be a model. But she had no interest in her looks—or men, much to Robert's relief. She was focused on helping her father and continuing her studies.

Tonka headed to the buffet and assembled a hamburger, then piled some potato salad, fruit, and some more of the candied bacon onto his plate before pulling out the empty chair next to Brick.

"Hey, everything good at the barn?" his friend asked with a raised brow.

"Yup. Thought I'd come up and grab some lunch," Tonka said.

"And?" Brick asked after a long pause.

"Can't I just come up here to eat?" he asked, stuffing another piece of bacon into his mouth. He had no idea how Luna made the stuff, but it was literally irresistible.

"Of course. But since you hardly ever eat with us, I'm naturally wondering what *other* reason you might have to visit," Brick said reasonably.

"I might have something I want to discuss with you and the other guys," Tonka admitted after a beat.

"Of course. Stone and Tiny should be here soon. They're giving our new housekeeper a tour of the place before leaving her with Carly and Jess to teach her the ropes."

"We have a new housekeeper?" Tonka asked.

Brick smirked. "This is why you should come up and hang out at the lodge more often. Yes. Alexis quit because some great-uncle or something died and left her some money. She moved back home to Georgia."

Tonka nodded. "Cool."

"Yeah, but we needed to replace her quickly. Alaska put up an ad and we interviewed applicants yesterday. Ryan was clearly the best choice. Today's her first day. Anyway, when they get here, we can talk...unless you want to wait for Spike and Pipe to get back from their hike?"

Tonka shook his head. "I can talk to them later."

"All right." Then Brick turned to the guests and said, "You might remember, but this is Tonka. He's in charge of all the animals here at The Refuge."

Tonka did his best to curb his impatience as he made small talk with the guests for the next ten minutes or so. When he finished his meal, he stood, and Brick told everyone he, Tonka, and Owl needed to get some work done, bidding them a good day before leading the way to a conference room.

He didn't miss the way Brick immediately sought out Alaska as they made their way across the lodge, as if wanting to make sure all was well with her. They smiled at each other, and even though he didn't detour over to the desk, it seemed as if they had a whole secret conversation from across the room.

He was happy for his friend. Alaska was perfect for him, and vice versa. Not to mention, she'd been a huge help at The Refuge too, taking over the administrative duties.

The three men walked into a small conference room, where Owl leaned against the table. "Do we need to sit for this?" he asked.

Tonka shook his head. "No, I'll be quick. It's about Henley."

Owl straightened. "Is she all right?"

"Yes," Tonka reassured him, torn between being pleased at his friend's concern...and somewhat worried that Owl might be reacting the way he was because he *also* had deeper feelings for her.

"It's her daughter. Well, I mean, sort of. She's fine. Jasna, that is..." Tonka sighed in frustration. He wasn't explaining this well at all.

To his relief, Brick just grinned. "Take a breath, Tonka."

"Right. So, we didn't even know Henley had a daughter. She didn't tell us about her until recently. And apparently her neighbor's been helping with childcare, but the woman had a stroke yesterday and will be moving to Albuquerque to be closer to family. With summer coming up, that leaves Henley without anyone to watch Jasna. So...I told her that she could bring her here.

"You guys don't have to worry about her," he continued quickly. "I'll make sure she doesn't get into any trouble, and when we have guests who've marked kids as a trigger on their intake form, I'll keep her away from them. I'm afraid if Henley doesn't figure out something affordable, we'll lose her. And she's too valuable to The Refuge and to our guests."

Tonka knew he was talking too fast, but he didn't want to give either of his friends a chance to protest. This was important.

"And I watched her yesterday—Jasna, that is—and she was great. I mean, she was sick, so she slept for a lot of the afternoon, but still. Before that, when she was awake, she was polite and courteous and super-interested in the animals. I'm sure I can keep her busy when she's here. And Henley says she's pretty self-entertaining. She likes to read and stuff, so I don't think she'd get in trouble."

Brick outright laughed now, and held up a hand. "Easy, dude. We aren't disagreeing."

Tonka stared at his friends, practically holding his breath.

"I think it's a great idea," Owl said with a shrug. "There're plenty of things around here to keep her busy. She could go on hikes with guests, or even shadow the employees if she wants to learn what they do—providing they're amenable. She could help with the housekeeping, although I'm guessing that probably won't be her favorite. Help you out in the barn or hang with Robert and Luna in the kitchen. I bet Hudson wouldn't mind her tagging along while he does the landscaping, and if she's interested, Jason could show her some of the simplest maintenance tasks."

"Alaska would love to show her some of the admin stuff she's doing. And while Savannah's accounting work might not be as exciting for a kid, I'm sure she also wouldn't mind letting her help, as well," Brick said.

Tonka let out the breath he'd been holding. "Thanks, guys."

"No need to thank us," Brick said with a shake of his head. "Henley's one of us, and if she needs help with her daughter, we're more than willing to step up. I'm still a little upset she didn't even tell us that she *had* a kid. We could've been helping her long before now."

Tonka agreed with his friend on that one. "I don't know what the schedule will be for her summer, or how often she'll be here. I think Henley said something about some camps she might sign Jasna up for as well, but I'll find out for sure. And school's not out for another week."

Owl nodded. "We'll figure it out." He turned speculative eyes to Brick. "Besides, I think it would be good to have kids around...you know...in preparation."

Brick rolled his eyes. "Alaska and I aren't planning on popping out babies tomorrow, Owl."

"I know, but eventually you might."

Brick just grinned.

"On that note, I'm out of here," Tonka said. "Henley should be here soon. She was going to go to the hospital to visit her neighbor then head this way. I'll let her know that Jasna's welcome to be here while she's working. That we'll keep our eye on her."

"If she can swing it, it really *would* be helpful if she could let us know ahead of time when she'll be here," Brick said. "Like you said, so we can keep our eye on anyone who might be triggered by children and make plans for both Jasna and the guests."

"Of course. I'll be sure she reaches out to both Alaska and myself with her schedule. We'll stay on top of it," Tonka said.

Brick nodded. "I think this is a good idea, Tonka. I personally like the idea of having kids around here. I mean, not screaming their heads off and running amuck, but you know."

Tonka nodded. He really *didn't* know, as he hadn't been around children much. But Jasna seemed pretty mellow. He didn't think she was the running-around-screaming type. Then again, he'd only been around her when she was sick. He could be wrong.

"She seems really interested in Melba and the other animals, so I'm thinking, at least to start, she'll probably be sticking pretty close to the barn," he told his friends.

"Sounds good. And, Tonka?" Brick added.

"Yeah?"

"It was great to have you at lunch. You're a huge part of our team, and it'd be nice to hang out with you more."

Tonka nodded. "I'll do my best."

"We haven't pressed, and we still won't. But if you ever want to talk about anything...we're here," Owl added.

Tonka had always been close-lipped about his personal demons. But perhaps it was time to loosen the iron hold he had on his past. If he couldn't trust these men, he figured there were few people he *could* trust.

Although, he wasn't the only one with pretty high shields around his emotions. Owl was a Night Stalker, one of the Army's elite helicopter pilots, when his chopper was shot down and he'd been taken captive. Stone was Owl's copilot, and the two men were held for several weeks before they'd been rescued. The experience had damaged them both. Neither of them were inclined to share the details of what they'd endured.

The Refuge had given them a chance to start over. To

conquer their demons...or at least drive them to the back of their minds. Tonka knew better than anyone that the bad memories never truly went away. They were always there, waiting to come into the light and fuck up a perfectly good day.

"I know...and I'm not ready," Tonka admitted to his friends. "But I'm trying to get there."

Both men nodded, and Brick clapped him on the shoulder. "It's progress," he said sincerely.

And it was. A year ago, Tonka wouldn't even have contemplated telling anyone about what he'd been through. For one, he didn't want to put it into words, reliving that day by actually talking about it. And for another, he was still processing everything that had happened, even though it had been years ago.

No one could understand the emotional agony that day had imprinted on his psyche. Even his close friend Raiden Walker, who'd been there with him, couldn't relate. He'd been unconscious throughout most of the horror. Yes, he'd lost his canine partner too...but Raiden hadn't seen what Tonka had.

No. He didn't think anyone would ever fully understand...but that didn't mean they weren't willing to listen.

Realizing he was getting sucked down into the past, Tonka did his best to turn his mind to something else. Something better. Henley would be here soon, and he'd get to tell her that Jasna could hang out at the resort this summer.

Of course, Tonka still needed to get the okay from the others, but he didn't think they'd have a problem with Henley's daughter being around.

They walked out of the conference room, and he

wasn't surprised when Brick went straight to Alaska. He watched as his friend put his hand on her cheek, leaned over, and gave her a kiss. He straightened a bit, but didn't drop his hand. He couldn't hear what they were saying, but it was more than obvious the two were madly in love.

Tonka didn't really understand that kind of connection. He loved his parents, sure, and he cared a hell of a lot about his friends...but deeply emotional love, the need to be near someone constantly, the innate urge to put your hands on them pretty much at all times, just to make sure they were all right...that wasn't something he'd experienced with another person.

However, he more than understood that kind of emotion when it came to animals. He would've done anything for Steel. Just as the dog would've done anything for him. Which was why what happened hurt so badly, even today.

Did he really *want* to feel that deeply for a woman? Losing his dog was difficult enough...

Shit. There he went again, getting sucked down into the pit of despair that had held him in its grasp for so long after that awful day.

To his relief, the front door to the lodge opened and around a dozen people entered. Spike and Pipe were in the lead—with whom Tonka assumed were the guests who'd been on the hike—followed by Stone and Tiny.

"Any food left?" Spike asked loudly.

The group all headed for the dining area, except for Tiny and a woman with shoulder-length black hair. Her head was on a swivel as she checked out the lodge. She obviously hadn't spent much time inside, if her wide-eyed reaction was any indication.

"Ryan," Alaska called as she scooted out from behind the desk and headed for the woman. "How was the tour? I hope Stone and Tiny behaved themselves. You aren't ready to quit, are you?" she joked.

The woman chuckled. "No way. This place is awesome! The cabins are adorable. And we didn't have time to go to the barn, but I can't wait to meet Melba."

Alaska laughed. "Yeah, she's a huge hit around here, for sure. Speaking of, this is Tonka. He takes care of all the animals."

He nodded in greeting, and Ryan offered an easy smile.

"Did you get to meet Carly and Jess?" Alaska asked the woman.

"Briefly, yes. They seem really nice."

"They are." Alaska looked at Tiny, as if just realizing he was still standing there. "What are you doing? Shoo," she told him. "Go eat. Or flirt with the ladies. You know you're the pretty one of the bunch."

Tiny rolled his eyes, then turned to Ryan. "As I said earlier, if you need anything, one of us is always around. I'm sure Jess and Carly will mention it, but once you get any rooms ready for incoming guests each day, you can take a break and grab some food. If the buffet's been cleaned up, just head into the kitchen. Robert or Luna will be happy to make something, or you can grab food on your own. Unlike most chefs, Robert's not territorial at all. Just be sure to clean up whatever mess you make."

Ryan nodded. "Thanks for the tour. Will you thank Stone for me too?"

"Will do. It's nice to meet you. Welcome to The Refuge family."

Tonka noticed a subtle pensive look cross the newcomer's face before she masked it and nodded. But any other observation he might've had about Ryan's reaction to Tiny ended when the door behind her opened—and Henley stepped inside.

"Was there a party I didn't get an invitation for?" she joked when she saw so many people standing just inside the door.

Alaska laughed. "Nope. The guys just got back from a hike with some of the guests, and Stone and Tiny were giving Ryan a tour of the place. Ryan, this is Henley. Henley, Ryan. Ryan's our new housekeeper."

"Oh! It's good to meet you," Henley said warmly, holding out her hand to the other woman.

"Same," Ryan said with a smile.

"Henley's our psychologist. She works mostly in the afternoons, and meets with our guests if and when they need it."

"Cool," Ryan said, not seeming weirded out in the least to be working in a place where the guests needed therapy while they were on vacation. But then again, she had to have done her homework on The Refuge before applying for the job, so it wasn't as if she wouldn't know what their mission was or why people came here.

"I'm gonna go have a word with the guys who just got back," Brick told Tonka meaningfully. "If you want to chat with Henley...?"

Tonka nodded, and because he hadn't taken his gaze from Henley, he saw the way she frowned and looked between him and Brick.

"A chat? Am I in trouble?" She smiled, but the concern was easy to hear even though she tried to hide it.

"No," Tonka said. "It was nice to meet you, Ryan," he

said a little belatedly, then held out his hand to Henley while gesturing to the conference room he'd just vacated. It took everything he had not to put his hand on the small of her back when she passed him, but Tonka didn't think that would be very professional, especially in front of the others.

He followed her into the room and shut the door. As soon as it closed behind them, Henley turned. Her back was straight and her expression concerned as she asked, "What's wrong, Finn?"

"Nothing's wrong," he told her. Not wanting her to stress a moment longer, he laid it out. "I talked to the guys, and they're fine with Jasna being here this summer when you don't have anyone to watch her. She can hang with me in the barn, and maybe even shadow the other employees. I forgot to talk to the guys about it, but if she finds she enjoys doing something in particular, I was serious about paying her for the work she does while she's here. Not a lot, since we can't hire her officially, but enough to make it seem cool to be hanging out with the housekeepers and vacuuming floors and stuff."

"I...I didn't think you were going to ask them *today*," Henley said.

"Why not?"

"Well, we just had the conversation about my childcare situation this morning."

"And?"

"I don't know. I just didn't think you'd immediately come back here and ask the guys about it."

"Well...here's the thing." Tonka ran a hand through his hair. "School's out really soon, and I...I *like* you, Henley." She looked surprised by his words, but he forged on. "I know I haven't shown it very well, but I do. And even though I just met your daughter yesterday, I like her too. You're a big part of what makes The Refuge special, and you know as well as I do that summer is busy for us. Losing you for a few months would suck. So..." He shrugged. "Me helping to solve your childcare issues is a win for everyone."

Tonka had kept his gaze on Henley while he was speaking, and he loved the small smile on her face when he'd first started...but by the time he was done, she was frowning slightly.

"Yeah, that makes sense. I wouldn't want The Refuge to lose any business if I wasn't here. Not that I couldn't be replaced. I mean, I could probably ask Mike, my boss, if he could talk to the other therapists in our practice and see if they wanted to work here this summer."

Tonka realized that she'd taken what he said the wrong way. Just like she had last night.

Henley had her head down, looking lost in thought, and he took a step toward her, putting his finger under her chin and forcing her to meet his gaze.

"That came out wrong," he said quietly, hardly believing he was touching her beautiful face. Her skin was smooth and warm, and it took everything in him not to cup the back of her neck and pull her closer. An image of Brick standing close to Alaska and kissing her popped into his mind, but he pushed it away. "What I *meant* to say was...I don't think I could go all summer without seeing you."

"Oh," Henley said softly, staring at him with wide eyes.

"Yeah. Oh." He frowned slightly. "Another reason why I stick to hanging out with the critters is because I'm not that good with words," Tonka told her. He hadn't dropped his hand, but she didn't seem to mind, so he kept his finger where it was.

"I think your words are pretty darn good," she replied.

Tonka stared down at her for a long moment. Should he kiss her? Did she want him to? Lord knew he wanted to lean down and see if her lips tasted as good as they looked. But he wasn't sure this was the time or the place. "I never did thank you."

She frowned. "For what?"

"When that guy came here looking for Alaska. I kind of lost it on you...and you helped. A lot. You didn't push me to talk, you were just there. I appreciate it."

Her eyes got soft. "You're welcome. Finn?"

"Yeah?"

Henley licked her lips, and Tonka barely held back the groan that threatened to escape his lips.

"I like you too."

Her voice was soft and low, and when she reached up and wrapped her fingers around his wrist, Tonka's resolve not to kiss her was seriously tested.

"Are we...doing this?" she asked before he could respond.

"This?" he asked.

She blushed, and Tonka thought it was adorable. They were grown adults, and yet somehow it felt as if he was a teenager fumbling his way through his first relationship all over again.

"Yeah. You like me, I like you..."

He smiled. It still felt rusty, but good. "Yeah. We're doing this," he told her. Then blurted, "You want to go to dinner with me sometime?"

She returned his smile. "Yes. Is it okay if Jasna comes?"

"Of course. I want to get to know her too. But I'm thinking there may be times when I wouldn't mind if it was just the two of us, as well."

Henley nodded. "I have to admit...I was beginning to think this would never happen. I mean, I've kind of liked you for a long while now. But I wasn't sure how you felt."

"I liked you too. But I wasn't in a headspace where I could do anything about it."

"And now you are?"

It was a fair question. Tonka nodded. "After what happened to Brick and Alaska, I kind of realized that I was letting the assholes in my past win. I'm not saying I'll ever be normal. I'm broken, Henley. And I know it. But I got mad. Angry that even though the man who caused my pain is rotting behind bars, I'm kind of rotting right along with him."

"I don't know what happened, and you don't have to tell me. I mean, I *want* you to, but I understand if you can't. But, Finn, you aren't rotting. Not by any stretch. You're an integral part of The Refuge. You're doing something that none of your friends can. Taking care of the animals is what you were born to do. Anyone who sees you with Melba and the goats, and *all* the other animals here, knows it. Our pasts shape who we are today, and while I hate that you obviously went through something awful, the man standing in front of me is anything but broken."

Her words were a balm to his soul. "There you go, being all psychologist-y on me," he said with another small smile.

Henley shrugged. "Hazard of dating a therapist. Does it bother you?"

"Honestly?"

"Always."

"A little. It's partly why I haven't let you know how attracted I am to you. But that night in the barn...it helped me understand that you'd never force me to talk about anything I don't want to. And maybe you knowing there's this huge thing in my past that I can't talk about will make me *want* to talk about it. Eventually."

Henley let go of his wrist and placed her palm on his cheek, and Tonka immediately tilted his head slightly, giving her some of his weight. Her touch felt so good. Grounded him. The last time he'd felt this at ease was when Steel was still alive, and he'd snuggled with his snoozing dog on the couch while he watched TV.

"Do I want you to tell me what happened to you? I won't lie. Yes. But do I *need* you to tell me in order to like you? To want to go out with you? To want to get to know you better? Absolutely not. We don't have to figure everything out right this second. Knowing you feel the same attraction is enough for today. We'll take the future one day at a time. Okay?"

Tonka nodded, loving how her palm stroked the short beard on his face.

"Thank you for talking to the others about Jasna. I promise I won't take advantage of all your generosity. And if things don't work out, if my daughter is more trouble than anyone is ready for, we can reassess."

"Henley, she's twelve. How much trouble can she get into?"

She laughed and dropped her hand. Tonka figured that was his cue to step away from her, but he hadn't expected it to be so difficult.

"She's almost a teenager, Finn. She's hormonal, and while we have a good relationship right now, I fully expect her to enter the 'my mom's an idiot' phase at any time."

Tonka shook his head. "Not gonna happen."

Henley simply shook her head. "Just promise that if things get weird, and it becomes more work to have her here than you expected, you'll let me know."

"I will," Tonka replied, but he had no doubt that Jasna would be just fine.

"Okay. I should probably get ready for my session so I can get back before Jasna gets home from school."

The thought of her leaving made Tonka frown, but he nodded anyway.

"Are you going to sit in on the group session today?" Henley asked.

He reluctantly shook his head. "There's stuff I need to get done down at the barn. But I'd like to see you before you leave...if that's okay?"

"That's okay," Henley reassured him with a smile. "I'll wander down to find you when I'm done."

And just like that, Tonka felt better. Knowing he'd get to see her again was enough to lift his mood. "All right. Have a good session. And if anyone gets too worked up, give one of us a yell."

Henley rolled her eyes. "I know the procedure. And everyone will be fine. How many times have the guests gotten out of control since I've been working here?"

Tonka shrugged. "Never."

"Exactly," Henley said with a laugh.

"But I'm thinking that's partly because I've made it a point to sit in on the sessions with some of the more...*wounded*...guests," Tonka told her.

Henley stared at him. "That's why?"

He nodded.

"I wondered."

"They all fill out a questionnaire before they arrive. We ask them to be honest about their triggers and their state of mind. When we have guests who've admitted they're struggling and have anger issues, I've made it a point to be there during the group sessions."

"I...I didn't know."

Tonka shrugged. "It might have taken me a long time to get up the courage to admit my attraction. That doesn't mean I haven't been trying to watch over you. And now that I've said it out loud, it sounds kind of creepy."

"It doesn't," Henley said immediately. "It's...nice." She smiled up at him.

"Right. So...I'll see you later then," Tonka said, uncomfortable with the emotions rolling inside him. He'd been going through life in a haze for so long, it was tough to deal with all the feelings he was having at the moment.

"Okay," Henley said.

Tonka backed up toward the door, not wanting to take his eyes from her until he absolutely had to. When he bumped into the door, she chuckled, and Tonka couldn't help but return her smile.

He reached for the doorknob and walked back into the great room of the lodge. Giving Alaska a chin lift, he headed for the back door, his steps feeling lighter than they had in a very long time.

CHAPTER SIX

Two weeks later, Henley sat in her CRV with Jasna in the back seat as they headed to The Refuge. This was Jasna's first day at the retreat—and Henley was full of warnings.

"Don't be a pest," she told her daughter. "If someone is busy or looks like they don't have time to answer your questions, leave them for another day."

"I will, Mom."

"And do your best to stay out of the way of the guests. We've talked about this, and while you're not a crazy kid, some of them have been through things that make seeing children hard."

"I know."

"And make sure you do what you're told," Henley said.

"Enough, Mom. I'm not going to be a hoodlum running around with a can of spray paint and yelling at the top of my lungs. It's going to be fine."

Henley chuckled. She had no idea where Jasna got these things.

Another school year was done and her daughter was

officially a middle schooler. Well, would be once school started again in the fall. She'd be going to Los Alamos Middle School as a seventh grader and Henley wasn't prepared. Not at all.

She remembered middle school being hell when she was her daughter's age. But then again, she'd still been dealing with the trauma of what happened to her mom, still unable to speak to anyone, *and* attempting to navigate the tricky hormonal waters of her pre-teens.

Henley was waiting for her daughter to enter the emotional seventh-grade-girl phase, but until then, she was still her sweet little girl. More interested in books and reading than in boys or her looks. Henley didn't know if it would last, but she hoped so, at least for a little longer.

"Finn's gonna be there, right?" Jasna asked.

Her daughter hadn't seen him since the morning he'd come to their apartment to return Henley's keys, but she'd asked about him every day. Wanting to know about Melba and the other animals and what was going on at The Refuge. When Henley informed her that she'd be spending a lot of her summer at the retreat, the girl had been overjoyed.

Now, Henley couldn't keep the smile off her face. "Yes," she told her daughter.

Every time she thought about Finn, she smiled. She'd gone from almost never seeing the man, to having him around all the time. When she arrived, he made a point to come up to the lodge to say good morning. He sat in on most of her group sessions. He still didn't participate, but he was there. Having his gaze locked on her was a little unnerving, but she couldn't deny she liked his attention.

He'd invited her to hang out in the barn with him on

the days she didn't need to get back to Los Alamos right away to meet Jasna when she got out of school, and once they'd even gone on a short hike together. Henley had wanted to see Table Rock since she'd first started working at The Refuge, but between her work schedule and wanting to be there when Jasna got home from school, hadn't really found the time. So when Finn had somewhat shyly asked if she wanted to go for a walk, she was all for it. And to her surprise, they hadn't had any problems coming up with things to talk about.

If someone had told her a month ago that she'd not only be hiking through the woods with Finn Matlick, but that he'd be chattering away as if he didn't have a care in the world, she would've said they were crazy.

And she couldn't help but love that Finn was almost as excited about today as Jasna. Yesterday, he'd asked three times about her visit, making absolutely sure she wanted to hang out in the barn with him, rather than stay inside the lodge with Alaska.

His nervousness was endearing, and because he wanted to make such a good impression on her daughter, Henley was even more touched.

The truth of the matter was, even without them having done more than hold hands as they hiked through the woods, Finn was a better boyfriend than anyone Henley had ever gone out with. He was constantly checking on her, asking if she was hungry, or too hot or cold. He called briefly each night to ensure she'd arrived home safely after work. He asked about Jasna. He was protective, making sure nothing untoward happened in the group counseling sessions he attended. He brought her bottles of water before her sessions, and on the few occasions they'd eaten together, Finn ensured she had everything she needed before he relaxed enough to eat his own meal.

In short...so far, Henley hadn't seen anything that would make her not want to see where their attraction could lead. Finn might be struggling with his demons, but even with his tendency to shy away from people, and his penchant for getting lost in his head more than most, he was still one of the best men she'd ever met.

"I'm so excited to meet the new calf!" Jasna said, practically bouncing in her seat. "And you're sure Finn said I could actually name her?"

Henley smiled. "I'm sure."

"That's so cool! I've never named a cow before. I'm gonna have to watch her a while to make sure I pick a name that fits. And I can't wait to see the kittens either!"

Henley grinned as they neared The Refuge. Jasna had been looking forward to this day ever since Henley explained she'd be going to work with her anytime she wasn't at camp.

With Mike's permission, they'd spend their mornings at the psychology clinic while Henley saw patients, then head off to The Refuge. Jasna wasn't exactly a morning person, so the schedule should work out well. She could read and do other low-key activities in the morning while she hung out in the break room, occasionally visiting with Mike and the other psychologists, and in the afternoons, she would be well awake enough to enjoy more physical activities.

"Mom?" Jasna asked.

"Yeah, sweetie?"

"I love Mrs. Singleton, and I'm sorry that she got sick and moved...but this is gonna be the best summer *ever!*"

Henley chuckled. "I hope you think that after a few weeks and you don't get bored."

"Bored?" Jasna asked, her brows arching up comically. "No way! How could I be bored with all the animals, and learning the ropes of how everything works at The Refuge? When I told my friends what I was doing this summer, they were all totally jealous! Most of the popular girls are all googly-eyed over the hot owners—their words, not mine—but I think I'm more excited to get to spend so much time with Melba."

Henley burst out laughing at that. Leave it to her kid to be more excited to hang out with a cow than people. Come to think of it, she and Finn had more in common than they probably realized.

"Well, just remember that Finn and the other guys like their privacy, as do the guests. So don't be taking pictures of them without permission."

Jasna rolled her eyes. "I won't. Jeez. But I can take pictures of Melba and the other animals, right? And my cow I get to name?"

The smile on Henley's face hadn't faded. "Yes, I think that's probably fine. But you should ask Finn first."

"I will," Jasna said happily.

As she pulled onto the road leading to the lodge, Henley realized she hadn't been this relaxed in a very long time. Raising a kid on her own wasn't easy. She constantly worried about Jasna, and grateful to Finn and his friends for allowing her to bring her daughter with her to work this summer. She just hoped their enthusiasm for having Jasna around wouldn't wane as the weeks went by. While she was generally an easygoing kid, she had a tendency to ask a million questions. Not to mention she was a pre-teen. This wasn't the easiest time in a child's life.

As she parked the car, Henley opened her mouth to give Jasna one more warning about being polite and not getting in the way, but before she could say anything, her daughter had opened her door and was running toward the barn faster than Henley had seen her move in a long time.

After getting out of the car, Henley looked toward the barn and realized Finn was standing at the open doors. When he saw her looking in his direction, he gave a little wave, then turned and followed an excited Jasna into the barn.

She wanted to go down and join her daughter and Finn, but she had an individual session to get ready for. And later she was having another group session. Jasna was getting more and more independent and would be perfectly fine with Finn. So she took a deep breath and headed for the lodge.

Her cell made a pinging noise, notifying her of an incoming text message. She wasn't sure who would be texting, since her most frequent texts came from her daughter, and she'd literally just dropped her off. Henley stopped and rummaged through her purse for the phone. A warm and fuzzy feeling filled her when she saw who the message was from.

Finn: Hey. Don't worry about Jas, we'll be fine. If I can pry her away from the calf, I'll bring her up for some lunch after your first session

Finn: Sorry, hit enter too soon. By the way...you look nice today. The highlight of my day is seeing you arrive safe and sound.

. . .

Gah. This guy. Feeling as if she was on cloud nine, Henley headed into the lodge.

* * *

Tonka stood outside the stall where the new calf was resting and watched with a smile as Jasna babbled nonstop to the little animal. She'd been full of energy when she'd arrived, and it had been a long time since he'd seen anyone as excited as she'd been to work. She did everything he told her to, including muck out the goats' stalls, without complaint.

Tonka had no doubt the chores would get old and the pre-teen would prefer to just do the fun stuff, like feed the kittens and hang out with the animals as she was doing now, but he wouldn't care either way. And instead of feeling as if his domain had been invaded, it was nice to have someone there who seemed to love the animals as much as he did.

At the moment, Jasna was sitting in the straw with the calf's head in her lap. She was muttering to herself, trying out different names. Tonka had been notified about the calf when he'd been in town a few days ago. A rancher had asked if he might be interested in taking her because the mom had died, and he had no time to take care of a newborn. If Tonka didn't want her, he was going to sell her to the butcher.

Once he heard that, the decision was easy. The Refuge didn't need another cow, but there was no way Tonka could let the calf be sold for meat. He hadn't asked his friends if it was all right to bring in another animal, but to his relief, they didn't mind. There would come a time when The Refuge couldn't sustain any more rescued animals, especially since Tonka was the sole person responsible for their care, but for now, they were doing all right. There were other ranchers around the area who took in injured and neglected animals, and if needed, Tonka was fairly certain he could contact them and they'd agree to take in some of the rescues.

But for now, seeing Jasna bond with the calf made his heart swell. The girl had been too excited to stop for lunch, and Tonka hadn't pushed. She'd eat and sleep well tonight, of that he had no doubt. He also hadn't wanted to leave her alone in the barn, so Jasna not wanting to take a break meant Tonka hadn't either.

Which further meant, he hadn't gotten to see Henley. He'd sent a few texts, letting her know they wouldn't be up for lunch and not to worry, but it wasn't the same as seeing her in person.

"Scarlet Pimpernickel!" Jasna exclaimed softly from inside the stall.

Confused, Tonka looked down at her. "What?"

"Scarlet Pimpernickel," she repeated. "That's her name. Scarlet for short."

Tonka chuckled. "Sounds good."

Jasna beamed up at him.

"You okay here for a while?" Tonka asked. The need to see her mom was almost overwhelming. He felt more comfortable leaving Jasna alone for a short time, now that she'd been here for a few hours and everything wasn't so new.

"Of course."

"I'll be back in a bit. If the goats come in wanting dinner, don't give in. They know when they eat but they'll do their best to sucker you into feeding them early. If you get bored, you can always go check on Chuck and his lady. Make sure they've got lots of peanuts and walnuts."

Chuck was the squirrel he'd rescued. The poor thing was missing two feet and had nearly been starved to death. Of course Tonka had fed him, and now the little guy was pretty tame, living with his girlfriend in a squirrel condo Tonka had built for them behind the barn.

"Bored? Are you crazy?" Jasna asked with a completely befuddled look.

Tonka chuckled. "Right. If you need anything, I'll be up at the lodge."

The girl nodded, but her attention was already back on the calf, who looked perfectly content to lay right where she was for the rest of her life.

Giving the girl one last look, Tonka headed for the exit. With every step he took, butterflies swam in his belly. He felt as if he was thirteen and about to ask a girl out.

He waved at Carly, Jess, and Ryan, who were folding sheets in the maintenance building located next to one of the cabins. He was glad the new girl was working out, since there really was too much work for just two people. And it was even more of a relief that the three women were getting along. They worked hard taking care of the lodge, and getting the cabins cleaned and ready for new guests. The Refuge didn't offer daily housecleaning during a guest's stay. If they needed new towels or wanted a change of bedding or whatever, they could simply request it. But no cleaning during a visit sometimes meant a lot of work for the women after guests left.

With Alexis quitting, the cleaning of the lodge itself had been left to the guys, and they were all relieved when Ryan had been hired and took over that duty.

Looking around their vast property, Tonka smiled slightly, pride filling him. When Brick had invited him to invest and be a part of The Refuge, he'd accepted simply because he suspected if he didn't...he wouldn't be around much longer. Tonka had been struggling to get out of bed each day, and the sheer volume of work required to get the retreat up and running had taken his mind off the shit that had happened to him.

But now, as he walked toward the lodge, satisfaction settled deep. It hadn't been easy to make The Refuge what it was today. But he and his friends had relentlessly made it one of the premier places in the country for people suffering from PTSD to get away from real life for a while. Because of their tenacity, and the hard work of the people who worked side-by-side with them day in and day out, they'd prospered.

He pushed open the door to the lodge and inhaled deeply. The smell of Robert's delicious chocolate chip cookies permeated the entire building. Tonka's belly growled. He'd had a quick bowl of oatmeal in his cabin before heading to the barn for his morning chores, and since he'd skipped lunch, he was definitely ready to eat something.

But more than food, Tonka needed to see Henley. Wanted to lay eyes on her and make sure she was good. He wasn't sure why the need was always so strong, but he knew he wouldn't be able to settle until he'd seen for himself that she was safe.

He peeked into the conference room she used for her

sessions and saw her sitting in a chair in front of three of their guests. She was nodding at something one of them said. One of the many things Tonka liked about Henley was that when someone was talking, every ounce of her attention was on them. She never made anyone feel as if she was bored or in a hurry. She made them feel as if they were the most significant people in the world and what they were saying was important.

Tonka had seen a few different therapists right after everything had happened, but he hadn't trusted any of them. One man had interrupted him mid-sentence and informed him their time was up and he could pick up where they'd left off next time. There hadn't been a next time. Another woman was so frequently distracted by her cell phone sitting next to her on the desk, Tonka finally realized she hadn't even been listening to him.

A third therapist had actually told him that he shouldn't be taking what happened so hard, since no *people* had died.

Those were extreme examples. He knew that. Most psychologists and therapists weren't so bad, were genuinely interested in helping their clients. But his experiences had soured him on the whole therapy thing, and after those three, he'd decided he was done.

And then Henley had arrived at The Refuge.

It had taken him months to join one of her group sessions, and even then it was only because he didn't like how one of the guests had been acting, so he wanted to make sure Henley and the guests were safe as she conducted the session.

But as he'd sat in the room and listened to her talk, saw how concerned she was for her patients...how she empathized and truly listened...Tonka understood just how different she was from the therapists he'd been to in the past.

She didn't offer platitudes. Didn't tell anyone she understood when there was no way she could know what it felt like to have to shoot another human being in the head in order to survive. She was tough but nurturing at the same time. She gave the guests permission to be sad, angry, and even scared.

And she made herself vulnerable. Opened herself up by sharing her own traumatic experiences, again and again.

In short, if Tonka'd had a therapist like her right after his own life had blown up in his face, maybe he wouldn't be so messed up today.

He forced himself back to the present and watched Henley through the window in the door for another ten seconds or so, enough time to ensure all was well, before turning and heading for the kitchen.

By the time he'd made himself a roast beef sandwich, eaten some leftover green beans from lunch, scarfed three of Robert's cookies, then wandered back out to the lobby of the lodge, Henley's session had ended.

She was just saying goodbye to one of the guests when she saw him. The way her eyes lit up and she smiled made Tonka feel ten feet tall.

"Hey," he said as he walked toward her.

"Hi," she returned. "You don't seem too battered and bruised after spending a few hours with Jasna."

He chuckled. "She's actually been a huge help. And she and Scarlet Pimpernickel have really bonded."

"Who?" Henley asked with a laugh.

"That's what she named the calf."

"Oh, jeez. I'm sorry. Don't feel as if you have to keep that name," Henley said with an adorable wrinkle of her nose.

"I wouldn't dream of changing it. She thought about it long and hard, all afternoon. We'll call her Scarlet. I like it," Tonka said. "And," he added, lowering his voice, "I have to admit that thinking up names is definitely not my forte, so she did me a favor. You wouldn't believe how much crap I got about Melba's name."

Henley laughed. "You thought that up?"

"Uh-huh. Thought it was awesome until the rest of the guys tried to veto it. I didn't care, really, but it was the principle of the thing. I had to stick to my guns. And I know without a doubt none of the guys will give your *daughter* crap for the name she decided on. Win-win for me."

"Well, I appreciate it. She's been looking forward to today for two weeks."

"Did you get lunch?" Tonka asked, changing the subject.

"I did. I don't know what Robert and Luna did to those green beans, but I'm not usually a fan and I had two helpings."

Tonka was constantly amazed at the joy this woman found in the simplest things. He'd struggled for years just to get out of bed, and she was extolling the virtues of green beans. This was why he'd been drawn to her almost since they'd met. And why he couldn't stay away from her now.

"What? Why are you looking at me like that?" Henley asked, brushing a lock of hair behind her ear self-consciously.

"You're amazing," he blurted.

A blush turned her cheeks pink, making her even prettier in his eyes.

"You are," he insisted. "You've raised a wonderful daughter by yourself. You're an incredible therapist. And when I'm around you, I remember what it's like to laugh and be happy."

Stepping into his personal space, Henley put her hand on his chest. "There's a guy who writes parenting books I really like. I'm not going to get this quote exactly right, but hopefully it'll be close enough. He said that life is awesome. Then it's awful. Then it's great again. Between the awesome and the awful, it's ordinary and boring. We should enjoy the awesome, hold on through the awful, relax and breathe through the ordinary, and rejoice when it's great again.

"I've been through the awesome, and the horrible, and the ordinary. What I know is that I wouldn't give up the great to make the horrible disappear. We're shaped by the things we go through...and I'd go through *everything* I've experienced all over again if it meant I'd be where I am today. With a daughter who gives me a purpose, a job I love, and the friends I've made here at The Refuge."

Tonka couldn't stop himself from wrapping an arm around her waist and pulling her against him. "I'm going to kiss you," he informed her gruffly.

"It's about time," she said with a smile as she linked her fingers together at the small of his back.

A part of Tonka had been waiting for her to tell him it was too soon, or that she wasn't comfortable with moving their relationship to that level yet, but at her words, pressure in his chest that he wasn't even aware was there melted.

Moving slowly, determined to draw this moment out, Tonka lowered his head. His fingers pressed slightly into her back as he held her close. She went up on her tiptoes and lifted her chin.

His lips brushed against hers once. Twice. And on the third pass, he nibbled on her lower lip. Henley let out a small moan and leaned against him fully, giving him her body weight as she opened for him.

Tonka didn't hesitate, sweeping his tongue inside her eager mouth. She tasted of wintergreen, the mints she liked to suck on. He'd kissed his fair share of women in his life, but nothing affected him like kissing Henley. If pressed, he wouldn't be able to explain what it was about this kiss, about *her*, that was so different. It just was.

She didn't passively let him kiss her. She gave as good as she got. Their heads moved from side to side slowly as they learned each other's taste, what made each of them moan.

When he finally pulled back, Tonka felt as if his entire life had changed in the few minutes they'd been kissing. He stared down at her, at a loss for words.

"Wow," she said after a moment, licking her lips.

"Yeah, wow," Tonka repeated in a semi-daze.

Someone cleared their throat behind them, and Tonka moved without thought, spinning and pushing Henley behind him.

At seeing Alaska and Brick standing there, he relaxed.

Alaska giggled. "Sorry, we didn't mean to, um...interrupt, but I wanted to know if Henley might be interested in staying the night Saturday. We had a cancelation, and I thought it would be fun if Jasna and Henley got to partici-pate in the bonfire we're planning."

Tonka turned to look at Henley, whose eyes were wide as she glanced back.

"Is that okay?" she asked. "I mean, it wouldn't be an imposition? I wouldn't want to put extra work on Carly, Jess, or Ryan."

"It's not a problem at all," Brick answered before Tonka could. "I've been thinking for a while about letting our employees stay in the empty cabins when they're avail-able. As both a thank you, and as a way to try to instill more pride in what we're doing up here. We all know how much the land heals us, and I figure it would be the same for just about anyone. You're more than welcome to stay. I should warn you though. While Al said we're having a bonfire, in reality, it's just a normal-sized campfire. We don't want to light anything too big and risk it getting out of control," he finished with a grin.

"I can't remember the last time I sat around a fire and relaxed," Henley said.

"There will be marshmallows too. Can't have a fire without s'mores!" Alaska told her. "Please say yes. As much as I adore Drake and his friends, I'd love to hang out with a woman."

"I'd like that too," Henley said with a shy smile.

"Yay! Now...you two go back to what you were doing when we interrupted," Alaska said with a sly grin. "Just pretend we were never here. Although you should know, I saw a group of guests headed this way. I think they just got done with a hike and are probably looking for a snack."

Brick gave Tonka a chin lift as he led Alaska back toward the front door.

Hoping Henley wasn't embarrassed about being caught kissing, he turned back to her. He didn't see any discomfort on her face. Instead, she was smiling up at him. Her lips were a little plumper than they'd been before, and Tonka couldn't help but feel possessive about how they'd gotten that way.

"You okay?"

"Why wouldn't I be?" she asked with a small tilt of her head.

"I didn't really mean to do that here. Where someone could see us."

"I'm not embarrassed to be with you, Finn. It's probably no shock to Alaska or the rest of the guys that I'm attracted to you, and have been for a while. You're all super observant. And I have to say...that kiss?"

When she didn't continue, Tonka prompted, "Yeah?"

"*Anytime* you want to kiss me like that, no matter where we are or who's around, feel free. Okay, maybe not around Jasna just yet. She probably needs to get a little more used to the fact that her mom is dating."

Tonka had no idea how he'd gotten so lucky. This woman was made for him. He knew it down to his bones. He just hoped he was worthy enough to deserve her.

"Speaking of which, I should probably go and check on her," he said after a moment, doing his best to control his urge to pull Henley back into his arms and continue kissing her. "Not that I think anything is wrong, but you know, it's her first day."

"Care for some company?" Henley asked.

"*Your* company, yes," he reassured her.

But before they could sneak out a side door, the lodge was suddenly full of half a dozen guests, and when they saw Tonka, they decided seeing the new calf was more important than getting a snack.

Tonka did his best not to resent their intrusion on his time with Henley, instead reassuring himself that he'd have plenty of time to spend with her in the future. She was going to be around all summer, and she'd be there that weekend as well. He'd have a chance to hang out with her all night, not just in the stolen moments they found between work.

CHAPTER SEVEN

The rest of the week went by smoothly and before Henley knew it, it was Saturday. She and Jasna had packed a bag and were excited to spend the night at The Refuge. Jasna had been bouncing off the walls, more hyper than Henley had seen her in a long time, so after a quick stop at her office in town, they'd headed out to The Refuge earlier than planned.

Henley'd had a brief chat with Mike about a few of their clients. He frequently spent a few hours in his office on Saturday mornings, so it was a good time to bounce ideas off of him and get his advice on how best to help those who were struggling most. She was grateful for how supportive her boss was of her work out at The Refuge, as well. She was truly blessed to have a job she loved so much.

Mike had brought up Christian Dekker again, once more warning Henley to be aware of her surroundings at all times. He admitted that he had no idea how viable the threat against them was, but it would be careless to dismiss the concerns of the boy's mom.

Henley couldn't imagine how awful Mrs. Dekker must feel. How horrible it would be to have a child you were truly scared of. Christian was sixteen, outweighed most kids his age and was almost six feet tall. He apparently came and went from his home as he wanted, and ignored all the rules his parents had tried to put in place in an attempt to control him. He'd also dropped out of school mid-year, and basically hung around town all day, making everyone he came into contact with nervous. His mom had mentioned he had some sort of fort in the woods behind their house, where he spent a lot of his time, but she had no idea what he did out there.

Henley had tried to help the boy, but she simply hadn't made any kind of connection that allowed her to find out why he was so angry with the world. He stopped letting her in fairly early in their sessions, spending most of his time attempting to mess with her head.

According to Mike, Mrs. Dekker had also taken her concerns to the local police, so they were aware that Christian could be a threat, but as of now, he hadn't displayed any sort of aggressive moves toward anyone or made any verbal threats...that they knew of. For now, they were just watching and waiting.

"Hey," Finn said, as he sidled up next to her near the as-yet-unlit firepit and wrapped an arm around her waist. He leaned down and kissed her lightly.

Henley was thrilled with how quickly they'd gone from friends, to dating, to being able to touch each other so casually. She leaned into him and said, "Hey."

"You looked like you were lost in thought. Everything all right?"

"Yeah. Just thinking."

Finn nodded. That was another thing. He never pressed her to talk. If she said she was good, he took her at her word.

"Jasna's down at the barn tucking everyone in," he told her with a small chuckle.

"So we might be able to light the fire in two hours or so?" Henley joked. Her daughter had taken to life at The Refuge like a duck to water. She never complained about the hard work to keep all the critters fed and their stalls clean. She wasn't grossed out by all the poo she had to shovel out of the barn, or the smell. She seemed to love every second she got to spend with Finn and the animals, and in regard to the former...Henley had to admit, she was a little jealous of her own daughter.

Finn chuckled. "She won't be too long. She's too excited about s'mores. And hanging out with the adults."

Henley nodded. That sounded like her daughter. She enjoyed being around people older than her. It was something she'd worried about more than once in the past. The last thing she wanted was Jasna getting in with an older, more mature crowd, and possibly being pressured into doing things she wasn't ready for.

"Holy crap, is Tonka really hanging out with us around the fire tonight?" Spike teased.

"Right?" Pipe joined in the ribbing. "I think the last time he blessed us with his presence was...oh, that's right, never!"

"Shut up," Finn said with a shake of his head. "I hang out with you guys all the time."

"No, not really," Stone countered. "When we have meetings about The Refuge, sure. When you want our input on something going on with the animals, yes. But simply chillin'? Nope."

Henley glanced at Finn and saw he looked extremely uncomfortable. She hated that. "Well, he's here now," she pronounced in a no-nonsense tone. "Who's gonna get that fire going? Jasna's been talking about making s'mores all day, and if there's no fire by the time she gets back up here, I think she might just try to build one herself."

Her declaration turned everyone's attention from Finn to getting the fire started, and making sure the ingredients for the s'mores were ready on a nearby table.

"Thanks," Finn said softly, leaning in to whisper the word directly in her ear.

She turned in his hold and looked up at him. "Of course."

"They're right, you know," he told her with a shrug. "This hasn't really been my thing in the past."

"If you don't want to stay, you don't have to," she felt obligated to say.

"Are you staying?" he asked.

Henley nodded. "Yeah. Jasna's been looking forward to this all day."

"Then I'm staying," he said firmly.

She smiled up at him.

"It's not that I don't like the other guys," he continued, even though Henley hadn't pushed him to explain why this was the first bonfire he'd been to. "It's just...I've gotten comfortable with the animals. They don't ask questions. They don't mind when I'm in a bad mood. I don't have to pretend to be...*normal* with them."

"Finn, none of your friends want you to be anyone but who you are. And if you don't think they feel the exact same way you do, you're wrong. I don't know their stories, but the reason you're *all* here is because of whatever happened in your pasts. On the surface, they might all seem to be perfectly happy and well adjusted, but I can tell you that most of the time, people do whatever they can to hide their pain from the ones they love the most."

Finn was silent for a moment before nodding. "Yeah."

That was all he said, just that one word. But Henley could tell he was really thinking about her words.

"Come on," she urged. "Let's get a good seat before they're all taken." She pulled him toward one of the huge tree trunks placed around the firepit to be used as seats.

Looking around the fire, Henley saw there were half a dozen guests milling about, some sitting, some standing. She'd met with all of them at one point or another, and knew none of them would be triggered by fire, probably one of the reasons the guys decided this was a good time for a bonfire. Two of the men had been in the military, another was a survivor of a shooting at his workplace, one woman had been carjacked, the other had been raped, and the last guest at the fire had lost his arm in one of the machines on the assembly line where he used to work.

All six were currently talking and laughing as if they didn't have a care in the world. Come to think of it, *everyone* was smiling. The gathering was a good reminder of how resilient the human spirit was.

She and Tonka were good examples of that as well. There had been times when she'd been a teenager that she didn't think she would make it. She'd felt so vulnerable and she'd been scared all the time. But Henley had survived.

She could only hope all the men and women she met at The Refuge would too.

"Incoming," Finn said softly from next to her as Jasna exited the barn and jogged their way.

"Did I miss it?" she asked in an excited voice as she got close.

Henley laughed. "Miss what?" she asked. "The lighting of the fire? Yes. The s'mores, no."

"Whew," Jasna said, wiping her brow exaggeratedly.

A few people around them chuckled.

"Everyone all settled?" Finn asked the girl.

"Yep. The goats are starving to death, but I told them they weren't allowed any more food today, that they'd be okay until the morning. Melba and Scarlet Pimpernickel are settled down and I changed out their water. The horses are good. The kittens nursed and are sleeping. The dogs are snoring so loud, I thought for sure you'd hear them all the way up here, and I even said goodnight to Chuck and gave him a couple extra nuts, just because."

"Awesome, thank you," Finn said.

"Jasna, you want to make the first s'more?" Alaska asked from across the way.

Quick as a flash, Jasna headed in her direction, obviously eager to partake in the sweet treat.

"She's gonna be bouncing off the walls tonight," Henley grumbled, but she had a smile on her face as she watched her daughter painstakingly put a huge marshmallow on a wire prong before stepping toward the fire.

"And you love it," Finn said.

Henley smiled. "Yeah. She's such a serious kid. I never have to get on her about doing her homework. She can entertain herself for hours by reading or making up stories in her head. Seeing her out here, enjoying herself, being social and carefree...it's everything I never got to experience. I'll do whatever I have to in order to give her experiences like this for as long as she wants them."

"Like the camps you've got her signed up for this summer," Finn added.

"Yeah. There are four of them. Two are day camps and the others are sleepover kinds. One of the day camps is an art thing, where she'll get to try out over ten different mediums...painting, drawing, wire art...things like that. The other day one is a theater camp. She wasn't so sure about that one, but I convinced her to give it a try. The overnight ones are typical summer camps...you know, with swimming, hiking, and campfires. She loves the swimming and boating parts, but not as much the bugs and hiking."

Finn chuckled, and Henley loved hearing it. "Sounds like she's gonna be busy this summer, between being here and all the camps."

Henley nodded. "I worry about her," she admitted.

"Why?"

"She doesn't have a lot of friends, and her preference is to hang out by herself. I want her to learn how to be social, to relate to her peers. While I love being with her and doing mother-daughter things, I think she needs to spend more time with kids her own age."

"You're an awesome mom," Finn told her.

Henley couldn't help but grin.

"What?" he asked.

"Like you're the best judge of that?"

But he didn't return her smile. "What I know is that Jasna is a kind kid. She's got compassion, she's polite, and she isn't afraid to show her feelings. She feels safe with you, and you've obviously talked to her about some of the dangers of the world because she's not reckless. She's not glued to her phone, doesn't whine about not being able to watch TV or scroll social media for hours watching thirty-second videos that'll rot her brain. I'm not a parent, but I know it's not easy to raise a kid in today's world. And it's even harder as a single mother. You've done an amazing job. You should be proud. Of yourself *and* Jasna."

Henley felt tears well up and turned to stare at the flickering light of the fire. She wasn't generally an emotional person...except when it came to her daughter. Finn wasn't wrong. Raising Jasna had been one of the hardest things she'd ever done, second only to overcoming what had happened to her mom. Having Finn praise her daughter felt like the best compliment she could ever receive.

Next to her, Finn stood, and Henley turned to see where he was going. But he simply stepped behind the large tree trunk and stationed himself behind her. He pulled her shoulders back until she was resting against him, essentially using him as a backrest.

She loved the feel of him, so sturdy and supportive, and she relaxed, giving him her weight.

Alaska came over and sat next to her, while Tiny joined Finn and started a conversation about the surprising number of donations The Refuge had been receiving lately.

"She's having a great time," Alaska said with a smile, motioning to Jasna. Spike and Pipe were standing near the fire with her, arguing over the best way to roast marshmallows. If it was better to light them on fire and blow the flames out so there was a black crust around the entire treat, or if they should only be lightly browned before putting it on the chocolate.

The other owners were standing and sitting around the fire with the guests, chatting quietly.

"She is," Henley agreed.

"I haven't had a lot of chance to talk to you lately," Alaska said.

"We've both been busy," Henley agreed. "I know the guys are all thrilled since you've taken over the administrative stuff."

The other woman chuckled, then leaned in and whispered, "Between you and me, it was a disaster."

They shared a smile. And for some reason, emotion almost overcame Henley and she blurted, "I'm so glad you're okay."

Alaska's expression softened. She obviously knew Henley was referring to the guy who'd come to The Refuge to hunt her down and kidnap her for his own nefarious purposes. "Honestly, I think you guys back at the lodge had it worse than I did," she told her.

Henley snorted. "I'm not so sure about that. You were hunkered down in the woods, scared to death, while Brick went off and looked for your kidnapper. I'm not sure I would've wanted to be in the woods by myself, wondering if I'd be found."

A look Henley couldn't read flitted across Alaska's face before she shrugged. "Yeah, but you guys were dealing with the fire, all the fireworks going off, and trying to keep the guests calm. And I heard Tonka had his hands full with the animals too. I'm thinking it wasn't fun for any of us."

She wasn't wrong, and Henley wasn't surprised the other woman was downplaying her own fears. From what she'd seen, Alaska was very even-keeled. And why wouldn't she be? She had a man she loved at her side.

"So, changing the subject...I don't know a lot about *you*. I know through the grapevine that you grew up on a reservation, but I don't know which one or where. Sorry," Alaska said, looking chagrined.

"I'm Zuni. I grew up in western New Mexico on a reservation out there. We were poor, but honestly, I didn't really notice. I don't have any brothers or sisters, it was just me and my parents. We were happy. But after my mom was killed, my dad wasn't the same. He'd lost the love of his life in a horribly traumatic way, and while he did his best to care for me...he never really recovered."

"I'm so sorry," Alaska said, putting her hand on Henley's knee. "I didn't mean to bring up such bad memories."

"It's okay. I mean, it's a part of who I am. Anyway, I didn't talk at all for many years afterward as I tried to deal with everything. My dad moved us to Albuquerque because he felt I could get better medical care there. And he was right. I eventually started speaking again, and because of a particularly amazing therapist, got interested in helping others the way she helped me."

"And your dad?" Alaska asked softly.

Henley gave her a sad smile. "He got to see me graduate from high school, but succumbed to his demons not too long after."

Alaska looked alarmed. "Man, I'm the *worst* in social situations! Here we are, trying to enjoy ourselves and have fun, and I'm making you dredge up all sorts of bad memories."

"Thinking about my dad makes me happy," Henley

reassured her. "I mean, I'm not thrilled that he's not around, he would've absolutely loved Jasna, but he's not in pain anymore. And I know he's watching over me. I'll see him again, and that helps."

"I never knew my dad," Alaska said. "And my mom's never going to win parent of the year. I'm in awe of you, Henley."

She tilted her head in question at the other woman. "Why?"

"Because you're like the Energizer bunny. You just keep on going, no matter what. You have a successful career, an awesome daughter, and you're just so darn...*nice*."

Henley couldn't help but laugh. "Believe me, there are days when I'm definitely not nice. You should've seen me the other morning when someone cut me off when I was on my way to work. I have to say, I'm not proud of the names I called him, but it sure felt good."

Alaska chuckled.

"Is it weird to live out here and be the only woman?" Henley asked.

"Honestly? No. I would live anywhere as long as Drake was there with me."

"Awwww," Henley gushed.

"I've loved him my entire life. I wouldn't care if he told me he wanted to live in a tiny house in Timbuktu. I mean, I *would* love female company. The housekeeping ladies are great, but they're too busy working to socialize much. But being here isn't a hardship. Not at all. I mean, look around us. It's beautiful. But more than that, if I don't feel like cooking, there's a professional chef. I don't have to drive to work and deal with people cutting me off. And this is literally the safest place to live...I'm surrounded by seven former military badasses. Not to mention Mutt, who guards me wherever I go. And while many people might think the guests are broken and would be zero use in any kind of dangerous scenario, I think my situation proved that isn't the case."

"All very good points," Henley said with a nod.

"Why?" Alaska asked, leaning in so Finn couldn't hear her. "Are you moving up here too? Please please please say yes!"

Henley laughed. "You sound so much like Jasna when you beg like that. And no, I was just curious."

"Darn," Alaska said, straightening. "But there's still lots of time," she said in a cheerier tone. "And if Tonka is anything like Drake, he won't mess around. Once he figures out how awesome you *really* are, he's not going to let too much time pass before he puts a ring on your finger and moves you guys into his cabin."

Henley blushed, praying Finn hadn't overheard.

"Mom!" Jasna called from across the way. "Check this out!"

Looking over at her daughter, Henley's eyes widened at seeing the humongous s'more Jasna had put together. She gave her a thumbs up, even as she groaned.

She felt Finn shift behind her before he leaned down. "That thing is bigger than her head," he joked.

Tilting her own head back, Henley looked up at the man. He looked especially good tonight. He had on the jean shirt he seemed to always wear, but the shirt underneath was a dark purple today, giving a splash of color to the otherwise usually neutral clothes he wore. His beard was neatly trimmed, as usual, and his brown eyes were focused solely on her.

"My kid can definitely eat her fair share of food."

"She's fairly tall, but skinny," Alaska observed from next to her.

Henley tore her gaze from Finn's and turned to the other woman. "She eats," she returned, a little defensively.

"I didn't mean anything by that. Not at all," Alaska said quickly.

"Sorry. I tend to be a little protective of her. Her metabolism is off the charts. She's kind of like a bottomless pit. But I'm watching it, now that she's almost a teenager and puberty is going to hit soon. I don't want her to get too heavy."

"Can we not talk about teenage girls and puberty," Tiny begged from behind them.

Both Henley and Alaska grinned.

"What's so funny over here?" Brick asked as he approached and sat next to Alaska. He immediately put his arm around her and pulled her into his side. Mutt raised his head from where he'd plopped himself in front of Alaska earlier, and after seeing the newcomer was his master, immediately lost interest and closed his eyes once more.

"Girls hitting puberty," Alaska informed him with a grin.

Brick's eyes widened. "Nope. No. We're changing the subject."

"You can't come over here and butt into our conversation and demand we talk about something else," she informed him.

"I can and will," he said. "Things are going well tonight, yeah? Everyone's having a good time."

Alaska shrugged and gave Henley a look that screamed

"what can you do?" before agreeing with Brick.

"She'll work off the calories tomorrow," Finn told Henley for her ears only.

"I know," she agreed.

"You want one?" Finn asked.

"One what?"

"A s'more."

"I was going to get up in a bit and make one," Henley told him.

"I'll get it for you. Burnt marshmallow or lightly browned?"

Henley still wasn't used to anyone doing so much for her. When the toilet broke in her apartment, she fixed it herself instead of waiting on maintenance. When her car had a flat tire, she took care of it. Her dad had taught her to be self-sufficient, and living on the reservation had also drummed that into her. Living there, they didn't have a big box store within ten minutes they could run to in order to get what they'd need to fix a window, buy a new broom, or anything else. They made do with what they had and improvised when they needed to.

"Hen?" Finn asked.

"Sorry. Thank you, I'd love a s'more. And lightly browned, please."

"You got it."

Henley shivered as Finn trailed his fingers across her shoulder and down her arm before headed for Jasna, who was standing at the folding table preparing to make another s'more.

As the evening went on, Henley managed to visit with everyone. They either came over to where she was sitting, with Finn hovering behind her, or she spent a bit of time with them while stretching her legs and walking around the fire.

Jasna finally seemed to run out of steam and was sitting on the grass in front of another tree trunk, seemingly lost in thought.

Eventually, Henley stood and turned to face Finn. "It's getting late, and Jasna looks like she's beat. We should head in."

"I'll walk you," Finn said immediately.

"You aren't going to try to convince us to stay longer?" Henley teased.

Finn shrugged. "I've about reached my limit of socializing for tonight myself," he said.

"You lasted longer than I thought you would," Stone said, clapping his hand on Finn's shoulder. The other men had also come over to say good night when Henley stood.

"I'm thinking we need to do this way more often," Alaska said. "Maybe invite all the employees. I bet they'd all love to hang out and chill too."

"I second that," Tiny said.

"I'll check the calendar and see when we can do it again," Pipe said from nearby.

"Thanks for inviting me and Jasna," Henley told the group.

"Should've done it before now," Owl told her. "You're an integral part of The Refuge, Henley, and I'm not sure we'd be nearly as successful as we are today without you."

She blushed, smiling at everyone. "Thanks. You all make this a perfect place to work."

"I don't know about perfect," Spike said with a chuckle. "But we've definitely got our moments."

Finn stepped over the log and gently took her elbow in

his hand. He gave his friends a chin lift and steered her toward Jasna.

"Are you in a hurry?" Henley asked him quietly as she let herself be led away.

"I know them. They would've sucked you into some random conversation and it would've been another thirty minutes before you would've been able to figure out a way to extricate yourself politely. I don't have to be polite, since they're my friends and they know my standoffish ways."

Henley chuckled. "Comes in handy, huh?"

"Yup," Finn agreed, and his lips quirked upward briefly.

"Aw...is it time to go?" Jasna asked as they approached.

"Yup. Morning's gonna come quickly," Finn told her. "And I'm hoping you'll want to help me with the paddock."

"What about it?" Jasna asked, her eyes sparkling with interest.

"I need to check the fence, make sure there aren't any weak spots or places where Scarlet could possibly escape. It'll be hard work though, so you might not be interested."

"I'm interested!" Jasna exclaimed. "What time?"

"Seven-thirty."

"I'll be there!" And with that, Jasna hugged Finn hard before turning and running toward the cabin where they were staying for the evening.

Henley turned to Finn as they walked more sedately behind her. "Do you really need help? Or did you make that job up?"

Finn shrugged. "It could be put off for a while, but I figured since she's here and willing, I might as well do it now."

They'd arrived at the cabin, and Henley could hear her

daughter moving around inside as she turned to face Finn.

"Thank you for tonight. I loved getting to know Alaska a little better and hanging out with you and your friends."

"I had a good time too."

"You sound surprised," Henley noted.

"I am a little," Finn said honestly. "It's become sort of a habit to hide out in my cabin every night. It's just easier. But you and Jasna have made me want to try to break out of the self-imposed funk I've been in for so long."

Henley's heart swelled. "I'm glad," she whispered.

"Not only that...but I think it's time I called an old friend of mine. See what he's been up to."

"Yeah?" Henley asked.

"Yeah. We were partners in the Coast Guard, and when we got out, I came here, and he went to some small town in Virginia. Believe it or not, he became a librarian."

Henley's eyes widened. "Really?"

"Uh-huh. I don't know how the call will go. It's probably a stupid idea. I don't even know what I'll say to him."

"How about starting off with 'Hi'?" Henley quipped.

"Smartass," Finn said with a shake of his head. Then got serious. "I don't know that I can be the man you deserve, Henley. But I want to be."

"You don't have to be anyone but yourself," she told him. "Because I like you, Finn. More with every day that passes."

"Same," he said.

The attraction sparked between them, and Henley pressed her thighs together, trying to control her desire. Her daughter was waiting for her to come inside the cabin, and everyone around the fire could see them if they bothered to look in their direction. But there was no doubt that Henley wanted Finn. Their attraction had been simmering under the surface for quite a while, and now that they'd started getting closer, it was harder and harder to keep her hands off him.

"I want to kiss you," he murmured.

"Then do it," she told him eagerly.

"I can't kiss you the way I want to here," Finn said, sounding so disgruntled it was all Henley could do not to laugh.

But she sobered quickly as she looked up at him. "It's been a while since I've been in a relationship," she blurted. "I don't know what the dating rules are these days."

"Dating rules?"

"How long a woman should wait before rounding the bases." Unbelievably, she found herself blushing. Henley hoped Finn couldn't see her reddening cheeks.

He smiled down at her. "The only thing I've been interested in for years is taking care of the animals here at The Refuge...until a certain therapist caught my attention. I'm thinking we can make our own rules," Finn told her. "We'll do what feels right."

"This feels right," Henley said as she stepped closer, plastering herself against him.

"Yeah," Finn agreed as he backed them into the shadows to the left of the cabin door. Then he lowered his head and kissed her. All the nerve endings in her body sat up and took notice, and she literally tingled all over.

As she and Finn made out, Henley forgot where they were. That her daughter was steps away. That guests were still at the fire. She couldn't think about anything other than the taste and feel of Finn. They were both breathing hard when he lifted his head minutes later.

One of his hands came up and he brushed his fingers against her cheek. "You have no idea what I want to do with you right now," he practically growled.

"If it involves getting naked and licking me from head to toe, I *do* know," Henley blurted.

She felt a moment of embarrassment before he made a quiet choking sound and said, "You aren't far off."

They smiled at each other.

"We're doing this," he whispered.

"Yes. Hopefully soon," Henley returned.

"When's Jasna's first overnight camp?" Finn asked.

Was this crazy? It hadn't been all that long since they'd both admitted to liking each other and had started texting and talking more. And kissing. She couldn't forget that. But the rush of emotions between them didn't *feel* crazy. They felt right. Henley sighed. "Four weeks."

"A month," Finn said with a nod. "Right. This is probably good. Gives us more time to get to know each other."

He was talking more to himself than to her, and Henley thought it was adorable. And he wasn't wrong. It was probably a good thing to put on the brakes a little bit.

"You want to come hang out with us at my apartment sometime?" she asked a little shyly. "I mean, it's not the fanciest place, but we—"

"Yes," Finn said, interrupting her.

Henley smiled. "Cool."

"And we can watch a movie or something here at The Refuge in my cabin too."

Henley nodded. "Four weeks," she whispered after taking a deep breath. Although that didn't exactly calm her libido. All she could smell was Finn. His earthy, woodsy scent. It was a mixture of hay, smoke from the fire, and something deeper that was all him.

"Four weeks," Finn repeated. Then he moved his hand to the back of her neck and tilted her head up to him. "This isn't a fling," he said sternly. "I haven't wanted to get close to anyone, ever, the way I want to get close to you."

"Same," she agreed.

"I said it before and I'll say it again—I don't deserve you. But I'm gonna try my damnedest not to fuck this up."

"You won't."

He gave her a look that clearly said he thought she was wrong, but Henley didn't push. She'd show him through her actions that he was worthy of love.

"It doesn't matter what time Jasna comes to the barn tomorrow. There's no need for her to get up at the crack of dawn."

"She'll be there," Henley said.

"Make sure she gets something to eat before she does. If the fence needs mending, it's gonna be hard work."

"I will. You too."

"Me too what?"

"Make sure you get a good breakfast in."

He stared at her for a long moment with a look she couldn't interpret.

"What?"

"It's been a while since anyone's cared about my well-being."

"Well, get used to it. Because I do."

Finn nodded. "Maybe, if it'd be all right, I could come and get Jasna around seven-fifteen or so? We could go up to the lodge and grab something to eat before heading to the barn for morning chores and checking the fence."

"Why wouldn't it be all right?" Henley asked in confusion.

Finn shrugged. "I don't want to overstep."

"You aren't. And she'd love that."

"All right. You want me to bring you a plate back here when we're done? That way you can sleep in a bit."

Henley's heart melted a little more. "Yes, please."

"Okay. I'll see you in the morning then. Henley?"

"Yeah?"

"I had a good time tonight."

"Me too."

"And for the record...I'd be the luckiest son-of-a-bitch in the world if you were mine, and came to live up here with me."

And with that unbelievable statement, he leaned down, kissed her once more, then turned and headed toward the barn.

She wasn't surprised he was going to check on the animals once more before settling in for the night. But she *was* surprised by his parting words. He'd obviously over-heard Alaska's comment earlier. Henley supposed she should be embarrassed, but how could she be when she heard the wistfulness and seriousness in his tone?

Feeling as if she were on cloud nine, Henley headed into the cabin to let Jasna know the plans for the morning.

* * *

Christian Dekker lay very still in the trees not too far from the bonfire at The Refuge. He'd gotten good at sneaking around the woods. He'd learned to remain still for hours as he stalked his prey...exactly what he was doing now.

It was easy to go unnoticed by the men and women gathered around the fire, as the rods and cones in their eyes were fucked from the bright light. Even if they did turn to look into the trees, they'd never see him.

His target was the woman. It wasn't time to make his move; first he needed to conduct a little more reconnaissance. Needed to learn everything there was to know about her. He'd been secretly watching her for a few weeks already.

And tonight, he'd decided the best way to fuck with her and make her suffer was to take away the most important thing in her life.

In the dark stillness of the woods, his mind went back to when he was thirteen, shortly before she'd dumped him on someone else. To the day he'd overheard the doctor talking to his parents about him, recommending intensive inpatient therapy. She'd wanted to strip him of all control, take him away from his family. Not that he liked his parents or sister. He didn't. But *no one* got to make decisions about his life except him. Especially not some bitch therapist who thought she knew what was best for everyone.

Christian's eyes followed the girl as she moved around the fire. Laughing. Clueless that a predator was watching. Excitement rose within him as he made plans in his head. The girl would be his first.

His first *human* kill.

He had to execute it perfectly. Had to make sure no one learned of or interrupted his plans. First, he'd gather the items needed to subdue her, to torture her.

She'd be begging him to kill her by the time he was done.

Christian watched his prey until she entered a cabin. He already knew the therapist and her daughter didn't stay the night out here in the boonies often, which was a good thing. He had to nail down their schedule. Make sure he struck at the right moment.

When the bitch and her boyfriend made out on the porch, Christian felt nothing. The only urge he had was for blood. Not sex.

He slunk away as silently as he'd arrived, with no one the wiser, backtracking to his car—the car his parents didn't want him to have, but he'd bullied them to the point they'd given in despite their reservations. Probably thinking if he had a vehicle, he'd be home less often. It took him a while to return to where he'd left it along a remote road, but it didn't matter. No one was waiting up for him. He had no curfew. He did what he wanted, when he wanted.

His parents were petrified of him, exactly how Christian liked it. He was master of his own destiny, and after he'd tasted the joy of taking a human life for the first time, he'd put this fucking town in his rearview mirror. He'd easily find victims in the city. Throwaway people. Starting with the homeless and prostitutes. No one ever missed them. He'd perfect his techniques, then maybe head to Los Angeles. Possibly Chicago or New York. The world was his oyster. He could go wherever he wanted.

A short time later, Christian smiled as he drove back toward town. His entire life was ahead of him, and he was more than ready to get started. But first he'd take care of business here in Los Alamos. Show the bitch just how badly she'd underestimated him.

CHAPTER EIGHT

Four weeks. Good Lord, what was he thinking? Tonka wasn't sure he'd be able to make it four *days* before being with Henley. Sex had never been a huge thing in his life. Yes, he'd had it and enjoyed it, but he'd never *needed* it. Since that first kiss, however, he wanted to be near Henley at all times. His skin felt as if it was too tight for his body. And he hadn't masturbated so much in his entire life as he had in the last two weeks, since the night of the bonfire.

Being around Henley was both heaven and hell. She made him feel like the man he'd been *before*. Before he'd learned what true evil was. He smiled more. He was more sociable. And he'd laughed more in the last month than he had since even *before* leaving the Coast Guard.

Henley was funny, positive, and so incredibly selfless. She put everyone before herself. The guests, always wanting to make sure they were okay emotionally. Jasna, of course. His friends, and even the other employees at The Refuge. She always had a nice word to say to her co-work-ers...a compliment about the cleanliness of the rooms or lodge, how nice the landscaping was, the delicious food... even how nicely the rocks on the damn driveway were spread.

As for himself, Tonka realized she was as in tune with him as anyone he'd ever met. He had his good and bad days. Having Jasna out in the barn with him most of the time on the days she was here was a good distraction, making the shit in his head easier to deal with. But Henley always seemed to know when he was having a tough day. She'd send Jasna to shadow one of the other employees, giving him the time and space he needed to attempt to overcome his demons.

He'd avoided talking about what happened to him for so long, it was now a habit to shy away from any situation that might lead to him having to think about it.

One day, while sitting in on a group session, it occurred to Tonka yet again that maybe she could help him. The thought of reliving what happened by sharing his story was physically painful, but he knew without a doubt that if he was going to talk to *anyone*...it would be Henley.

"Hey," she said softly as she leaned against the door to the barn.

Tonka jerked in surprise and turned in her direction.

"Sorry, I didn't mean to startle you. I thought you heard me."

Tonka set aside the shovel he'd been using to clean out a horse stall and strode toward Henley. She straightened a bit where she stood. He didn't say a word. Not "good morning" or "it's okay" or anything else. He simply took her face in his hands when he got close enough and tilted her head up. Then he kissed her. Long and deep. Telling her without words how glad he was to see her.

By the time he forced himself to lift his head, Henley's hands were flat against his chest, her fingernails digging into his skin, and her cheeks were flushed pink. He could see a hint of cleavage from the v-neck blouse she was wearing, and it was all he could do not to bury his nose in the tantalizing flash of skin there.

"Finn," she breathed.

Tonka loved how his given name sounded on her lips. He hadn't understood why Alaska called Brick solely by his name until recently. There was something personal and comforting about Henley and Jasna being the only ones to call him Finn.

"Missed you," Tonka blurted.

She smiled. "You were at my apartment hanging out with me and Jasna just last night," she reminded him.

Tonka shrugged. "It's been about twelve hours since." He was being sappy but couldn't help it. "Jasna's okay at her art camp thing?" He hadn't let go of her face. Couldn't. "She seemed excited about their project for today."

"Yeah. They're making sculptures with things they find in nature, and she was talking nonstop about how she was going to see if she could make a portrait of Scarlet with sticks, rocks, and moss," Henley said with a smile. "I know a lot of twelve-year-olds would scoff at stuff like that, probably think it was too babyish, but I'm grateful she can still find pleasure in such simple things. That she's not all boy crazy."

Tonka frowned at the thought of Jasna dating.

As if she could read his mind, Henley chuckled. "Don't worry, I don't think dating is on her radar yet."

"I'm thinking when it is, you need to bring any boy she's interested in out here, so we can all make sure he understands that if he doesn't treat Jas like gold, he'll have to answer to *us*."

To his alarm, tears filled Henley's eyes.

"What?" he demanded. "What's wrong? Too fast? I'm sorry, I—"

But Henley was shaking her head as she cut him off. "No! It's just...it's been me and her for so long. The idea of Jasna having men like you and your friends watching out for her caught me off guard. In a good way."

Tonka dropped his hands from her face, wrapping an arm around her and steering her into the office. Normally he would be annoyed by an interruption in the middle of a job. But Henley could interrupt him any day, any time, and he'd drop whatever he was doing to talk to her. To make sure she was good.

He sat her on the sofa, the same one Jasna had slept on when she'd been sick the first time she was here, and where Tonka himself had slept on more than one occasion simply because he didn't want to return to his empty cabin. He knelt in front of her and put his hands on her knees. She immediately covered them with her own.

"Jas's father isn't around? At all?" he asked. He'd long suspected he wasn't, but he wanted to know more about Henley's past and wasn't sure how to ask.

Henley shook her head. "When my dad died, I was struggling to find my place in the world, and was still a little angry about everything that happened to me. I desperately wanted to be loved, to feel safe, and was trying to ease the stress of college. I was in toxic relationship after toxic relationship. Jasna's father and I had been dating about two months, and pretty much the only thing he was good at was sex—

"Um...sorry...you probably don't want to hear that part. Anyway, I had told him I wasn't on any birth control. Pills messed with my hormones too much, and I didn't like the idea of an IUD. He always bitched about having to wear a condom. And one night...I guess we were both too drunk to really think about it. I was as much to blame as he was." She shrugged.

"Afterward—when we realized what we'd done—he wasn't concerned. Kept insisting that I was being paranoid. That the sex was better without the condom. Of course, I was worried about getting pregnant, but I also wasn't thrilled because we weren't exclusive. I had no idea how many other women he was having unprotected sex with. When I realized I was pregnant, he told me in no uncertain terms that he didn't want to be a father, and that I couldn't prove it was his kid."

"Of course you could," Tonka said in disgust. "A paternity test could clear that up in a heartbeat."

"I know, but honestly, I was kind of relieved. And I *had* slept with my share of men before him," she said a little sheepishly.

"He's still a dick," Tonka said firmly.

"I could've fought him, forced him to pay child support, but I knew having to deal with him for the next eighteen years would only bring more stress into my life, so I decided to raise Jasna on my own. I also didn't want a man like him around my kid. It probably wasn't fair to deny Jasna a male figure in her life, no matter how lacking. But I still think I did the right thing. I knew it wouldn't be easy to be a single mother, but I loved my baby with everything I had in me from the second I realized I was pregnant.

"I also stopped using sex to deal with my stress and pain. Jasna's been my entire life from the moment I learned she existed. I'll do whatever it takes to keep her safe. I even took the job in Los Alamos because it seemed safer than living in the city."

"You've done a remarkable job with her so far," Tonka said immediately. "Jas is beautiful, caring, smart, unselfish, and you should be proud, *so* proud, of the young woman she's becoming."

"Finn," Henley said softly.

Tonka rose from his crouch and sat on the cushion next to her. He took her hands in his and said earnestly, "This probably isn't the time or place to be having this discussion, but fuck it. I'm completely in awe of you. You've worked your butt off for years to give Jas a safe and happy environment to grow up in. And as far as what that asshole said, about sex being better without a condom, he's wrong. I know without a doubt that being inside you will be the most amazing thing I've ever experienced in my life. I don't mind being the one responsible for birth control. I'll never forget to wear one when I'm with you. It'll be my honor to protect you."

She blinked a few times as she stared at him. Then blurted, "How are you still single?"

"I'm moody. There are stretches of days when I don't even want to talk to anyone. I like animals more than people. I live like a hermit. I'm—"

But Henley cut him off before he could continue. "You're loyal, considerate, protective, gentle, gorgeous, and you make me happy simply by being near me. I don't expect you to be perfect, just as I hope you don't expect the same from me."

"You know I don't," he told her.

"Right. So, we've had a few years to get to know each other, and in that time, I haven't once been afraid of you, or not wanted to hang out with you. In fact, I desperately *wanted* to spend time with you, but I didn't know how to make that happen. Now that we've finally acted on this attraction we've had toward each other...I'm happier than I've been in a long time, Finn."

"I'm not sure I know what happy is anymore. All I know is that I feel itchy and unsettled until you arrive, and the second you leave, that feeling returns until I see you again and know for certain that you and Jasna are safe and content."

She tilted her head as she studied him quietly.

"What?" he asked.

"I want to say something, but I don't want you to think I'm putting my therapist hat on and analyzing you."

Tonka's lips twitched. "Go ahead. Say it. I promise I won't think that."

"I'm thinking you feel that way because of whatever happened in your past."

He nodded slowly.

"You don't have to talk to me about it, but I get it, Finn. I do. After my mom was killed, I was afraid to let my dad out of my sight. Whenever he had to go to work, even years after the murder, I felt physically sick until I saw him again. I want to tell you that nothing will happen to me. I can't," she said sadly. "But I'm careful. I'm a single woman with a young daughter. I've had to be more watchful of my surroundings because of how the world works."

Tonka took a deep breath and nodded. "I know. My brain knows that you're a grown woman who's been on her own for a long time. I just…I couldn't bear it if anything happened to you. I had to stand by and watch a loved one hurting, and I can't do it again."

It was as close as Tonka had ever gotten to sharing what happened on that awful day so long ago—and surprisingly, it didn't bring back any more awful memories than he already carried in his head and heart.

Henley didn't say anything for a long while, but she did hold his hand a little tighter. Eventually, she said, "I hope one day you can share what happened. If not with me, then with someone you trust."

"I trust you," Tonka said immediately, not wanting her to feel differently.

She smiled at him, then thankfully changed the subject. "And I appreciate you not being weird about the condoms."

"Of course not," he said. "It wouldn't be smart of either of us to get involved in a sexual relationship and not use them. But again, even once we're comfortable with each other and our relationship progresses, as I hope it will, I'll continue to use protection until we either decide to find an alternative birth control method, we break up, or we decide we want children together."

She inhaled sharply at that. "You want kids?" she asked.

Tonka shrugged. "Honestly? Before you, I would've said no way in hell. I didn't want to be responsible for another helpless being ever again. But now that I've gotten to know you and Jasna better, I'm thinking…maybe."

Tonka was aware that he'd let a big clue to his personal demons slip, but suddenly it didn't seem quite so crucial to keep Steel's memory locked away any longer.

"It's almost overwhelming to think of going through

raising a child again after all these years...but like you said, with the right person by my side, I don't think it would be nearly as difficult. So, I'm a maybe as well."

Tonka brought one of her hands up to his mouth and kissed her fingers. "I'm thinking it would be a good idea to stop talking about sex and babies. I'm not going to make love to you for the first time in the barn," he said. "You probably have work to do, and I have shit to shovel."

"Oh, yeah, that's a mood killer," Henley said with a roll of her eyes.

Tonka chuckled. As always, the sound was a little rusty, but it felt good. He stood, pulling Henley up with him. Then he kissed her again. Their hands wandered freely, and just feeling her curves under his palms was exciting and pushed his control to the limit.

One of her hands had delved under his shirt, and she was rubbing one palm over his nipples, the other holding his butt cheek in a death grip. To be fair, he'd pushed the neck of her blouse aside and was tracing the edge of her bra with his thumb, while holding her against him with his other hand at the back of her neck.

When they finally pulled back and stared at each other, neither removed their hands. Tonka couldn't find the strength to stop the movement of his thumb against her creamy skin. He looked down, wanting to put his mouth where his hand was more than he'd wanted anything in a very long time.

"Two weeks," she said breathlessly, as if reminding herself, as well as him.

Tonka liked knowing she wanted him as much as he wanted her. The anticipation was a kind of aphrodisiac for them both. If she put her hand on his cock right that moment, he had little doubt he'd explode in seconds. It was one thing to masturbate with his own hand, but having her touch him would be a completely different experience. Something he couldn't wait to feel.

"I'm not with you for sex," Tonka told her, his thumb still brushing back and forth slowly. "If you told me right here and now that sex was off the table permanently, I'd still want to be with you."

The shy smile she bestowed on him made Tonka's heart crack a little.

"Same. Although, for the record...sex is definitely *not* off the table. I want you, Finn. And you should know...I like sex. A lot."

Tonka groaned. "Right. On that note, we need to stop."

She giggled that time and squeezed his butt cheek once more before removing her hand from under his shirt, being sure to brush against every inch of his abdomen as she did. "What are our plans for after work?" she asked.

For a moment, Tonka had the urge to ask if she wanted to go to his cabin, but decided that probably wasn't smart. He loved being alone with her, but didn't think either of them would be able to keep their hands to themselves. And while Jasna was eating dinner at her camp, she needed to be picked up at six-thirty. That wasn't nearly enough time for Tonka to do what he wanted to every inch of Henley. Especially not the first time they were together.

"Robert and Luna are making a New Mexican dinner tonight. Stacked red chile enchiladas, green chile stew, chiles rellenos, chicos, carne adovada, and sopaipillas and horno bread for dessert."

"Oh my God, I think I gained ten pounds just listening to you say that," Henley moaned.

"So you want to stay here and eat with me and the others, then go pick up Jas?"

"I'd love to. Will you come with me to get her? You can come back to the apartment with us for a while."

Tonka had planned to start work on the new lean-to he wanted to put in the paddock, so the animals could have some shade for the summer and protection from snow in the winter, but spending time with Henley and her daughter sounded a lot more fun. "Yes."

"Finn?"

"Yeah?"

"People like to say that our pasts don't define us, but they're wrong. They totally do. What happens in our lives shapes us into who we are today. And you, my friend, are a hell of a man."

Her words sank into his soul, making him feel ten times lighter. "Go," he said a little gruffly. "Or the first time we make love *is* gonna be right here and now in this barn, where anyone could walk in and disturb us."

She grinned and pretended to contemplate whether or not to take him up on his threat, before backing up. "See you later," she said, still smiling.

Tonka's throat was so tight, he couldn't respond. So he gave her a little chin lift. He stood where he was long after she'd disappeared from view. When he finally had control over his emotions, and body, he took a deep breath and headed back to the stall he'd been mucking when she'd arrived.

He hated that it had taken him so long to let Henley know he was interested, but then again, he wasn't the same man now as he'd been when she was hired. Back then, he wouldn't have even contemplated opening up enough to let her in.

Now? He thought he and Henley might have a better-than-average shot at a future together.

What had changed? There was more time between now and losing Steel, which was probably the biggest factor. And he'd witnessed how happy Brick was with Alaska. If his friend could overcome losing his entire SEAL team—and his guilt about not being able to save them—enough to have a healthy relationship with the woman who'd been his friend for most of his life, it gave Tonka hope that he might one day be able to have a healthy relationship as well.

Then there was Jasna. How could he continue to hold himself back emotionally when the girl was constantly telling him how happy she was? Showing him without words how much she enjoyed spending time with him and the animals he loved?

The two had cracked his heart open...and it didn't hurt as much as Tonka had feared. Of course, being around them didn't mean his worries were gone. There were just as many evil people in the world now as there were before. And Henley and Jasna could be taken from him just as easily as Steel had.

But the difference was, Tonka would fight to the death, *his* death, to make sure they were safe. Unlike before... when all he'd been able to do was bear witness as Steel was tortured and killed. Now, Tonka vowed to fight any person who dared put one finger on anyone he loved. And every single animal at The Refuge was included in that sentiment. Even the ornery goats who irritated him more often than not.

And if one of his friends was threatened? He'd go to Hell and back to be at their side.

Shaking his head as if he could remove the dark thoughts from his mind, Tonka picked up the shovel he'd propped against the wall earlier and did his best to concentrate on the task at hand.

CHAPTER NINE

One week.

Henley told herself that she could hold out for another week. Seven days. Ten thousand minutes. Six hundred and four thousand seconds.

She sighed. It was getting harder and harder not to give in and tell Finn she didn't want to wait until Jasna was at her sleepaway camp for him to make love to her.

The day camp last week was a hit. Jasna really enjoyed herself. She even met a girl, Sharyn, who she'd clicked with. They'd met up one night this week, going to a movie...with Henley and Finn sitting in a row in the back of the theater, keeping their eyes on the two girls. The great thing was that Sharyn was also going to the sleepaway camp Jasna was attending toward the end of the summer. Henley hoped the relationship continued to grow, as the girls were the same age and would be in the seventh grade together at the middle school in the fall.

As for her own work...today, for something different, Spike and Pipe had arranged for an "employee appreciation day" of sorts. The lodge was off limits to the guests for two hours so everyone could relax and not worry about being "on" for a short while.

To be honest, The Refuge didn't have a ton of employees, but that made working there all the more intimate. The nine employees, other than the seven owners, were all in attendance...Henley, Carly, Jess, Ryan, Savannah, Luna, Robert, Hudson, and Jason. Alaska was also included as an employee, even though she and Brick definitely had a wedding in their future.

The guys had gotten each of them a huge gift basket filled with treats, gift certificates, and even cash. Spike had ordered a cake from a bakery in town, and also catered in a meal—much to Robert's dismay.

Jasna was there, thrilled that she'd been included in the celebration. She'd gotten her own gift basket, and was currently flitting around the room talking to the men and women she'd gotten to know over the last few weeks.

Henley's gaze caught on Finn's from across the lodge, and he smiled at her. Every time she looked up, he was watching her. If anyone else had been so attentive to her every move, she probably would've called them a stalker and been freaked out. But she couldn't be upset that he kept track of where she was, because she did the same thing with him. It was as if they were magnets, constantly being pulled toward each other.

And of course, the sparks between them had only gotten more intense with each day that went by. She was getting to know the man better every time they talked, and she hadn't found a single thing that turned her off yet. Yes, he had demons from his past, but so did she.

It might be wishful thinking on her part, but Henley

couldn't help but notice the more time she spent with Finn, the more he opened up to her. No, she still didn't know exactly what had happened to him, but she had gleaned enough information to understand he'd lost his canine partner, Steel, to some horrific incident. He had intense guilt over what happened, and as a result, had backed off from interacting with...pretty much everyone. Preferring the company of animals to people.

But he was slowly and surely changing before her eyes. He made more of an effort to hang out with his friends at the lodge, and he no longer looked quite so uncomfortable around the guests or at social events like this one.

"So...you and Tonka, huh?" Ryan asked.

Henley didn't even bother to deny it. Why should she? She wasn't embarrassed to be dating Finn, and neither of them had any reason to keep their relationship a secret. Especially not from the men and women they worked with. "Yup," she said, hearing the pride in her own voice.

"You guys are adorable together. And he's so good with Jasna."

"He really is. She's a good kid, but still, even I get over-whelmed with all her questions sometimes. And he answers all of them without seeming to get irritated in the least."

"She *does* ask a lot of questions," Ryan agreed with a chuckle.

"Sorry if she's been bothering you," Henley said, wrinkling her nose with chagrin.

"Oh, no, not at all. I love when she helps. She makes the day go by so much faster."

"Well, if she ever slows you down or you aren't in the mood, don't be afraid to say so."

"She's fine. Promise. I mean, being a housekeeper isn't exactly rocket science."

Henley glanced at the woman, assessing her with new eyes. When Ryan had been hired a few weeks ago, Henley immediately thought she didn't fit the mold of someone who might apply to be a maid at a motel.

That was stereotyping, she knew...but during her time at the retreat, the men and women who'd been in and out of the housekeeping job had all been marking time at The Refuge while they looked for something that paid better. It was typically a pretty short-term gig. Carly and Jess had also admitted being here wasn't a long-term thing for either of them. Carly was working for extra money while she went to school, and Jess's husband had been laid off, so she'd taken the job to keep their family afloat until he found work.

Ryan hadn't said much about her background at all, or why she was there. She'd mentioned she was grateful for the job and frequently cited how much she loved the atmosphere. She was somewhat mysterious, actually... which made Henley all the more curious about her.

"So...what about you? Got your eye on anyone? Do you have a boyfriend already?"

Ryan laughed. "Oh, no. I'm single and happy as a clam." But something in her eyes belied her carefree words.

"Oh, come on, we're surrounded by gorgeous single men. You're telling me not *one* of them has caught your eye? Pipe has the whole biker thing going on—and who hasn't fantasized about being on the back of a hot biker's motorcycle? Not to mention his sexy British accent. Or there's Stone, with those glasses and his whole scholarly-looking thing. Oh, wait! I know—you're holding out for

Tiny. He's such a pretty boy, but with those huge muscles," Henley teased.

To her surprise, Ryan blushed. Her gaze flicked briefly to the right, where Tiny was currently standing, talking to Luna.

"Ahhhh, so it *is* Tiny you've got your eye on," Henley said with a smile.

Ryan's gaze immediately dropped before she looked back at Henley. "Nope. I don't have my eye on anyone. I like being single. I can do what I want, go where I want..."

There was almost a hint of desperation in the other woman's tone, and Henley knew she'd pushed enough. She didn't want to make Ryan uncomfortable. She'd learned from her years as a therapist when to back off. "Good for you," she said, then changed the subject. "I know Alaska was thrilled you were willing to start on such short notice. After Alexis left so quickly, Jess and Carly were working overtime to keep up."

"I love it here. It's so beautiful," Ryan said.

Henley nodded. "It really is. It's almost ridiculous."

The two women smiled in agreement.

"Ryan, can I bug you for a second?" Alaska asked as she approached.

"Sure, what's up?"

"You were so cool about helping me last week when the computer at the front desk was acting up. You really seem to know what you're doing with electronics. My cell phone quit ringing yesterday...or making any noise, really. I'm also not getting notifications, even though the settings all seem right. I already checked to make sure I didn't bump the silent button on the side, and I didn't. Now I'm getting frustrated because I don't want to miss any texts or calls from guests while I'm working, but I am already."

"I'm sure it's something simple," Ryan said, holding out her hand.

Alaska gave her the phone with a sigh of relief. "I mean, I would've asked Jasna, because you know, kids these days seem to be experts at anything having to do with technology, but I haven't had a chance yet."

"I wouldn't say I'm an expert," Ryan answered, "but... here ya go. All fixed."

"*Seriously?*" Alaska asked, taking her phone back. "You had it for like two seconds! What was wrong?"

Ryan laughed. "You somehow turned on the 'do not disturb' function. When it's on, there's a little moon icon on the home screen."

"Oh! I saw that, but just thought that was an icon showing me my alarm was set."

Henley laughed this time, along with Ryan. "Nope."

"I swear, I have no idea how in the world I can be so good at admin tasks, even with the website, but be so clueless with stuff like this. Anyway, thank you so much!"

"You're welcome," Ryan said with a wide grin.

Alaska turned to head back toward Brick, and Henley couldn't help but look in Finn's direction once more. Just like always, as if he could feel her gaze on him, he turned his head and smiled.

"You guys are too dang cute," Ryan said with another chuckle. "Well, time for chow, I think. I'll talk to you later," she added, before heading for the food table.

"Hey, Mom!" Jasna exclaimed as she appeared out of nowhere next to Henley. She put her arms around her and leaned close.

Henley wrapped an arm around her daughter's shoulders and asked, "How you doin'?"

"Great!" Jasna said happily. "I love it here so much."

"I'm glad."

"I know you told me all about the animals, but I can't believe you didn't tell me how awesome everything else was. I could've been hanging out here every summer!"

Henley chuckled. "I did tell you it was great, but you weren't interested in hearing it because it was Mom's workplace."

Jasna laughed. "Okay, you're right. But seriously, how could I have known The Refuge wasn't anything like your office downtown?"

Henley wanted to roll her eyes and remind her daughter how many times she'd talked about the retreat for people who needed a break from the world, but she didn't. She was simply glad Jasna was having a good summer. Losing Mrs. Singleton, and thus her childcare, had been a huge concern, but everything was working out extremely well so far.

"If I can have your attention!" Spike called out from across the room.

Everyone turned to him, and he continued.

"We just wanted to tell all of you how much we appreciate the work you do here. We couldn't keep The Refuge up and running as well as it does without you. We talked about it the other night, and we want you all to know you're more than welcome to stay in the empty cabins, anytime there's one available. We try to have bonfires on one or two Saturday nights a month, which you can always attend, and of course you're more than welcome to take advantage of the hiking trails. We want you to feel as much pride in what you're doing here as we do. Just get with Alaska if you want to stay in a cabin, and she'll let you know when there's a cancelation or an opening. Unfortunately, it'll probably be a late-notice kind of thing, but we hope this might be a welcome perk for you all."

Everyone around them let out a cheer, and Henley smiled. She and Jasna had loved staying at The Refuge, and she knew the others would too.

"Now that that's out of the way...feel free to hang out for as long as you'd like. We'll open the lodge to the guests in another half hour or so, but that doesn't mean you have to leave. Oh, and take as much of the leftover food home as you want. Robert won't be upset if it's all gone by the time he serves what he calls a 'real dinner' tonight."

Everyone laughed, and Robert shrugged as if to say Spike wasn't wrong.

"As always, if you need anything—anything at all— never be afraid to ask any one of us," Spike went on. "Brick, Tonka, Pipe, Owl, Stone, Tiny, and I want you all to be happy during your time here. You're truly changing lives, even if you don't think what you do is important. The men and women who come to The Refuge need a place to relax while trying to heal from whatever they're going through. They want a stress-free vacation, and every single one of you helps provide that. And now I'm done being sappy. Thank you all again!"

Everyone clapped, and Jasna looked up at her with a serious expression on her face. "Mom?"

"Yeah, baby?"

"I don't like to think about anything bad happening to Spike. Or Finn. Or any of the other guys."

"I know. I don't either," Henley said softly.

141

"They were all in the military, right?"

"Uh-huh."

"So they probably had to kill people? And people were trying to kill them?"

"I don't know about that. Not everyone who's in the military has to actually shoot anyone," Henley said diplomatically. The truth of the matter was that she didn't know all the guys' stories. Even though she was The Refuge's therapist, the owners didn't sit down with her and tell her all their secrets. Finn was proof of that. She was dating the man, and she still didn't know what exactly had happened to make him want to invest in The Refuge.

"I know killing people is bad, but I don't think anyone here would do that on purpose. And if they did...the person probably deserved it."

It was fascinating to watch her daughter grow up in front of her eyes. To see her mature intellectually. "I agree," she said after a moment.

"And if anyone tried to hurt me, or you, I think they'd do whatever they could to help us."

Henley frowned. "Has someone said or done something to worry you, Jasna?"

"No," she said with a shrug. "I just feel safe here. And before you say it, I know bad things happen anywhere, but when I'm around Finn and the others...I just know no one can hurt me."

And with that bombshell, Jasna hugged her mom, then pulled out of her hold and bounced over to visit Savannah, the woman who did The Refuge's taxes and accounting.

"You okay?" Finn asked as he took Jasna's place against Henley.

She gave him her weight as she kept her gaze on her daughter. "I don't know," she said honestly.

"What's wrong? Talk to me, Hen."

Taking a deep breath, she looked up at the man at her side. "It's just that Jasna said some stuff that worries me."

"Like what?"

"About how she knows she's safe here at The Refuge. That even though you and your friends might've killed people, she was all right with that because they were probably bad."

Finn didn't say anything for a moment, then finally he nodded. "She's not wrong. On both counts."

"Should I be worried that she brought it up? I mean, maybe she doesn't feel safe in our apartment?"

Finn turned her and put a finger under her chin, tilting her face up. "I think she's a twelve-year-old girl who's experiencing her first bit of freedom this summer. She has the run of this place and loves every second of it. I think she's just trying to express her happiness, and let you know that she trusts us."

Henley nodded. "Of course she trusts you and your friends. Why wouldn't she?"

He studied her for a moment. "You're so amazing."

She frowned up at him. "Finn, we're talking about Jasna and her trust in you guys," Henley protested, even though she loved getting compliments from the man.

"And you said she trusts us without a second of hesitation. I know you're aware that most people would think twice about letting their daughter hang out with a bunch of former military guys who are suffering from PTSD. Not to mention all the guests who have the same issues," Finn told her.

"I'm not scared of you or your friends. Even the guests. That they're here at all means they're trying to figure out how to live with what happened to them. I worry more about the people out in the world who are driving drunk. The entitled people who think they have the right to berate hardworking employees in service jobs. People who don't care if they go to work or school when they're sick, with no regard for others. I'd rather Jasna hang out here with you and your friends than have her mind rotted by watching so-called reality TV or hanging out with mean girls from school." Henley stared intently at Finn, hoping he understood what she was trying to say.

"One week," Finn said as he stared back.

Henley's lips twitched. "One week," she echoed.

They shared an intimate look, and Henley swore she could feel his heart beating against her hand where it rested on his chest.

"Mom!" Jasna shouted from across the room.

The mood between her and Finn was broken with her daughter's summons, but his fingers against her back as she turned still sent goose bumps down her arms.

"They're gonna build a library here at the lodge! And Spike said I could help pick books!" Jasna said excitedly.

"That's great. But we're all standing right here. You don't have to yell as if I'm on the other side of the property."

"Sorry," Jasna said with a small grin. "I'm just excited."

The rest of the afternoon went by quickly, and the more Henley thought about her daughter's words about being safe, the better she felt about them. It was simply Jasna's way of trying to tell her mom not to worry. That she was happy.

Everything Henley had done in the last twelve years had been with Jasna in mind. The jobs she'd taken, the food she bought, the movies they watched on TV. The most important person in her life was her daughter. Knowing she loved The Refuge as much as Henley did felt really good. And she wasn't wrong. The men who owned the retreat *were* special. Yes, they probably had killed in the past, but that in no way made them unworthy—or untrustworthy. She'd trust her life to them. More importantly, she'd trust Jasna's life, if it came down to it.

Tonight, Finn had invited her and Jasna to walk out to Table Rock before it got dark and view the sunset. She'd been there before, and the hike out to the picturesque spot wasn't too difficult. It pretty much didn't matter what she and Finn did together, he could ask if she wanted to sit in an empty room and stare at the wall with him and she'd be more than happy to agree. Just being around the man made her happy.

One week, she reminded herself silently. Piece of cake.

CHAPTER TEN

Tonka couldn't stop looking at his watch. He'd gotten a text from Henley earlier, letting him know she'd dropped off Jasna at her adventure camp and was going to her office for a session with a client, then she'd head his way.

He prayed that he'd be able to control himself when Henley arrived. As far as he knew, she didn't have any sessions planned with guests at The Refuge today or tomorrow. Which meant they'd have plenty of time for just the two of them. Tonka was totally looking forward to that.

He loved Jasna, and was learning to truly enjoy spending time with his friends, but he wanted more one-on-one time with Henley. They couldn't exactly have deep conversations with her daughter listening or his friends hovering.

Giving each other these last four weeks to really get closer had been the right decision. With sex off the table, Tonka found he was able to relax and not worry about anything other than enjoying his time with Henley and Jasna.

They'd watched TV, went bowling one night, had gone to the movies a couple of times, and simply enjoyed being around each other. He'd laughed more than he had in many years. It was stunning that in a few short weeks, he'd learned to actually enjoy being around humans once again.

There had been a time, right after that awful incident, when Tonka had felt as if he wanted to move to the middle of nowhere and never talk to anyone ever again. The Refuge was as close to that as he could get, even though Brick and the others wouldn't let him be a *complete* hermit.

But hanging out with his friends more and more over the last month, he rediscovered the joy of having someone at his back. He'd missed the comradery of fellow military men. They understood him in a way others couldn't. And *this* group of men understood when he was having a bad day. When his memories were overwhelming. They gave him the space he needed.

Brick had literally saved his life when he'd invited him to join his PTSD retreat venture. It had taken many years, but Tonka finally felt as if he was crawling out of the pit he'd been in for way too long.

And Henley and her daughter were a big part of why he'd found the strength to do so. He wanted to be the kind of man they could count on. He wanted to make them happy, and he couldn't do that if he was moody and standoffish. The animals at The Refuge had been his sanity, but Henley was his guiding light. His reason to continue to try to fight his demons.

He looked at his watch again. Two minutes since the last time he'd checked.

Shaking his head, Tonka pressed his lips together and got back to work. If he was going to take some time off to spend with Henley and not worry about the animals, he needed to get shit done.

The rest of the morning went by excruciatingly slowly. Just when Tonka thought he was going to lose his mind with impatience, he heard the sound of a car's tires on the gravel outside the barn. He realized he was smiling as he quickly went to the wall and turned off the water he was using to refill troughs. He walked outside in time to see Henley step out of her CRV.

The second she saw him, she broke into a jog as she headed his way. She didn't slow, nearly knocking him over as she threw herself at him when she got close. Tonka went back on a foot, still smiling.

She hugged him hard, then pulled back just enough so she could look up at him. "Hi!" she said happily.

"Hi, yourself," he returned. "Have a good morning?"

She wrinkled her nose adorably. "It seemed to last forever. I'm now officially on vacation. At least for the next day and a half. Do you know how long it's been since I've had absolutely no responsibilities or anywhere I needed to go?"

"I'm guessing a while."

"You'd guess right," Henley said. Then she hugged him again, resting her cheek on his chest, and it was all Tonka could do not to haul her off to his cabin right that moment. For weeks, they'd been dancing around their attraction. Yes, they'd made out plenty of times, but they always knew they couldn't go any further because they didn't have the time or privacy they both wanted.

But now? Knowing this woman was all his for two

nights? That he wouldn't have to stop just when things were getting interesting? Tonka couldn't wait. But he supposed dragging her to his bed the second she arrived probably wasn't cool. "You hungry?" he asked after a long moment.

"Starved," she said, looking up at him with an expression that probably mirrored his own.

"Need to feed you," Tonka said gruffly. "Because once I get you in my bed, it's going to be a long damn time before I let you leave...and I have no idea what I've got to eat at my cabin."

Henley grinned, then rested her forehead against him. In a muffled voice, she said, "All I've been able to think about today is you. I should probably be a little cautious, but I don't want to." She lifted her head and looked up at him once more. "You're a good man. The best I've ever met. You've given me time and space to get to know you. You've been nothing but patient and kind to my daughter, who I know can be a little overwhelming occasionally. You're so damn handsome, there have been times I've had to pinch myself to make sure I'm not dreaming, that you seem to want *me*."

"I want you," Tonka reassured her.

"This is either gonna be epic, or the biggest letdown in the history of sexual encounters," she teased.

"I vote for epic," he said with a small laugh.

"Me too. Come on. Let's go eat, say hi to everyone, then we can disappear without guilt until tomorrow afternoon."

Could this woman get any more perfect? Tonka didn't think so. He reached for her hand and rushed toward the lodge. Her giggle was the sweetest thing he'd ever heard.

Lunch was a long lesson in restraint. Henley couldn't seem to keep her hands to herself...which was definitely all right with him. When he was about to take a bite of pasta salad, he felt her hand on his leg, which she immediately shifted so her fingertips caressed his inner thigh. One inch higher and she'd be touching his cock.

All the while, she was deep in conversation with Owl next to her about the library they were attempting to build along one entire wall in the great room of the lodge. His little minx was driving him crazy, and she knew it.

He retaliated when they were eating brownies with ice cream for dessert, by slipping his hand under the leg of her shorts and running a single finger over the crotch of her panties.

She hadn't been able to keep her reaction under control, and she jerked—hard. She mock glared at him and grabbed his wrist to try to keep him from moving, but her hold was no deterrent. Stone asked her a question about a last-minute group session she'd agreed to do tomorrow afternoon, and as she did her best to be coherent, Tonka continued to drive her as crazy as *he* felt.

He'd never been so grateful to finish eating. He had a feeling Henley was torturing him on purpose by dragging out her goodbyes to their friends and the guests who'd eaten with them. By the time he wrapped his arm around her waist to lead her out of the lodge, Tonka was at the end of his rope.

Henley giggled as he practically force-marched them toward his cabin. The sound was carefree and happy, and it wormed its way under his shields, permanently shattering them. This woman had been to hell and back, and here she was, laughing and practically skipping next to him. Tonka wanted to be like her. Wanted to find joy in a world that had completely let him down. She was the key to his happiness, he had no doubt.

"In a hurry?" she teased as she slipped one of her hands under the waistband of his cargo pants. The feel of her fingers skimming the crack of his ass made his already hard cock even stiffer. He needed her. Right this second. He thought he was going to die if he didn't get inside her body.

Tonka fumbled with his keys as he approached his cabin. Up here, there wasn't much reason to lock his door, but he'd seen too many crime documentaries that started with something like, "the community was safe and no one locked their doors," before an hour of murder and mutilation commenced.

As he attempted to get the key in the lock, Henley lifted his shirt from behind and tweaked one of his nipples. Hard.

The door swung open, and Tonka grabbed Henley by the waist and dragged her inside. He slammed the door with his foot, not willing to let go of her for even a second. At the same time, he pushed her back against the door, his head already lowering.

He was too far gone to stop. Or to slow down. And thankfully, it seemed Henley was on the same page. Her hands immediately went to his zipper. He grabbed the hem of her shirt and lifted. She had to let go of him to raise her arms so he could remove the top. The second the material was gone, Tonka reached for her bra and pulled one of the cups down and latched his lips to the erect nipple begging for his attention.

Henley moaned and one of her legs flew up. He

grabbed her thigh, pulling her harder against him even as he sucked hard on her nipple. Her back arched, and she made that sexy little moan in the back of her throat once more.

"Finn," she said in a throaty whine. "I need you."

"And you're gonna get me," he assured her gruffly as he yanked the cup away from her other tit.

She wiggled and writhed in his grip, and Tonka had never felt so desperate in his life. He wanted to kiss her. Put his mouth between her legs. Fuck her. He wanted to do it all at the same time, and he also wanted to slow down. Show her how much she meant to him by worshiping her properly.

But the time for slow had passed. Neither of them wanted that at the moment.

Henley's hands returned to his pants, and she desperately tried to get them undone and shoved down. Tonka was breathing hard as he reached for his wallet. He barely got it out of his pocket before his pants were at his ankles.

The feel of Henley's hand on his cock almost made him come right then and there. Tonka pushed her hand off him a little roughly and ordered, "Pants off, Henley. *Now*."

She grinned at him and reached for her zipper. As she did that, Tonka tore open the condom he'd taken from his wallet and clenched his teeth as he pushed his underwear down just far enough to roll the thing over his throbbing cock.

The second Henley kicked off her shorts and underwear, Tonka's hand was between her legs. Thank *fuck* she was soaking wet. The last thing he wanted to do was hurt her. Especially their first time. He backed her against the door again until there was no space between them. His erection trapped against her belly.

"Jump up," he growled as he put one hand on her ass.

Still grinning, Henley didn't hesitate. She hopped a little, Tonka lifting her, and then she was in his arms. Bracing her against the door, he reared back a bit and reached for his cock. It took a little maneuvering on both their parts, but finally, after what seemed like an eternity, the head of his cock breached her pussy.

He paused then, and swallowed hard. Tonka wanted nothing more than to shove himself inside her as far as he could get, but he couldn't. Needed to make sure she was as desperate for him as he was for her.

Looking down, he was almost overwhelmed by how sexy the woman was. She still had on her bra, her generous tits pushed over the cups, her nipples hard as her chest rose and fell with her quick breaths. Her legs were spread wide around his hips, and he could see the tip of his dick just inside her body.

"Finn?" she asked. "What are you waiting for?"

"I need to make sure this is what you want."

She chuckled, and Tonka felt the reverberations move up his cock.

"I want this," she reassured him. "I *need* this. Need you. Fuck me. Please!"

That was all it took. Tonka moved before his brain could even send the proper signals to his limbs. One second he was admiring how sexy his woman was, and the next he was balls deep inside her. The shock of how good she felt around his cock almost made his knees buckle. But if he fell, Henley could be hurt, so he somehow managed to stay standing.

"Oh my God!" she exclaimed.

"Did I hurt you?" he asked, worried.

"No! Hell no. Please, more. I need more!"

"Hold on to me," Tonka ordered.

Her fingers dug into his biceps and her legs squeezed his hips even tighter.

Tonka couldn't have held back if his life depended on it. He fucked her. Hard. Against his door. This wasn't how he'd imagined their first time. He'd wanted to go slow, show her how much she meant to him. But they'd both been holding back their desires for a while, and this was the result.

With every thrust, Tonka felt as if he was returning to the man he'd once been. Confident. Content. Even a little cocky.

How could he not feel a little arrogant right this second? He had the most beautiful woman he'd ever seen writhing in his arms, begging for more. And if his Henley wanted more, she'd get it.

Balancing her ass on his forearm, Tonka shifted and reached between them with his free hand. The first time he flicked her clit as he pounded into her, he felt her muscles clamp down on his cock.

She jerked in his grip, thrusting her hips forward with his next thrust.

"You like that."

It wasn't a question.

She nodded and licked her lips as her gaze zeroed in on his face. "I like everything, Finn."

Tonka wanted to gaze into her eyes, wanted to see them glaze over as she orgasmed, but he couldn't stop himself from looking down as he fucked her. The sight of his cock glistening with her copious juices as he entered and retreated from deep inside her was the most carnal thing he'd ever witnessed.

He wasn't going to last. He'd wanted her for too long. Much longer than the five or so weeks they'd officially been dating. He'd been drawn to her the first time they'd met, but he hadn't been ready.

He increased the pressure and speed of his thumb against her clit and couldn't help feeling immensely satisfied by her reaction. Her hands tightened and she groaned. Her head went back and hit the door behind her, but he was pretty sure she didn't feel any pain.

Her hips rocked rhythmically against him, and he stopped thrusting so he could concentrate on making her come. So he could feel every muscle spasm and jerk around his cock.

It didn't take long. Her belly tightened and her back arched right before she began to shake uncontrollably. Tonka tightened his hold on her and watched in awe as she came apart in his arms. And he hadn't been wrong. She squeezed his cock so hard, it felt as if it would break right off inside her.

His balls tightened and, amazingly, with just the feel of her coming around him, he flew over the edge himself. Groaning, Tonka came so hard, he thought he'd never stop. No sex in his life had ever been better. And his masturbation sessions *certainly* weren't this fulfilling. They were both panting harshly, and he could see Henley's heartbeat in her neck.

He never wanted to move. Wanted to stay inside her forever. But he could feel his thighs shaking, both from the massive orgasm he'd just had and from holding Henley against the door. Not only that, but he could feel his come leaking out of the condom and onto his balls. He'd never come so much that he'd completely filled a condom.

Remembering that Henley wasn't protected from pregnancy, it took every ounce of strength he had to pull out of her body. But he didn't let go of her, simply turned and shuffled awkwardly toward the perfectly good bed in the bedroom across the cabin.

Her clothes were strewn across the floor, his keys and wallet lying forgotten in the mess, but all Tonka could think about was getting her to his bed and continuing where they'd left off. He usually wasn't raring to go twice in such quick succession, but he had a feeling Henley was rewriting everything he'd ever known and experienced when it came to sex.

* * *

Henley was having a hard time breathing. Or thinking. Or doing anything. Luckily, Finn seemed to be functioning a little bit better. She hated that he'd pulled out of her so quickly, but couldn't muster up the energy to ask why.

They'd almost reached the bedroom when she roused enough to open her eyes. And giggled at what she saw. Finn was shuffling rather than walking because his pants were still down around his ankles. He had on his shirt, his socks and shoes, and even his underwear was hanging around his thighs. She was naked except for her bra, which was cutting into her chest, now that she thought about it.

But somehow, the moment felt just right. Neither had been able to wait another second to be with the other. The anticipation had escalated over the last few weeks to its explosive conclusion.

And if she thought she'd feel less needy, less desperate after they'd finally had sex, she'd been wrong. If anything, Henley wanted him even more, now that she'd experienced everything that was Finn Matlick. In her younger days, Henley had loved sex. But she couldn't remember it ever being so intense.

They reached his bed, and he slowly leaned over and set her on the mattress. She leaned back and rested her weight on her elbows as she ran her gaze up and down Finn's body. As she stared, he began to strip. His shirt went up and over his head, and Henley's mouth literally watered. She'd seen him without his shirt on before, but there was something so sexy about Finn baring himself for her now, while she was mostly naked and he'd just been inside her.

He took off his boots and pants and shoved his underwear off. Then, as she watched, he removed the condom from his still half-hard cock. Beads of come dripped from the ruddy tip as he leaned over to grab a tissue from the small table next to the bed.

Henley moved without thought. She went to her knees in front of him and grabbed the base of his dick with one hand, taking as much of him as she could into her mouth.

"Shit!" Finn exclaimed as she moaned deep in her throat. Giving head had never been a favorite activity of hers, but with Finn? She felt ravenous. One of his hands thrust into her hair, but he didn't push her down or try to control the pace. He simply held on as she licked and sucked every trace of the orgasm that lingered on his skin.

He tasted a little like latex and was a tad bitter, but

Henley was more focused on the way his thighs shook as he separated his legs to balance himself. How good he smelled as her nose buried itself in his pubic hair when she took him down her throat. How the moans and groans that left his mouth sounded so desperate and needy as she pleasured him.

She used one hand to hold the base of his cock as she slurped and sucked, and the other she moved between his legs to fondle his balls. They were large and swung freely as his hips swayed with her movements. She caressed the sensitive sac and felt him grow even harder in her mouth.

She couldn't hold back a slight smile as she bobbed up and down. Having this man at her mercy, someone larger than life, someone who could control a thousand-pound horse or cow with merely a sharp word, was empowering, and she loved every second of being on her knees in front of him.

Just when she was getting into it, when she thought she might get to experience him coming down her throat, Finn moved.

He lifted her off his cock and off her knees as if she weighed nothing and practically flung her back onto his bed. She bounced a little, and didn't have time to do anything more than lick her lips before he was shoving her legs apart and diving in.

Henley's back arched as he practically attacked her. He licked and sucked as if he were a starving man. She'd never had anyone go down on her so voraciously before. She tried to shift her hips away from his hungry mouth, her clit still sensitive after her last orgasm, but he tightened his hold on her hips, holding her right where he wanted her.

"Finn!" she exclaimed as she clutched his hair. At first she tried to pull him off, but when he started sucking her clit, she pushed his face harder against her. Her brain was as confused as her body, apparently.

It wasn't long before she felt another orgasm rising. Her heart was beating so hard in her chest she would've been a little scared she was having a heart attack if she could think clearly.

Finn was making slurping noises and desperate sounds deep in his throat as he ate her out, and Henley couldn't do anything but hold on. As good as his tongue and lips felt, she was still empty. She'd *loved* having an orgasm while he fucked her. As much as she'd always enjoyed sex, including being filled, she didn't recall ever coming with someone inside her. Her orgasms were always clitoral, either before or after her partners got off. And her vibrator was no substitute for the real thing.

For Finn.

But she didn't get a chance to beg him to enter her before she was falling over the precipice once more. She half sat up as she clung to Finn's head and her body quaked with pleasure. And when he pushed two fingers inside her, she soared even higher.

"That's it. Fuck, you're gorgeous. Come on my fingers. That's it, baby. So beautiful and sexy. You're mine, Henley. All fucking mine."

She barely heard him through the ringing in her ears. Had sex ever been this good before? No, definitely not. A fine sheen of sweat coated her body, and Henley felt as if she'd run a marathon. Not that she knew what running a marathon felt like, but she imagined the aftermath had to feel something like *she* felt right now. Boneless, exhausted, and oh so satisfied.

And Finn wasn't done. Henley hadn't even realized he'd moved until he was rolling her over and urging her onto her hands and knees.

"Ass up, Hen," he ordered, pulling her up with a hand on her belly.

She looked back and saw that, while she'd been recovering from the latest orgasm, he'd put on another condom and was fully erect once more.

She let out a sound somewhere between a moan and a whimper as she arched her back and lifted her ass. She felt his hands at her back, and then her bra blessedly loosened around her. She didn't have time to lift her hands to throw it to the side before she felt his cock against her soaking-wet folds once more.

He didn't hesitate, but sank balls deep in one slow and steady thrust.

They moaned in unison that time.

"You have no idea how amazing this feels," he said in a strangled tone as his hands caressed her ass and lower back.

"Oh, I think I do," she said dryly.

Then he began to thrust. But instead of pounding in and out of her, as he had earlier, he kept his movements slow and gentle. It felt good, but Henley needed more.

On his next glide in, she thrust back against him, making his balls slap against her as he bottomed out.

He grunted. When he pulled out and pushed back in, she did it again. She bucked against him over and over, until he was holding onto her hips and fucking her hard. Almost frantically.

Henley went down to her elbows, changing the angle so he was hitting her G-spot with every stroke.

She couldn't think. Couldn't do anything but moan into the sheets under her as Finn took her on the ride of her life. And when he curled over her back, resting one hand on the mattress next to her face and the other between her legs, to pluck and rub at her clit, she completely lost it. Bucked against him so hard he actually slipped out when he pulled back at the same time.

His cock landed on her ass, but he never stopped playing with her clit. He straightened so she couldn't feel him against her back anymore. She felt the loss of his heat and was sad for a moment, but when she heard him let out a long groan, felt liquid heat hit her ass and back, she realized why he'd lifted off her.

He'd taken off the condom and was ejaculating on her skin. It could've felt degrading. Or gross. But it was the sexiest thing Henley had ever experienced. She immediately came once more as Finn continued to flick her overly sensitive bundle of nerves.

Her legs finally collapsed, and Finn fell with her, rolling to his side and taking Henley with him, cradling her as they both tried to catch their breath. Minutes later, he pushed her forward, back onto her belly, and his hand gently massaged his come into her skin.

Henley floated as if her soul had left her body. She'd never been turned inside out so deliciously.

Neither of them said a word, she just lay still and let Finn caress her. The scent of sex was strong in the air, and normally right about now, Henley would be craving a shower. Would even want the guy she'd been with to be on his way. But when Finn lay down again and pulled her close, her back against his chest, his flaccid cock against her ass, Henley could only sigh in contentment.

She must've dozed off, because when she woke up, she could tell it was much later. The light coming through the curtains was subdued. She was on her back, and turning her head slowly, she saw Finn lying next to her. One hand on her belly and the other propping up his head as he stared back at her.

Instead of feeling self-conscious, Henley felt sexy. When he realized she was awake, his hand moved upward until he was lazily playing with one of her nipples.

"Hey," she said softly.

"Hey," he repeated.

"How long did I sleep?"

Finn shrugged. "A couple of hours. You obviously needed it. You work too hard."

She smiled. "I think it was all the orgasms," she countered.

His lips twitched. He kept his gaze on hers, but his fingers didn't stop moving. He circled her nipple, and Henley could feel it tighten under his ministrations. He didn't seem as if he was gearing up to make love to her again. At least not yet.

"Did I hurt you?" he asked softly.

"No. Not at all. Did I hurt *you*?" she countered.

He grinned. "No. Although I don't think I've ever had anyone go down on me that...enthusiastically before."

Henley felt her cheeks heat. "Should I apologize?"

"No. *Fuck* no."

"Good. Because I liked that. A lot. Although you pulled away too soon."

"I was two seconds away from shooting down your throat," he said.

"I know. As I said, you pulled away too soon." With Finn, it didn't feel slutty saying such things. It felt perfect. Erotic.

"You want that?"

"Yes," she admitted without hesitation.

He moved then, rolling over until he was on top of her. His elbows on the mattress by her head, his body resting heavily against her own. She could feel his cock hardening against her belly, and she spread her legs, giving him more room.

Leaning down, Finn kissed her. It was a soft and loving kiss, and it made Henley melt even more under him. She wrapped her arms around his neck and kissed him back.

"You make me feel normal," he said after a moment.

"What's normal, Finn?" Henley asked. "We all make our own normal."

"True," he agreed. "You want to shower?"

Henley shrugged.

"No? You aren't grossed out by what I did?"

"Not at all. It felt good. Right."

"I liked doing it. Felt like I was marking you as mine."

She rolled her eyes a bit at that. "You're such a guy."

"Glad you noticed," Finn said. Then he rolled off her, and when Henley started to turn onto her side to snuggle into him, he put a hand on her belly and kept her on her back. "I want to do something. Will you let me?"

"Yes." She had no idea what he had in mind, but by the look of lust in his eyes, she had a feeling she would enjoy it, so it didn't matter.

"Lie still. Whatever you do, don't move," he ordered in a low, growly tone.

Henley never would've guessed this man was as sexual as he was when she'd first met him. The fact that he had such a high sex drive was a huge turn-on. She'd been a mom for so long, hadn't had the time or energy to think about anything other than raising her daughter. It felt as if she was coming out of a long, deep sleep.

Finn sat up, sitting cross-legged next to her, and Henley couldn't help but look between his legs. His cock was big. She'd known he was larger than normal when she'd taken him into her body...into her mouth...but she hadn't fully noticed how long and thick he was until right that moment.

"Close your eyes," Finn ordered with a chuckle. "Don't want you distracting me."

Henley huffed out a breath, but did as he asked.

For a while, all she felt was his fingers brushing up and down her body. It felt good, kind of ticklish but nice. Then without warning, one of his fingers slowly pushed inside her. Her hips automatically lifted, but he *tsked* in his throat and used his free hand to push down on her belly.

"Stay still," he ordered.

"Finn," she whined, but he simply held his finger still deep inside her pussy until she took a breath and relaxed against the sheets.

"You're so gorgeous. So small. I can't believe you were able to take me as easily as you did. But you get incredibly wet. I love that. It's such a turn-on. Even now, right after you've woken up and before I've even touched your clit, you're creaming all over my finger."

He kept talking. Henley had no idea dirty talk would turn her on so much, but it definitely was.

"I want to make you come like this. With you staying completely still and with nothing but my fingers. Will you do that for me?"

Henley's heart was beating hard once more. She licked her lips and nodded.

"Good girl." His finger began to move, slow at first, then faster, and it took every bit of control Henley had to stay completely still. One hand gripped the sheet at her side, and the other reached for Finn. She loved this, but she wanted to touch him too. Needed that connection. He didn't seem to mind when she put a hand on his thigh and held on for all she was worth.

"That's it. Hold on to me. Listen to my voice. Know that it's *me* making you feel like this. It's me inside you. It's me watching you come undone."

Henley had seen Finn do this before...well, not *this*, of course. But she'd heard him use the same calm, controlling tone. They'd gotten a new horse recently who was completely skittish from a trauma Henley knew nothing about. Finn had stood in the corral and talked to the animal for hours. Just letting it get used to his voice, understand it was safe and cared for. He'd made the horse feel relaxed enough that Finn was eventually able to approach and lead it into the barn.

She felt like a little that horse. Completely under Finn's command.

The sound of his finger moving in and out of her soaking folds was loud and obscene, and should've been embarrassing, but since she was with Finn, it wasn't.

"You hear that? That's your body's way of telling me

how much you love this. Getting ready to take me. You were made for me, Henley. Honestly...at first, you scared me. I think I knew you were going to get under all the shields I'd put up, and I wasn't sure I wanted anyone there. Now that you are, I never want you to leave."

Henley felt a tear escape her closed eyes. She wasn't sure why she was crying. Maybe because of how good she felt. Of how hard it was to stay completely still. Because of what he was saying. She wanted to tell him that he'd gotten under her shields as well, but was finding it hard to form words.

She felt as if she were floating. Finn was being extremely gentle. This sexual experience was nothing like what they'd done so far. It had been fast and hard earlier, but nothing about this slow build was any less pleasurable than when he'd been pounding into her.

"That's it. I can feel your muscles tightening around me. It's the most incredible feeling. Seriously. How about if I do this?" He moved the hand on her belly downward, until his thumb was gently brushing over her clit. He didn't press hard. Didn't tug or pull. He simply brushed over her again and again with a super-light touch.

She wanted more. Needed more. Wanted to press up against him, force his fingers to move faster. Harder. But he wanted her to stay still, so she clenched her teeth and tried to do what he wanted.

"Damn, Hen, you're amazing. Letting me do this. Your nipples are so hard, I bet they're throbbing, aren't they?"

They so were. She nodded.

"Hang on just a little longer. I promise to get you there."

A little longer turned out to be way too many minutes

for Henley. This was both torture and heaven at the same time.

When her orgasm hit, it was almost a surprise. One second she was gritting her teeth, doing all she could not to move, and the next her entire lower body felt as if it was on fire.

"So damn gorgeous," Finn breathed—a moment before he added a second finger inside her body and turned his hand. He pressed against that spot deep inside her that made Henley jolt in his grip.

All thoughts of staying still flew from her mind and her body convulsed as Finn caressed her from the inside out. Liquid shot from between her legs, soaking the sheets and Finn's hand. Henley would've been mortified if Finn wasn't so completely thrilled.

"Yes! *God yes*, Hen. Jesus, that's amazing. *You're* amazing. That's it...so good. You smell delicious. I could eat you up."

Henley had a feeling she'd kind of passed out there for a moment, because the next thing she knew, Finn was lying next to her, one hand covering her pussy possessively.

She roused enough to say, "Your turn?"

"Shhhh. I'm good. That was the most erotic thing I've ever seen. Thank you for giving that to me."

"Um, I think I should be thanking *you*. Do we need to change the sheets now?"

"Why bother when we're just going to get them all messy again later?"

Henley forced her eyes open at that. "Again?" she asked incredulously.

"I'm never gonna get enough of you, Hen. And since you now have a session tomorrow afternoon and I'll have to let you out of bed, I'm going to make the most of our time together."

Henley smiled and snuggled into him. "Okay."

"Okay," he agreed, the fingers over her pussy moving now, petting her.

Henley would've grinned again, but she was already nodding off. Besides, it felt good to have him hold her like this.

The last thing she felt before she fell asleep once more was his lips against her temple.

CHAPTER ELEVEN

Tonka felt like a completely different man than the one he'd been before he and Henley started dating. And it was all because of her. She gave him the strength to push the shadows to the back of his mind and concentrate on the here and now.

The morning after their all-night lovemaking session had been just as comfortable and easy as all the days leading up to it. Which was a relief, because the last thing Tonka wanted was Henley feeling embarrassed about everything they'd done together.

He'd never felt so free to do what he wanted sexually as he did with Henley. She trusted him implicitly, and as a bonus, enjoyed making love as much as Tonka. They'd both been insatiable throughout the long night and the following morning, and she'd barely made it to her appointment on time.

They'd showered together, did the laundry—which began innocently enough and ended with Tonka taking her while she was sitting on his washer—made a large breakfast, and even snuggled on the couch for a while, watching a random zombie show before making love once more.

She was everything Tonka had ever dreamed about in a woman, but never thought he'd find.

The night Jasna got back from camp was harder than he'd thought it would be. He missed Henley. Yes, the sex was out of this world, but it was the intimacy that he missed most of all. Even after just the few nights they'd spent together, he'd gotten used to looking over on the couch and seeing her. Waking up in the middle of the night and having her snuggled up against him. Getting out of the shower and smelling coffee brewing. Coffee that he hadn't had to make himself.

He'd been alone for so long, he'd figured it would be extremely difficult to get used to someone else being in his space. But that hadn't been the case at all. Henley fit into his world as if she'd always been there.

And being able to go to his cabin with her after work, knowing he wouldn't have to say goodbye, was something he hadn't even realized he'd needed.

So it sucked big time that first night after camp when she and Jasna had hung out in his cabin, then she'd stood up around eight o'clock and said they had to get going.

Tonka treasured every moment he got to spend with Henley and Jasna. He'd learned the hard way that nothing in life was guaranteed. He'd assumed he had many more years with Steel. He thought the dog would be retired from service from the Coast Guard, and he'd get to live out his years comfortable and pampered by Tonka. While Steel had "only" been a dog, he'd also been Tonka's best friend. They'd spent every minute of their days together.

Which was why it hurt so bad to have him so violently and suddenly torn away.

Shying away from his memories, Tonka returned his focus to the discussion going on around him. He and the rest of the guys were having their monthly business meeting about the goings-on with The Refuge. Revenue was up ten percent and donations had increased a hundred and forty percent since Alaska had first suggested adding a donation button to the website.

Savannah, their accountant, had just left after giving her report, and Jason was currently talking about the cabins and the needed repairs and upgrades to keep them looking as inviting as possible for their guests. Hudson and Robert had already given their reports, and thankfully there hadn't been any surprises with either of them as far as the landscaping and food preparation was concerned.

Before he knew it, it was Henley's turn. Tonka couldn't take his eyes off her. They hadn't made love since Jasna's overnight camp had ended, but truthfully, he was content simply to be around Henley. Did he like the sex? God yes. Did he *need* it? No. He enjoyed spending time with her because she was witty, and kind, and she made him feel like his old self again.

In the past, Tonka had barely paid attention in their monthly meetings because all he really cared about was the animals and making sure their needs were being met. He trusted his friends and co-owners to make good decisions about everything else. But today he found himself more interested than usual. The Refuge was his home, after all, and now more than ever, he wanted to make sure he was doing his part in keeping it a safe and happy place for everyone, not just their paying guests.

"I think the increase in people making their way to The Refuge outside the military is an interesting trend," Henley said. "While veterans are largely our focus, there are so many more outside the military who experience trauma, who also need help coping, and they're discovering The Refuge. Just last month, for example, we had eight guests who'd been sexually assaulted, two who'd been bullied so badly as kids they still struggle to cope today, four who survived a workplace violence episode, and three who'd been stalked and traumatized by a former spouse... and no, they weren't all female. Males can be traumatized by their wives just as easily as women can be by husbands."

"That *is* an interesting trend, and a great point," Pipe said. "What can we do to make them feel just as welcome as our veterans? We've worked hard to market this place toward veterans with PTSD, but as you pointed out, there are plenty of people who've experienced trauma unrelated to military service. Word of mouth has apparently brought plenty of people to The Refuge who haven't served in the Armed Forces, but I agree that we could do more."

"I'm not bringing this up as a criticism of anything you guys are doing or not doing. Just as an interesting point. While things like firecrackers and cars backfiring are still valid concerns, there are other things that could be triggers—for those outside the military—that aren't so obvious."

Spike frowned. "So we should update our intake form."

Henley nodded. "I can probably help with that, as I talk to most of the guests. I have a pretty good grasp of what could be triggering and what we might want to ask."

"What else?" Owl asked, leaning forward.

As Tonka listened to his friends and Henley discuss the

best ways to make sure all their guests were as safe as possible while they were here—both mentally and physically—he couldn't help but be impressed by his woman all over again. She was using her experiences to understand and help others. While he was...

What *was* he doing?

Avoiding thinking about Steel altogether. Hiding out as much as possible. Keeping his distance from some of the very people who would understand what he was going through more than anyone else.

He'd sat in on Henley's sessions and listened to guest after guest share what they'd been through. And not once had he tried to recognize the similarities between his own experience and theirs. He'd stubbornly taken the stance that nothing they'd been through was as bad as what *he'd* faced.

Pressing his lips together, Tonka suddenly felt... ashamed. Henley herself had gone through something most would argue was twice as traumatic as what he'd experienced, and at a significantly younger age, and she was coping a hell of a lot better than he was.

"You've given us a lot to think about, Henley," Brick said, jerking Tonka back to the discussion. "Any other suggestions you can give for what we should be doing differently in terms of guest recovery, please don't be afraid to bring it to our attention. Even if it's not at our monthly meetings. When we opened this place, we just wanted it to be a refuge for people. A safe place where they could get some much-needed peace for at least a little while. And if we're doing anything that makes that less possible, even unintentionally, we want to know about it."

"I will. And I think this place is incredible. Almost all

of the guests I've met with have said they've felt a tremendous sense of relief simply being on the property. They aren't judged for their mental health issues, which in itself is a huge deal. And as you know, we have a lot of repeat customers."

Brick and the others nodded, but Tonka could only stare at the woman across the table who was now standing and gathering her papers. She glanced at him, offering a small smile before she left the room.

"Right, so...that leaves us. What are everyone's thoughts about what we've heard from the others and how the place is doing? Anything we need to change?" Brick asked.

Everyone went around the room and gave brief reports on the things they'd been working on and gave their opinions about the business in general.

When it was Tonka's turn, for the first time in five years, he didn't talk about the animals.

"I want to thank you all for putting up with me for so long," he said solemnly. "I haven't pulled my weight when it comes to the everyday operations, and I'm sorry."

All six of his friends spoke at once, trying to deny his words, but Tonka held up a hand, stopping them.

"I appreciate you giving me time and space to work through my shit, although I'm sure you didn't expect it to last five fucking years. I haven't talked much about what happened to me...but maybe it's time."

Now it was so quiet in the room, Tonka could hear the clock ticking on the wall above their heads. "I can't go into detail...not now, and maybe not ever. But I had a canine partner. He was a Belgian Malinois and his name was Steel. I trusted him, and he trusted me. We were a well-oiled machine. He was my best friend. Well...a mission went bad. Bad in a way you can't even imagine, and I lost him. The man we were trying to bust for drugs got the drop on us and killed him in a horrific way.

"After that, I guess I just decided I preferred to interact with animals because they don't know how to be deceitful. How to be evil. They don't turn on you without reason. As long as they aren't hungry or cold, have adequate shelter, aren't beaten...they're perfectly happy to be your friend and they're completely loyal. I'd seen first-hand how evil humans can be, and after losing Steel, I painted almost everyone with the same brush.

"I know that's a fucked-up way to see the world, and I'm working on it. Thank you all for not giving up on me, and for putting up with me being so standoffish."

Tonka stared at the men around the table. He respected each and every one of them. He'd kept them at arm's length even though they'd been nothing but support-ive. He didn't know how they'd react to what he said— plenty of people thought his grief was bullshit because he'd lost a dog—so he braced for anything.

"Holy shit. Henley truly is a miracle worker," Spike said into the silence.

For a moment, everyone stared at him in shock—then they burst into laughter. Tonka couldn't help but join in. His friend wasn't wrong.

"Right?" Pipe said. "She's turned our grunting animal man into a pile of mush!"

Tonka threw his pen at Pipe, chuckling when it bounced off his forehead.

"Ow!" he exclaimed, bringing a hand to his head.

Everyone laughed harder.

"I mean, I know Alaska changed *me* into a better man, but jeez," Brick said with a shake of his head and a fond grin.

"Where can I find me a Henley?" Spike asked. And while Tonka and everyone else knew he was kidding, there was an undercurrent of wistfulness in the question that was easy to hear.

"It's been really great having you around more," Tiny told him.

"Agreed," Stone said with a nod. "I mean, I'm guessing you're never going to volunteer to run a karaoke night or anything, but seeing you at meals and at some of the nightly activities has been awesome."

"And having Jasna around this summer has been a ton of fun," Owl said.

"I second that. She's so inquisitive and full of wonder. You forget how healing that alone can be. And some of the guests have even mentioned how they've loved chatting with her in their reviews," Pipe agreed.

"We should talk about that," Brick said in a more serious tone of voice. "When we started this place, we agreed that no children were allowed. We didn't want to have undisciplined or unruly kids running amuck. Not to mention, crying babies could be a trigger for some people. But do we want to revisit our stance on the kids thing?"

"You asking for any particular reason?" Stone asked with a grin.

Brick smiled. "Maybe. I mean, I'm not saying Alaska and I are going to pop out a baby tomorrow, but there might come a time when we want to have children. And hopefully someday you guys will find your own women and possibly want kids yourselves. It seems a little unfair to have a no-children rule when our own could be running around someday."

"And opening the place up to kids would let more single parents take advantage of what The Refuge has to offer," Stone said.

"But here's the thing," Pipe said. "As far as our own children go, we have a say in how they're raised. We can teach them to be respectful and not bring them up to be hooligans. If we open The Refuge to kids, we have no control over how they'll act. I mean, we can have guide-lines and stuff, but what do we do if one of them is a holy terror?"

"Good point," Stone said.

"And crying babies could still be a trigger," Tiny added. "I think our cabins are far enough away from the others that if we had babies, they wouldn't always be heard by the guests."

"So, what? Alaska and Brick won't be allowed to bring their baby to the lodge?" Owl asked. "Just in case it might cry and make someone uncomfortable?"

"No, I'm not saying that," Tiny said.

"What if we started off by saying children over the age of eight will be welcome, but with certain rules? Like they have to be accompanied by an adult at all times?" Spike suggested.

"Or maybe we could have certain *weeks* where children are welcome. That way, anyone making reservations would know when there might be kids around, and can decide on their own if they want to come at that time," Tonka added, speaking up for the first time.

"That's a good idea," Brick said. "We could also come up with age-appropriate activities and stuff, maybe hire someone to entertain the kids while the parents take some time for themselves or when they're in therapy sessions. Down the line, we could even add a building that's specifically for kids."

"I have to admit, I like the adult vibe we have going on here," Spike said. "This isn't a theme park or a summer camp. We started this place with the intention for our guests to have a place where they can relax. No matter how well-behaved the kid, having children around brings a different vibe to the place. I think we've seen that with Jasna around this summer. And don't get offended, Tonka, I'm not saying I haven't enjoyed her being here. Just that it's different."

Tonka nodded. His friend wasn't wrong.

"However," Spike continued, "what I love even more about this place, and working with all of you, is that we aren't afraid to make changes. To keep up with new needs and demands. So many other businesses would refuse to do anything different, especially when they're making a profit. I like that we can talk about the pros and cons of things and come to a reasonable agreement."

The others agreed with Spike, as did Tonka. Hell, he was just glad to be involved in the discussion. It might have taken five years for the fog in his head to begin to clear, but he was lucky to have landed here in New Mexico with these men. Any other employer would probably have fired him by now. Not wanting to put up with his idiosyncrasies.

"Okay, we'll need to come up with some verbiage for the website and figure out what weeks we want to open the place to people with children. I'll have Alaska look at the reservations and see if there're any weeks that seem better than others. This summer and next are already pretty booked up, but maybe we can find time in the fall and spring that will work," Brick said.

More nods around the table, before Brick changed the subject.

"So...I take it things are going well with Henley?"

"Yeah, they are," Tonka said with a small smile.

"Good. You deserve to be happy," Brick said. "And before we get all mushy again, you want to talk to us about how the calf is fitting in? What'd Jasna name her again?"

"Scarlet Pimpernickel," Tonka said with a grin.

"Good Lord," Owl groaned with a smile and a shake of his head.

"Scarlet for short," he informed them. "And she's good. A little on the thin side, but we'll fix that in no time. Although she's gonna grow up to be just as big or bigger than Melba. We're probably going to need to expand the paddock. Especially with the horses and goats and who knows what else we'll take in."

The next twenty minutes were spent discussing how much space there was in the barn and how many more animals they could reasonably house before the barn itself needed to be expanded as well.

"If we keep expanding, we might need to hire someone to help Tonka," Stone said. "I mean, I know the barn is his domain, but there are only so many hours in the day."

"That'll be up to Tonka," Tiny said firmly. "The barn is his domain. I would never want to bring someone in who might disrupt his routine."

The others all looked to him for his thoughts, and once more, Tonka was thankful for these men. They might all be former military, and a little rough around the edges, but they were considerate and loyal. And instead of feeling panicked at the thought of sharing his animals with someone, of allocating some of his workload, Tonka thought about how much more time he'd be able to spend with Henley. "I'd be open to having some help," he said simply.

Brick grinned, as if he could read Tonka's mind. "I'll put out some feelers when the time comes, but you'll be in charge of interviewing and hiring, all right?"

Tonka nodded. In the past, he would've balked. Would've told Brick to hire whoever he wanted. But today, he felt confident enough to make such an important decision for himself.

"I don't know about you guys, but I'm about meeting'd out," Stone said. "Anyone want to check out the bunkers with me? We haven't done it in a while, and after what happened with Brick and Alaska, I figured it might be a good idea to make sure they're all good."

"I'm game," Spike said as he stood.

"I can take anyone interested on a hike to Table Rock, to keep them from possibly following you guys and seeing something they shouldn't," Pipe volunteered.

"It's also about time to check all the bird feeders around the property. I'll ask Jasna to recruit some volunteers to help her refill them. That'll keep a few people occupied until dinnertime," Tonka volunteered. He wanted to do his part to help his friends, but giving Jasna the job would thrill the girl—and give him and Henley a moment to be alone at the same time. She didn't have any sessions scheduled this afternoon, and he knew she'd come down to the barn to hang out until he was finished with chores and they could go eat.

"Perfect. Thanks, everyone. I'll keep you updated on

everything we talked about," Brick said as he scooted his chair back and stood.

Tonka got up quickly and made his way to the door. He felt good about opening up to his friends, but he couldn't wait to see Henley. He still didn't fully understand his compulsion to be around her all the time, but he didn't fight it either. She made him feel good. In general and about himself.

When he exited the conference room, he saw Henley and Ryan talking to Alaska. The three women had gotten closer over the last couple of weeks, and Tonka was happy for Henley. She'd admitted one night that she didn't have a lot of friends, and while he didn't know Ryan all that well, he liked and respected Alaska.

"Thanks again for helping me clean up the computer," Alaska told Ryan as the other woman smiled at her. "I can't believe all the websites Becky was visiting and all the cookies and tracking shit it ended up putting on the machine."

Tonka recalled that Becky was their last administrative assistant, and just like the many people in the position before her, she hadn't worked out. They'd all gotten lucky when Alaska took on the job.

Ryan nodded. "Of course. Now you know which folder all that stuff gets stored in, so you can empty it every now and then yourself."

"Yup. We're still on for shopping and lunch next week, right?" Alaska asked her.

"Absolutely. I'm off on Thursday and would love some girl time," Ryan answered with a smile.

"I can't wait," Henley said. "I can't remember the last time I had a girls' night out."

"Well, it's more like a girls' afternoon, but I'm okay with that," Alaska said with a laugh.

"On that note, I need to get moving. I've got one more load of sheets and towels to fold, then I'm out of here," Ryan told them.

"I thought Jess was on laundry duty today," Alaska said with a frown.

"She was. But her husband is sick, so I took her shift and sent her home." Ryan shrugged. "It's not a big deal. See you guys tomorrow. Hey, Tonka," she greeted with a smile as she walked past him toward the front door.

He came up beside Henley and put his arm around her waist, lowering his head to kiss her lightly.

"Hey," she said, leaning into him. "The rest of the meeting go okay?"

"Yeah. I wasn't trying to eavesdrop or anything, but Jasna's got that theater camp next week, right? You want me to pick her up on Thursday, so you can enjoy your afternoon off and don't have to worry about cutting it short? I can bring her back here so she won't be alone with me in your apartment."

Out of the corner of his eye, Tonka saw Alaska stepping away from the desk to greet Brick, but all his attention was on Henley.

She frowned. "Why would I care if you guys were alone in my apartment?"

Tonka gave her a look. "Because I'm a guy and she's your daughter."

It took Henley a moment to understand what he was implying. To Tonka's surprise, her brows furrowed and she looked mad. At *him*. Stepping out of his hold, she turned to him with her hands on her hips and asked, "Are you kidding me?"

"Um...no?" he said in confusion.

She frowned even harder for a moment, then grabbed his hand and towed him toward the door.

"Bye, Henley! Talk to you later!" Alaska called out.

"Definitely. I have to talk some sense into this idiot. I'll tell you about it later!" Henley responded loudly without slowing her stomping march toward the exit.

Tonka had no idea what she was all riled up about, but he couldn't keep the grin off his face. She was adorable when she was being all tough. While he was a little worried about what he'd done to irritate her, he already knew he'd do or say whatever was necessary to fix it.

She towed him all the way to the barn and the second they were inside, she turned on him. "Finn Matlick, why the hell wouldn't I trust you with my daughter? Are you going to hurt her?"

"What? No!" he exclaimed.

"Are you going to do perverted things that'll make me have to run you through with a sword?"

"No," he repeated, trying not to laugh at that visual.

"Have you, or have you not, spent time alone with her in this barn?"

"I have, but that's not the same."

"Why?" she asked, with her hands on her hips.

"Because. We aren't really alone."

"So the other day, when she was here for three hours with you while you taught her how to tie proper knots, you weren't alone?"

"We were, but guests could come in at any time when

we were in the barn. Taking her to your house, where we're *really* alone, behind closed doors...it's different."

Henley shook her head. "No, it's *not* different. Finn, I trust you with the most precious thing in my life—my daughter. I see the way you look at some of the guests when they get too close to her. If you could, you'd snatch her up and carry her away, simply to keep her safe. No matter what demons might get in your head, you're a good man. You've made my life so much easier this summer, but more than that, you've made *Jasna's life* richer simply by being in it. She adores you."

"You need to stop talking," Tonka said quietly.

But she didn't. "I don't trust easily, especially when it comes to my daughter. I've seen firsthand the bad things that can happen in life. But I would, with no hesitation, trust both my life *and* Jasna's life to you."

"Seriously, stop," Tonka begged.

"No, I won't stop. You need to know that whatever happened to you wasn't because of something you failed to do. If you could've stopped it, you would have. Your hands must have been tied. I know that without fail—because you would've rained hellfire down on whatever asshole was hurting you and those you loved if you could've."

She couldn't truly know how spot-on her comment was about his hands being tied, but Tonka couldn't handle any more of her sweetness. He stepped into her personal space and took her shoulders in his hands, backing her up until she hit the door of Melba's stall. The cow was out in the paddock at the moment, but Tonka didn't even think about that. All he could do was kiss her to make her stop talking.

She didn't push him away. In fact, Henley grabbed hold

of his shirt and took handfuls of the material in her fists and yanked him closer. Their kiss started out desperate and almost angry, but immediately morphed into a sensual, passionate embrace.

Tonka had never experienced this kind of immediate connection. She understood him on a level no one ever had. And the trust she had in him, when he didn't have it in himself, was humbling and overwhelming.

Even though he wanted nothing more than to take her against the stall, Tonka was well aware of their surroundings. He'd never do anything to embarrass her—or Jasna, who could wander into the barn at any moment.

He pulled back, breathing hard, trying to find the will to let go. He had one hand tangled in her hair, holding her still for his kiss, and the other was on the small of her back, clutching her against him.

"Damn, Finn," she said with a smile as she looked up at him.

"Sorry—" he began, but she shook her head.

"Oh no, you don't get to be sorry about that," she told him.

Her lips were wet and swollen and she looked as if she'd just been ravished. Tonka couldn't help but love that look on her.

"As I was saying, if you want to pick up Jasna next week while I'm out with Alaska and Ryan, I'd be grateful. If you want to take her to my apartment, that's fine. But I'm guessing she'd prefer to come here and hang out with you and your animals. I can meet you back here and we'll figure out dinner. I can stop and grab something after my shopping trip, we can eat at the lodge, or we can go back to your cabin and make something. I honestly don't care. I just want to spend time with you."

She was being sweet again, and it took a moment for Tonka to feel as if he could talk without his voice cracking. "How about we play it by ear and I'll text you and let you know what the plan is?"

"Perfect. When I drop Jasna off at camp, I'll let them know you're on the approved list to pick her up."

Tonka blinked. He hadn't even thought of that. There were so many little things he had no clue about when it came to raising a kid. "Okay," he told her quietly.

"Finn?"

"Yeah?"

"It might take some time to sink in...but no matter what happened in your past, the man I'm looking at right now is pretty damn awesome."

"I want to tell you," he blurted. "I told the guys some of it this afternoon. I just... Be patient with me."

A hand came up and palmed his cheek. "Take all the time you want. I'm not going anywhere."

And as he'd thought before, that was one of the biggest reasons why she had him in the palm of her hand—literally and figuratively. She wasn't pushy. Didn't insist he open up and spill all his secrets. She took him exactly the way he was. And the reassurance that she wasn't leaving only made him want to open up to her all the more.

Henley went up on her tiptoes and tugged on the back of his neck. He obliged and leaned down so she could reach him. She kissed him quickly and nodded. "Right, so now that we've settled the fact that I trust you, what do you want to do for dinner tonight?"

Tonka grinned. "I've got about two hours' worth of stuff to do here since I took time off for the meeting."

"No problem. I saw you had some ground beef in your fridge. You want me to make meatballs? Or we could have sliders?"

"Meatballs sound awesome," Tonka said.

"Cool. I'll see if I can find Jasna. She's around here somewhere. I'll get her to help me. That'll give you space to get things done here without her tagging along."

"I was going to have her go around and refill the bird feeders on the property with any guests who want to help," Tonka said.

"Cool. I'll tell her to come to your cabin when she's done and she can help with the meatballs."

"Sounds like a plan," Tonka said.

Henley smiled at him and shook her head.

"What?" he asked.

"It's just that if someone had told my ten-year-old self that I'd be this happy twenty-five years in the future, I would've told them there was no way. Take your time, Finn. I'll text you when dinner's close to being ready."

Tonka nodded, as he couldn't get any words past the lump in his throat. He watched as Henley walked away. She turned at the barn door, waved, then was gone once more.

How long he stood there, trying to get control of his emotions, Tonka wasn't sure. But eventually he roused himself enough to get moving. The faster he got done here, the faster he could get home and spend time with Henley and Jasna.

CHAPTER TWELVE

Henley was ridiculously excited about today. And since Finn was picking Jasna up from her camp that afternoon, she didn't have to worry about anything but having fun with Alaska and Ryan. Their plan was to eat lunch at Blue Window, which Henley had heard a lot of great things about, then go shopping.

Henley was generally a frugal person, she'd had to be raising a child on a single income, but The Refuge paid generously and her bank account was fairly healthy. Granted, Los Alamos didn't exactly have huge malls and designer shops, but Henley was happy enough to be out with friends.

Over the years, she hadn't had many. She'd been too consumed by school then work, and raising her daughter. So the fact that Alaska had even asked her to come today felt really good. Ryan was quickly becoming a good friend as well, and with each day that passed, the more content Henley felt.

Alaska held open the door to the local restaurant and

they all filed in. They were seated quickly and it didn't take Henley long to decide on the green chile BLT sandwich.

"So...I have to say it...you and Tonka are absolutely adorable together," Alaska said with a smile as she leaned on her elbows over the table after they all sat down.

"He's awesome," Henley said, nodding. "I've been attracted to him since the first day I started working at The Refuge, but honestly never really thought we'd be where we are today."

"He's pretty closed off," Alaska said.

Henley didn't take offense, since she wasn't wrong. "He's only said a few things here and there, but I gather whatever happened to him while in the Coast Guard was really awful. I know he had a canine partner, and that something happened to him, but I don't know the details."

Alaska nodded. "He's so good with all the animals at The Refuge. He's got a special touch when it comes to them, for sure."

"I think Jasna's got that same touch. I saw her the other day behind the barn and she actually had Chuck, that messed-up squirrel Tonka adopted, in her lap and was hand-feeding him."

"Wow, really?" Alaska asked. "I tried to get him to come to me and the second he saw me from twenty feet away, he bolted into that little house Tonka made. Did you guys know Tonka once compared me to that pathetic thing?"

Henley and Ryan chuckled.

"I'm serious! He said I reminded him of Chuck, and then went on to describe how pathetic and ugly the thing was," Alaska told them wryly.

Henley frowned. "I'm sure he didn't mean that in a bad way."

"Of course he didn't. His point was that Chuck was brave, and he thought I was too." Alaska shrugged. "I couldn't be offended because it was Tonka. He's quiet and introspective...and kind. I like him."

Even though her friend wasn't complimenting *her*, Henley still felt a wave of warmth flood her body.

"Me too," Ryan said just before the waitress put their lemonades on the table.

They all took long sips of the cool, refreshing drink, and then Ryan continued.

"I'm still really new to The Refuge, and sometimes it's hard to fit in when everyone around you has known each other and is used to the ins and outs of the way things work. He was nice enough to track me down when I first started and tell me the best times to go to the kitchen to get fresh cookies," she said with a smile. "And he said that if I brought Robert a box of Little Debbie Christmas Tree Cakes, he'd bend over backward to make sure I was always fed."

"Wait, what?" Alaska asked in confusion. "Christmas Tree Cakes?"

"Yeah, they're usually only out around December. I don't know why they're so good, but they are. I think it's the little green sprinkles on top or something. Anyway, I went online and was able to find someone selling them. I brought Robert four boxes and I literally thought his eyes were going to bug out of his head. He declared me his best friend, and I have to say...any chance of losing weight while I'm here is now officially shot to hell."

The women all laughed.

"I had no idea," Henley said with a shrug. "And I've been here a lot longer than either of you two. I'm gonna have some words with Finn when I see him next about not letting me in on that little secret."

"Anyway, my point is that Tonka went out of his way to welcome me when I started, and I appreciate it," Ryan said with a shrug.

"It has to be hard dating when you have an almost teenager," Alaska said.

Henley shrugged. "I mean, it's not the easiest thing I've ever done, but I think it's probably better now than when she was four or five. Back then, she needed constant supervision and entertaining. I swear I feel a little guilty now, because from the time we pull into the parking lot at The Refuge, Jasna's leaping out of the car and I don't see her again until it's time to leave. I appreciate both of you humoring her and letting her hang out with you and watch what you do."

"I'm not sure my job's too interesting to her," Alaska said with a small laugh and shrug. "But she does enjoy watching YouTube videos."

Henley wrinkled her nose. "I try to limit her screen time. Usually she's cool with it, content to read or play a game with me, but every now and then she gets sucked in and it's hard to tear her away."

"I'm surprised at how happy she is working with me," Ryan said with a small smile. "I've never seen a kid actually enjoy cleaning before."

"She doesn't slow you down too much?" Henley asked with concern. "I know how hard you, Carly, and Jess work, the last thing I want is her being a distraction."

"She's not!" Ryan exclaimed, sounding so genuine,

Henley was relieved. "She actually helps a lot. She thinks it's fun to steer the laundry cart back and forth from the rooms to the laundry. And aside from that one time, when she used twice as much detergent as she should've and we had bubbles floating across the parking lot, she's been great."

All three women laughed. Henley had been horrified when she'd looked out the window during one of her sessions and saw all the bubbles. She'd just had a gut feeling that her daughter was somehow involved with whatever had happened. And she hadn't been wrong. But everyone had taken the incident in stride and laughed at the odd inconvenience.

"She's a good kid," Ryan said after a moment. "She's well loved, that's easy to see. You've done an amazing job with her."

Henley felt her throat get tight. Hearing compliments like that made all the stress and frustration of single parenthood worth it. "Thanks," she said.

"You're welcome."

The waitress returned with their lunches and they all dug in.

"So...please tell me Tonka's good in the pleasure department," Ryan said with a wicked grin.

Henley almost choked on her sandwich, but managed to swallow without incident. "Pardon?"

"I mean, is it *really* a girls' day out if we don't bring up sex at least once?" Ryan asked with a laugh. The woman was refreshingly direct and funny—and Henley realized with a start she had no idea where Ryan came from or why she was in the middle of nowhere, New Mexico. The Refuge wasn't exactly on the beaten path, and someone as outgoing as Ryan seemed out of place with the rest of the mostly subdued staff at the retreat.

"Hell no, it's not," Alaska agreed.

"Should we talk about *your* sex life then?" Henley asked the other woman.

Alaska simply grinned. "We can. It's incredible. Drake knows what he's doing in bed, that's for sure."

"Shit, maybe I shouldn't have brought up the topic. It's been waaaaay too long for me," Ryan groaned.

"So?" Alaska prompted. "I'm guessing Tonka's the slow and steady type. Let's you take the lead. Am I right?" she asked with a grin.

Henley couldn't help the snorting laugh that escaped. "Um...no."

"Really?" she asked, her eyes lighting up.

Henley hadn't been prepared to talk about her sex life, but she trusted these women. "Really. Our first time? We barely made it into his cabin."

"That's kind of romantic," Ryan sighed.

"Well, it actually wasn't. We were standing up, he took me against the door, he was fully dressed, and neither of us lasted very long," Henley said with a small smile. "But it was also the hottest experience in my entire life. Pretty much every time we get together it's like an inferno between us. We haven't done things slow and romantic very often, but I'm guessing at some point we'll both be less desperate and will be able to take our time."

"Hot damn!" Alaska exclaimed. "I wouldn't have guessed that in a million years."

"Me either. But I'm so deliriously happy, I'm waiting for the other shoe to drop," Henley admitted.

"I felt the same way when I first got with Drake. I

mean, I'd loved him for most of my life, and it was so hard for me to believe he was into me."

"That's what she said," Ryan said.

Both Henley and Alaska looked at her with furrowed brows.

"What?" Henley asked.

"It was so hard...into you..." Ryan said with a sheepish look. "That's what she said."

For a moment, Henley just stared at the other woman, then she burst out laughing. Alaska did the same.

"Oh my God, you didn't just say that!" she exclaimed.

"Sorry, it just popped out," Ryan said with a little grin.

"Is this when I say, 'that's what she said'?" Henley quipped.

That got them all laughing again.

When they had themselves under control, Henley smiled at her friends. "All I can say is that Finn is everything I looked for years ago, before I had Jasna. I've always been a fan of sex, probably too much, but I've never been with a man who makes sure I'm completely satisfied before he sees to himself. It's sexy and makes me feel so cherished. And the way he is with Jasna...well, let's just say, when he tires of dating a woman with an almost-teenager, I'm going to be heartbroken."

"Who says he's going to get tired of you?" Ryan asked. "From where I'm standing, he's head over heels for you both. I have the distinct feeling that if *you* aren't sure whether or not you want things to become permanent, you should probably work on backing off and slowing things down."

"You think so?" Henley asked softly, trying not to get her hopes up too high.

"If that man isn't already head over heels in love with you, I'd be completely surprised. You can see it in his eyes. The way his gaze follows you wherever you go. The way he looks at Jasna. How attentive he is at all times. The way he can't stop touching you when you get close."

"She's not wrong," Alaska agreed. "Tonka looks at you the way Drake looks at me."

Henley was blushing, but she didn't care. "*Really?*" she couldn't help but ask again. She knew the answer. She'd seen all the signs herself. But, well...sometimes she needed assurances as much as the next woman.

"Yes!" both her friends said at the same time.

"You don't think we're moving too fast?" she couldn't help but ask.

"Do what feels right," Ryan said. "Life's too short to have regrets."

"What are you, a freaking Hallmark card?" Alaska teased, then turned to Henley. "But she's right. Besides, you've known Tonka for years, it's not as if you met one day and were in bed the next. I'm guessing it's a little difficult to navigate the dating waters with Jasna around?"

Henley nodded. "But I can't deny I love watching them together. He doesn't get irritated that she asks a million questions. I admit that I don't exactly like not being able to be with him as much as I want, if you know what I mean, but when he cares so much for Jasna, it makes my frustration seem like not such a big deal."

"Jas has another overnight camp coming up in a couple weeks, right?" Alaska asked.

Henley nodded. "Yup. And I can't wait."

All three women grinned at each other.

"Okay, I'm thinking that's enough sex talk, especially since I'm not getting any," Ryan complained.

"Well, there are five other single guys at The Refuge," Alaska told her. "Why not go after one?"

Ryan's cheeks flushed, and she looked down at her plate as if it was the most interesting thing she'd ever seen.

"Wait, you *do* like one of them? Who?" Alaska pressed.

"Nope, no, I don't. I'm not getting involved with anyone. I'm single and I'm staying that way," Ryan protested.

But Henley could hear the pensiveness in her voice.

"Why?" Alaska asked. "They're all really good men."

"Yeah, and they're all former military," Ryan replied without hesitation. "I know the type. Badass super-soldiers who're nosey and bossy as hell, and I'm guessing most of them would never be satisfied with a fling. They'd want to know everything about me and my history, and they probably all want to be knights in shining armor or something. I don't want or need any of that. So I'm going to stay as far away from them as I can. I'm happy to have a job, and that's all."

Ryan was definitely protesting too much—and now Henley was concerned. She'd seen enough of her patients attempt to deflect and skirt around the issues that were the root causes of their mental struggles. While on the surface Ryan seemed happy and easygoing, Henley had a feeling she was anything but.

Unfortunately, this wasn't the time or place to try to delve deeper. Also, Henley had made the decision a long time ago not to psychoanalyze her friends.

"Anyway, I'm happy for you both, but I'm good. Promise," Ryan said. "So...where are we shopping today?"

Recognizing the attempt to change the subject, Henley nodded. "I thought maybe we could check out the consignment shop over near the Central Shopping center. I've found some pretty cool stuff there in the past, and I'm still on the lookout for that two-dollar Navajo blanket someone drops off that's actually worth millions."

Alaska laughed. "Is that really a thing?"

"It's happened. Maybe not around here because too many people know how valuable those things can be. But still..."

"I'm up for a good thrift store scrounge," Ryan said. "I've found some pretty awesome things others have basically thrown away."

With the decision made on their next stop, Henley finished the rest of her sandwich. There was a little argument about who was paying for lunch, but in the end, they all agreed to pay for their own meal...and to over-tip their waitress, who'd been so prompt and friendly throughout lunch.

By the time the three women were shopped-out hours later, Henley was tired and her feet hurt, but she couldn't remember an afternoon when she'd laughed so much or had such fun.

They were standing in the parking lot of an adorable gift shop named Bliss as they said their goodbyes. Henley had bought so many British chocolates and other goodies from the specialty shop that her bank account was crying. But she couldn't even bring herself to care. Jasna would love everything she'd bought for her today, and she hoped the little things she'd gotten for Finn would bring a smile to his face as well.

"I had fun today," Alaska said.

"Me too," Henley agreed.

"Me three," Ryan said. "When I took the job here, I never thought I'd actually make friends."

"Why not?" Alaska asked with a small frown. "You're funny, considerate, you work hard, never leave the crap jobs to Carly or Jess, and you're always offering to help others—like me—when they need it."

Ryan shrugged. "I don't know. I've kind of kept to myself in the past."

It was on the tip of Henley's tongue to ask why, but she swallowed the question at the last second. Instead, she stepped forward and hugged the other woman. "Well, there's no need to do that anymore," she said firmly.

Alaska hugged Ryan as well.

"Thanks, guys. Anyway, I guess I'll see you both tomorrow," Ryan told them.

"We should do this again soon," Alaska said firmly.

"I'd love to," Ryan said. "Maybe we could invite Jess and Carly. Even Luna."

"That's a great idea," Henley said with a huge smile. "I'd love to get to know them better."

"It'll have to be a little later in the day though," Ryan warned. "It's not like all three of the housekeepers can just up and leave work at the same time."

They all chuckled. "True. Okay, we'll play it by ear. Maybe we can do an afternoon shopping trip, then have dinner somewhere."

"Margaritas!" Ryan exclaimed happily.

"That sounds awesome," Alaska agreed. Then she turned to Henley. "You headed home then?"

"Yeah. Finn picked up Jasna from camp. The original plan was for them to go back to The Refuge, but they got sucked into a show and decided to watch some more episodes, so they're still at the apartment. I texted earlier and asked if they wanted me to bring home something for dinner, but Finn said they had it covered."

"Are you scared?" Ryan asked with a grin.

Henley laughed. "Actually, no. I mean, Finn's not the best cook in the world, but I trust him."

"That's awesome," Ryan said, the longing back in her voice. "That you trust him, I mean."

"Yeah," Henley said.

"All right, we could stand here all night, but I'm sure Drake's anxious for me to get back to The Refuge. See you guys tomorrow. Drive safe!"

"You too!" Henley and Ryan said at the same time.

All three shared a smile, then headed for their vehicles. They'd shared a car earlier when they'd been going from place to place, but before coming to the quirky gift shop that sold all things British, they'd agreed it would be their last stop and they'd all driven here individually.

Henley looked at the cargo area of her CRV through the rearview mirror and smiled. There were a ton of bags back there and she couldn't wait to share everything she'd gotten today with Jasna...and Finn.

She desperately wanted to have some alone time with him, but she knew when they were able to find the time to be intimate again, it would be worth the wait. She'd never been a fan of anticipation in the past, remembering how torturous it was waiting for Christmas morning, but now she was learning how fun it could be. How much better it made any moments alone with Finn.

Still smiling, Henley pulled out of the parking lot and headed for her apartment.

* * *

Christian Dekker drove out of the parking lot behind the shrink. He'd been following her all day, his anticipation building. He was tempted to make his move right then, take the bitch doctor instead, but he'd forced himself to wait. The anticipation was the best part. He'd been over and over what he was going to do in his head.

He'd scoped out a small, deserted cabin not too far from town. No one else was around for miles and he could do whatever he wanted, for as *long* as he wanted. There would be no reason for anyone to check the cabin when the kid went missing. And no reason to suspect he was behind her disappearance.

Thinking about how frantic and upset the shrink would be when no one could find her kid made him flush with pleasure.

He'd actually liked her when they first met. Had contemplated trying to change with her help. Suppress his desire to kill animals. Try to get along with his parents and sister. Yes, he'd gone out of his way to shock the therapist, say things that would scare her...but deep down, he'd actually liked going to her sessions.

Until she'd turned on him. Tried to get him sent away. And she'd pawned him off on that asshole she worked with. He'd felt betrayed in a way he hadn't experienced before—and Christian hated it.

She was going to pay for making him think she was different. That she wasn't just getting paid to talk to him, but truly cared.

His revenge had been a long time coming, but he was disciplined enough to wait for the perfect opportunity.

The bitch and the kid were spending a lot of time at that fucking motel place on the outskirts of town. They had cameras all over the property, so he couldn't risk grabbing her there. Not to mention, he was well aware the men who owned the place were former military. Everyone in town knew. They made a big deal out of the "heroes" who were helping others, and it sickened Christian.

He'd almost grabbed the girl earlier this week. She was at some bullshit camp, and at one point during some group activity, she'd gone to the bathroom. He'd almost made his move. But then another girl went into the bathroom, and Christian hadn't wanted to risk there being any witnesses. Yes, he could've taken both girls, but he wanted to concentrate on the shrink's kid to start. She would be his first. That was the plan. And he didn't want to do anything to risk fucking it up.

He already had all the tools for what he had in mind stored in the vacant cabin. Pliers, hammer, rope, handcuffs...he'd even stolen money from his dad's wallet to purchase the roofies. He was ready. He just had to find the perfect time to snatch the girl.

As the shrink pulled into the parking lot at her apartment, Christian saw the truck owned by the guy she was now apparently dating. The fact that the dude was always around made things more complicated, but not impossible. The asshole wouldn't stop him from doing what he was born to do.

Christian Michael Dekker would be the most famous serial killer the country had ever seen. Even more famous than John Wayne Gacy, Jeffrey Dahmer, Charles Manson, or Ted Bundy. And his body count would be higher than any of theirs. Much higher.

Everyone had to have a first, and the kid would soon be his. Maybe he'd specialize in killing children. That might be a cool angle, might make him even more infamous. Yes, a couple other serial killers had primarily targeted kids...but he'd do it better. More often and in more gruesome ways. Christian wanted to stand out. Make his mark on the world.

Anticipation grew within him once more as he drove past the apartment complex toward his house. He hadn't been back there in a couple of days, and he knew his parents and sister were probably relieved. Well, they'd be rid of him soon enough. Something they'd wanted ever since they realized he was different. They were still on his list of people who had to die, but he rather liked the thought of them looking over their shoulder for years, wondering if or when he'd strike.

He'd get to them soon enough, when they least expected it. When they'd let down their guard and thought he was gone forever. But first...the shrink's kid.

He couldn't wait.

CHAPTER THIRTEEN

The summer was flying by. On one hand, Tonka was glad. The Refuge was always packed in the warmer months and he much preferred the slower pace of the winter. But he was also a little sad because fall meant Jasna would be going back to school. He wouldn't get to spend his days with her at the barn.

Her curiosity was refreshing and inspiring, and she never balked at any of the messier chores that needed to be done with the animals. She'd actually had a blast while using the backhoe to scoop shit out of the corral.

As for Henley, he'd never imagined that being in a relationship would be so...easy. She was the perfect girlfriend. That didn't mean she was a perfect person. She spent too much time worrying about others, she worked too much, was a little too lax when it came to her own personal safety, and had a tendency to put regular chores off so long that by the time they absolutely had to be done, they were almost overwhelming. Laundry, taking the trash out, doing the dishes.

Tonka shook his head, remembering the last time he'd been at her apartment and saw the sink literally over-flowing with dishes. She'd merely shrugged and said there were more important things in life than keeping a tidy house. Like spending time with Jasna.

He couldn't exactly disagree. He was learning to appre-ciate each day as it came instead of dwelling on the past.

But still...today was a tough one for him. He was having trouble shaking off his funk.

It was the anniversary of Steel's death, and it still felt as if it happened yesterday instead of years ago. Memories had bombarded him since waking this morning. He was strug-gling not to get sucked down into the depression and anger he'd felt nearly every day before starting things with Henley.

Luckily, Jasna was shadowing Jason for the day and was off planting trees and trimming bushes, so she didn't have to be affected by his bad mood.

When Tonka realized he'd just yelled at one of the goats for doing what she always did—trying to eat some-thing she shouldn't—and had smacked Scarlet's rump a little harder than he should've while trying to get her to move faster, he knew he needed to get out of the barn. The last thing he wanted was his mood to physically hurt one of the animals. Or to psychologically damage them further than they already were.

He headed for his cabin, needing to be alone.

Tonka hadn't been there for thirty minutes before his phone vibrated with a text. He'd been sitting on his couch, staring into space, reliving the worst day of his life and second-guessing what he'd done and not done. Looking down, he saw it was from Henley.

. . .

Henley: Where are you?

He typed out a quick response.

Tonka: My cabin.
   Henley: Are you okay?
   Tonka: No.
   Henley: Can I come see you?

He appreciated her asking first. Taking a deep breath, Tonka contemplated what to say. On one hand, he desperately wanted to see her. But he also didn't want to drag her down into the abyss. He wanted her to stay the way she was. Happy. Clean. But she was probably the only person in his life at the moment who could make him feel even the tiniest bit better.

Tonka: Yes.

She didn't respond, but he knew without a doubt she was on her way. If the roles had been reversed, nothing would've kept Tonka from getting to her. She didn't know what today was. Didn't know what happened, but it didn't matter. She'd help him any way she could. And not just because she was a psychologist. Not because they were dating. She'd do it for any of her friends.

A few minutes later, a light knock sounded on his door.

"Come in," he called out.

Then she was there. Henley didn't say a word, simply sat next to him, grabbed his hand, squeezed hard, and put her head on his shoulder.

Tonka didn't know how long they sat like that, but eventually the hold the past had on his tongue began to loosen the tiniest bit.

Without prompting, his mouth opened...and he began to talk.

"When I was in the Coast Guard, you know I had a canine partner. Steel was my best friend. I was matched with him when he was only six months old, and we did everything together. Ate, slept, played, worked. I didn't go *anywhere* without that dog by my side. I could read his body language as if he was speaking English.

"We were on a mission with my friend and co-worker. His name is Raiden—Raid—and his dog's name was Dagger. We came up on a suspicious boat and boarded, as we often did. We fucked up by not waiting for our backup to arrive, but the boat wasn't that big. We both thought we could handle whatever situation we found. But things went to shit from the second we stepped onboard. Raid was almost immediately knocked unconscious, and I couldn't order Steel to attack because one of the guys had a gun pointed at Raid's head.

"They tied me up...and it was then that I learned we'd come across one of the most notorious drug lords in South America, Pablo Garcia. We'd been so cocky. And we were going to pay for it."

Tonka took a deep breath and stared off into space. He vaguely felt Henley squeeze his hand, and her touch was the only thing that was keeping him from breaking into a million pieces.

"They tortured Steel and Dagger. How fucked up is that?" he asked quietly, agony in his tone. "Garcia laughed as he hurt them. I won't go into detail, because it's not something I can ever talk about again. I didn't beg for their lives, knowing it would egg him on more, but even today...even knowing it would have made things worse...I hate myself for that. All I see when I close my eyes is Steel's amber gaze, begging me to help him. I was his best friend—and he couldn't understand why I wasn't doing anything to make his pain stop. Their legs had been zip-tied together, and they were completely helpless to anything Garcia wanted to do to them.

"Their whimpers and yelps are burned into my brain. And Dagger kept looking at Raid, but he was out cold. It was horrible...and every time I close my eyes, I relive it." Tonka whispered that last part before clearing his throat and continuing. "When Garcia got tired of his games, he threw my best friend, my partner, the dog I loved more than life, overboard while he was still alive. He'd tied some weights around them and threw both dogs into the water as if they were nothing more than trash."

Tonka heard Henley's sob, but he pushed himself to keep talking.

"His intention was to do the same to me and Raid, but he didn't get the chance. Our backup showed. There was a shootout, and I was hit with some stray rounds, but honestly, I question every day why I survived when Steel didn't. Something within me broke that day. And I'm not sure I can ever be put back together completely. The fact that Garcia is behind bars is the only thing that lets me get any sleep at night.

"People have questioned why I've had such a hard time coping with what happened. They can't understand why I have such bad PTSD when no one died. And of course, they mean when no *people* died. But to me, watching Steel suffer, seeing his pain, his confusion, was so much more horrifying. So soul-crushing that I'm not sure I'll ever fully recover.

"I envy Raid. He was unconscious throughout the entire thing. He didn't see Dagger, didn't see what that monster did to him. I'm sure he feels guilty enough about that. But I have guilt too."

When he didn't continue, Henley asked, "About what?" Her voice wavered, but her grip on his hand never loosened. Not even for a second.

"I used to wish it had been *me* who was knocked unconscious. So I wouldn't have had to see what I did. But that would've left Steel alone. And what kind of asshole wishes his friend was the one to see what I did? I should've done something to help Steel, Dagger, and Raid. But I didn't. I sat there and let that asshole hurt my best friend. Torture him."

"You already know if you'd shown him how badly you were hurting, he would've been even more sadistic," Henley said quietly.

Of course Tonka knew that. But it didn't lessen the guilt still choking him like a yoke.

"And *fuck* those people who insinuated you shouldn't be so upset that Steel was murdered. The fact that you're still struggling to deal with what happened proves how deeply you loved him. It doesn't matter that Steel was a dog. As you said, he was your partner in every sense of the word. Your best friend. I think I'd be more worried about you if you *weren't* having a hard time dealing with his death. Finn? Look at me."

He didn't want to. He was falling apart, and he hated her seeing him like this. When he felt her hand on the side of his face, Tonka took a deep breath and turned in her direction.

When he stared into her beautiful hazel eyes, all he saw was sorrow and pain...for *him*. There was no judgement. No pity. No exasperation. He swallowed hard.

"Hearing what happened helps me understand so much," she said quietly. Her eyes filled with tears as she stared at him, but she didn't stop talking. "It explains why you prefer the animals' company to humans. They can't hide what they're thinking or feeling. They aren't hiding a black heart like the man you encountered. And what you went through explains why you and Jasna get along so well."

Tonka frowned.

"Kids are a lot like animals. They depend on us for *everything*. For food, safety, shelter, comfort. The younger they are, the more they need us. Jasna isn't five anymore, but she's still vulnerable. I think deep inside you recognize that, and you're doing what you can to teach her, protect her, nurture her...just like you did for Steel. Jasna's not a dog, I understand that, but there are similarities that can't be ignored."

Tonka was stunned—because she was validating how he felt the first time he'd seen Jasna. When he'd compared her to his best friend. "She's safe," he added after a moment. "She's too young to be as evil as Garcia. Not that

I'm saying your daughter could *ever* be like him, but I feel more comfortable around her than most adults."

A weird expression came over Henley's face. One he didn't understand. Until she continued.

"I used to think that people were born a blank slate. They were neither good nor bad. That their environment dictated how they turned out. You know, the whole nature versus nurture thing. I was firmly in the nurture camp. But about four years ago, I was assigned a new client. A boy. He was twelve and his parents were at their wits' end with him. He wouldn't listen to anything they said, he was prone to angry and violent outbursts, and they were actually afraid he was going to do something to hurt either them or their other child, a girl who was four years younger than her brother. I was determined to get to the root of his issues, to learn how he'd become the way he was. But you know what I found out?"

"What?" Tonka asked.

"Nothing. I found out *nothing*. He didn't have any trauma in his past. No abuse, his parents' marriage was healthy. He hadn't lost anyone close to him, wasn't being bullied at school. By all accounts, this kid should've been happy and carefree, like any twelve-year-old. But instead, he was...dark. That's the only word I can use to describe him. And honestly, he scared me too. He was calculating, manipulative. Even so young, he knew how to play sick mind games. And the darkness I could see in his eyes was terrifying. I talked to Mike, and we agreed he'd take over the kid's sessions. I'm ashamed to say that all I felt was relief. He quit coming several months after that, but he still lives in Los Alamos."

She shivered, and Tonka frowned. Then she took a

deep breath, wiped the tears off her cheeks, and shifted so she was sitting in his lap. Her arms went around his neck, and she stared into his eyes.

"You're allowed to feel how you feel, Finn. Losing Steel was traumatic, and that Garcia guy knew that hurting him would cause you pain. Don't let *anyone* make you feel as if your trauma isn't as deep or important as someone else's. I don't know if anyone's ever given you permission to grieve for Steel as much as you would if he'd been a human partner...but that's exactly what I'm doing."

Incredibly, those words loosened something inside Tonka.

Her permission, her understanding, gave his feelings *legitimacy*.

He'd tried to convince himself over and over through the years that Steel was "only" a dog. That he needed to snap out of it and get on with his life. But that only made him feel worse. Steel had never been *only* a dog. Not to him. And seeing him suffer so horrendously had been the most painful thing he'd ever experienced.

"Thank you," he whispered, gripping Henley's waist.

"You're welcome. And because I am who I am, I have to ask this next thing. Have you talked to your friend, Raid, since it happened?"

Tonka winced. "No. I told you the other day that I was thinking about calling him, but I haven't yet."

"I think you should. He may not have been conscious, but he lost his partner too. Dagger, right? I'm guessing he's hurting just as much as you are. In a different way, but there's no right or wrong way to grieve for what you've both lost."

Tonka thought about his partner. Raid was goofy. He

was the tallest guy he'd ever worked with. He towered over people, and if that didn't make him stand out enough, he had red hair and pointy ears. He was also a nerd, preferred to sit home and play games on the computer than go out with the guys. But he was loyal, smart, and he'd been a damn good Coastie.

"He joined a search and rescue team in the foothills of the Appalachian mountains," he told Henley. He closed his eyes tightly. "Today's the anniversary," he admitted quietly.

He felt and heard Henley's surprised inhalation. "Do you have his number? I bet he'd really appreciate hearing from you," she replied quietly.

Tonka wasn't so sure about that, but the more he thought about it, the more he wanted to know what his old friend was up to. Needed to know that he was okay. Especially today.

"I have his number," Tonka admitted.

"I can give you some space if you want to call him," Henley said.

Tonka felt her muscles shift, as if she was going to climb off his lap. He tightened his hold and his eyes popped open. "No!" he said desperately. "If I'm going to do this, I need you with me."

"Okay. I'll stay right here," she soothed.

Tonka took a deep breath. Could he do it? Could he call Raid? He hadn't thought he'd ever voluntarily tell anyone again what happened that day, and yet he'd done just that with Henley.

"Who else can truly understand what you're feeling better than him?" she asked gently.

She was right.

Without a word, Tonka leaned over and grabbed his

phone, which was sitting next to the couch on the end table. He clicked into his contacts and stared at Raiden's name for a long moment before taking a deep breath and clicking the number.

Bringing the phone up to his ear, he heard it ring once, twice, then a third time. Just when he thought Raid wasn't going to answer, a deep voice said in his ear, "Tonka?"

"Hey," he said.

"You all right? Everything good?" he asked bluntly.

"Yeah. I just...I was thinking...you know...because of what day it is...and thought I'd reach out. See how you were doing." Tonka's words sounded stilted even to his own ears. This was even harder than he'd thought it would be.

"I'm as good as I can be today," Raid said.

"I miss Steel," Tonka blurted.

"Same. Dagger should be an old man right about now. Caring about nothing more than sleeping and chasing the squirrels that dare infiltrate his backyard domain," Raid answered.

To his surprise, Tonka chuckled. He hadn't thought he'd be able to find anything funny today. "Right? Damn. And Steel loved balls so much, he'd probably have a fucking huge trunk full of the damn things by now because I spoiled him so much, couldn't stop myself from buying a new one every time I was at the store."

Henley shifted off his lap, but didn't leave his side. He moved his arm so it was around her shoulders, and she rested her cheek on his chest.

"Remember when Dagger and Steel snuck out of the room when we were in a meeting? And when we were done and went to find them, they'd actually opened the refrigerator in the break room and had taken out our lunches and eaten every scrap? They didn't take anyone else's meals. Just ours."

Tonka chuckled. He'd forgotten about that. "They were such brats sometimes," he said.

The next ten minutes were spent reminiscing about both dogs. Surprisingly, it felt...good. Nice to remember the good times, rather than dwell on the bad thing that had happened to them on this day all those years ago.

"How're *you*, man?" Tonka asked. "You still with the SAR team?"

"Yeah. Found our two-hundredth missing person the other day."

"That's awesome."

"Yeah. And I've got Duke to thank," Raid said.

"Duke?"

"My bloodhound. You know, I had no intention of ever getting another dog after losing Dagger. Even the thought of it hurt. But then Duke came into my life. He was a tiny puppy, and he'd literally been thrown away in the trash. He's nothing like Dagger. I think that made it easier."

Tonka nodded. He knew exactly how his friend felt. He hadn't wanted another dog either. Taking care of the dogs in the barn was one thing, but he couldn't imagine ever having another as a partner, like Steel had been.

"Duke's literally the laziest mutt I've ever seen. Except when it comes to a search or food. Of course, I used food to scent train him, so that's probably why," Raid said with a laugh. "He slobbers everywhere, sleeps twenty-two hours a day, and he's exactly what I needed to get my head out of my ass and live again."

Without thought, Tonka said, "You need to get yourself a woman."

Raid chuckled. "Have *you*?"

Tonka looked down at the woman in his arms and said quietly, "Yeah."

"You know I live in Fallport...there aren't exactly a ton of choices when it comes to chicks here," he joked.

"No one?"

"Well, there's my pain-in-the-ass assistant," Raid said with a laugh. "But we snipe at each other more than we actually talk, so yeah, the situation looks kind of bleak."

Tonka could swear he heard more than irritation in his friend's voice when he mentioned his assistant, but it had been a long time since he'd seen or talked to Raid, and he might be misreading the situation.

"Anyway, I'm happy for you, brother. I've thought about you a lot over the years. Worried about you."

"Yeah. Same. That situation was fucked up," Tonka said quietly.

"It was," Raid agreed. "But that asshole's behind bars where he can't hurt anyone else."

"He's probably going to get out one of these days," Tonka warned. "With how crowded the prisons are, I'm guessing he'll be let go way before either of us are ready."

"Well, let's just hope that'll be a long time from now."

"Definitely. Anyway...I wanted to reach out today because I was thinking about what happened and had the urge to make sure you were all right."

"I'm hanging in there," Raid said. "Some days are better than others, but I love what I do, and being a librarian suits me. As does Fallport. It's quiet. Nothing much happens here."

"Famous last words," Tonka said with a small huff of

laughter.

"True. Forget I said that," Raid said. "And...it's really good talking to you. I wouldn't mind if we kept in touch a bit better."

"Same. And you're always welcome to spend time here if you're ever in the area. I know New Mexico and Virginia aren't exactly driving distance apart, but..."

"Thanks. I've heard awesome things about The Refuge. You and your friends have really gotten a good reputation. What you're doing is definitely needed in today's world."

"It is," Tonka agreed. "I'm gonna let you go. But, Raid?"

"Yeah?"

"Thanks. I needed to remember Steel and Dagger the way they were...not how I last saw them."

"Anytime, brother. They were great dogs."

Tonka was too choked up to say much more. "Talk to you later."

"Later."

He clicked off the phone and put it back on the table next to him. Then he wrapped his other arm around Henley and buried his nose in her hair. He held her as tightly as he dared.

"That sounded like it went well," she whispered against his shirt.

"Yeah. I miss him."

"Raid?"

Tonka shrugged. "Steel."

"Sounds like he was kind of a goofy dog." He could hear the smile in her voice.

"He was. But he was also smart as a whip, loyal, and deadly as hell when he needed to be."

"Tell me about him?"

If it had been anyone other than her—and probably any other time than right now, when he was feeling nostalgic and his guard was down—Tonka would've refused. But after reminiscing a little with Raid, he found he was almost eager to tell Henley some stories about his beloved Steel.

He didn't know how long he talked, just that Henley stayed against his side and listened without interruption, only asking a few questions here and there. The pauses between the memories of Steel got longer and longer, and Tonka realized how exhausted he was.

"Sorry...I'm so tired," he said after a while.

"It's okay. Sleep, Finn."

"Will you stay with me?" he asked. He should've been ashamed by the neediness in his tone, but he wasn't. He felt safe showing his raw emotions to Henley.

"Yes. I need to call Alaska and check on Jasna though."

"Shit, I forgot about her. What time is it?" Tonka asked.

"Shhh. It's fine. She's fine. Close your eyes, Finn. Relax."

"Are you sure?"

"Yes."

"Okay." And with that, Tonka closed his eyes. He wiggled around a bit so he was more comfortable and let himself sleep.

* * *

Henley let her tears flow once she was sure Finn was asleep, his breaths deep and even under her cheek. Her heart felt as if it was breaking for him. Hearing what had happened to his cherished dog had been horrifying, but she finally understood more about why he'd held himself so remote for years. She was appalled people had actually told him he shouldn't be so traumatized because Steel was just a dog.

People could have just as strong bonds with animals as they did with other humans. And losing his partner how he had would've broken anyone.

Taking a deep breath, and moving slowly so as not to wake Finn, Henley eased out of his hold and, once sure he was still sleeping, looked at her watch.

Crap! It was eight-thirty. She and Finn had been talking for hours.

She grabbed her phone from the kitchen counter where she'd left it when she arrived and dialed Alaska's number.

"Hi, are you all right?" she asked in lieu of a greeting.

"I'm so sorry," Henley told her.

"Don't be. Jasna's fine and she's been an angel. I'm more worried about you and Finn. When you called to see if I could look after Jasna because he was having a bad day, I wasn't sure what to think."

The thing about working at The Refuge was that, unfortunately, both Alaska and Henley were used to people having "bad days." PTSD could rear its ugly head anywhere, anytime.

"Today's the anniversary of him losing his canine partner," Henley shared. "He's struggling. Would you mind if Jasna stays the night with you guys? I'm so sorry to spring her on you like this but—"

"No need to apologize," Alaska said, interrupting her.

"And of course it is."

"Thanks. Is she there? Can I talk to her and let her know what's up?"

"Yeah. Anything you guys need, we're here," Alaska said.

Henley took a deep breath and did her best to get control over her emotions. It was so good to have such wonderful friends. That *Finn* had such wonderful friends.

"I'll go grab Jas for you. Hang on."

A few seconds later, Jasna's voice sounded in Henley's ear. "Mom? Is everything all right?"

"Yeah, baby. I'm over at Finn's cabin. He's having a hard night, and I'd like to stay here with him...if it's okay with you. I already asked Alaska and she said it was all right if you stayed there with her and Brick. Are *you* okay with that? I can meet you at the lodge in the morning for breakfast and we can run back to our apartment and grab some clothes to change into. Then I can either bring you back here, or you can hang out at the office with me while I meet with a couple of clients. Then we'll both come back to The Refuge and make sure Finn's all right. How's that sound?"

"Sure, Mom. Is Finn okay?"

"He is. He just needs some time. He's missing his dog he used to work with when he was in the Coast Guard. And his memories are a little overwhelming right now."

"Steel, right?"

"You know about Steel?" Henley asked, surprised.

"A little. He doesn't talk about him a lot, but he's told me a couple stories about how smart he was and how many bad guys and drugs he sniffed out."

Henley felt tears well in her eyes once more. Her

daughter's words were more proof of how Finn was more comfortable around kids than adults. "Yeah, that's him. Anyway, if you need anything, don't hesitate to let Alaska know. I'm sure she can give you a shirt or something to sleep in tonight. And I'm not too far away if you need me too. Be good, and I'll see you in the morning."

"Okay, Mom. Love you."

"I love you too. Good night."

Henley hung up the phone and wandered back into the living room. She probably should find something for them both to eat since they'd skipped dinner. But she had a feeling Finn probably wasn't hungry, and truthfully, neither was she.

She sat back on the couch, and felt all warm and fuzzy when Finn immediately lifted his arm and gathered her against him once more. Even half asleep, he was being sweet.

Henley dozed for a while before her phone vibrated in her hand, waking her. She hadn't put it down after she'd talked to Jasna earlier. Concerned, she looked at it and saw her daughter was texting.

Jasna: I can't sleep. Can I come over there?

Henley: Yes. But I'll come get you.

Jasna: It's not that far. Brick said he'd watch me from the door to make sure I got over there all right.

Henley was relieved Brick knew she was leaving. The last thing she wanted was either of them to wake up and find Jasna gone and think she'd been kidnapped or something.

And even though Henley felt perfectly safe at The Refuge, she still didn't want her twelve-year-old daughter wandering around the property at—she looked at the time on her phone—one-thirty in the morning. She didn't know why Brick was awake, or, for that matter, why Jasna was, but if her daughter was asking to see her so late, she had a good reason.

Henley: See you soon.

She eased out of Finn's arms once more, a little worried when he didn't even stir, and went to the door of the cabin. She unlocked it and stepped out onto the porch. She could see the lights from Alaska and Brick's cabin through the trees. Each of the owners had their own cabin, set apart from the guest accommodations. They were all within sight, but they still had plenty of privacy because of the trees.

Within seconds, she saw Jasna jogging through the trees toward her. The girl ran up the stairs and threw herself into her mom's arms. Henley stepped back and flicked the porch light a couple of times to let Brick know Jasna had arrived safely. She saw his own light blink twice, then she turned her attention to her daughter.

"Are you all right?" she asked.

Jasna nodded and looked up at her. "I couldn't sleep. I was too worried about Finn. I'm so sad that he's missing Steel."

"Me too," Henley said. "Come on, let's get inside."

She led them into the cabin and made sure to lock the

door behind her. Then she realized that there wasn't really any place for Jasna to sleep. Finn didn't have a bed in the guest room of his cabin, and there was only one bed in the master. She could settle Jasna there, but she had a feeling the girl wouldn't want to be far from either her or Finn.

"Shhhh, he's sleeping," she said quietly as they neared the couch.

Jasna frowned as she stared at Finn. "I don't know what to do to help him," she said, her voice breaking.

"You're doing it. You care enough to want to be here for him," Henley said.

"But he doesn't know that."

"He will in the morning," Henley reassured her. "Come on. Come sit with me." She sat on the couch next to Finn once more, and just like earlier, he mumbled something in his sleep and pulled her into his side.

Jasna didn't even blink at the way Finn snuggled Henley against him. She'd seen them kiss more than once in the last few weeks, and Henley was relieved her daughter wasn't grossed out, and didn't really even seem to care.

She sat next to Henley on the couch and leaned into her, yawning as she did so. Henley reached over and took Finn's other hand, which was lying on his belly, and twined her fingers with his. Then Jasna placed her hand on top of both. They were connected, all three of them.

Before too long, Henley heard Jasna's small snores as she fell asleep on her shoulder. She was sandwiched between the two people she cared about most in the world. How she'd fallen so hard and fast for Finn, she had no idea, but it felt more than right. He was a good man who didn't deserve the hand he'd been dealt. Then again, did anyone deserve the bad things that happened in their lives? Did she deserve to lose her mom the way she had in such a violent attack? No. But you could either get mired down in your tragedies, or you could choose to rise above them.

She'd chosen to rise, and she hoped and prayed that Finn was finally getting to a point where he could too.

Henley fell asleep feeling a little sad after everything she'd heard that night, yet still content.

* * *

Tonka wasn't sure what woke him, but one second he was dreaming about Steel, running and playing with one of his balls, and the next he was blinking at the darkness around him and feeling a slight weight against his side.

It only took seconds for him to realize where he was and the source of the weight. Henley. He could smell her. He'd also recognize her body against his own anywhere and anytime.

There was a bit of a glow coming from the hallway, where he'd left a light on earlier, and when he looked over at Henley, he was glad for the illumination. To his surprise, Jasna was sleeping against her mom, squishing her against him even harder. He looked down to his stomach and saw that not only was Henley holding his hand while she slept, her daughter's tiny hand was resting on top of their clasped fingers.

Emotion threatened to overwhelm him once again. First he felt panic. If he couldn't even keep a dog safe, how the hell could he keep a kid from getting hurt?

But then determination rose within him. He'd learned

his lesson after what happened with Garcia. Never again would he sit back and let shit hit the fan in front of him. He had no idea what would've happened if he'd fought back against Garcia and his flunky on that boat, despite being restrained. He probably would've ended up dead, along with Steel and Dagger.

But...maybe he could've saved them. Or maybe they wouldn't have suffered as much as they had at Garcia's hands.

If there ever came a time when Henley or Jasna were in danger, he sure as hell wouldn't just sit back and let the chips fall where they may. No, he'd fight tooth and nail to keep them from being hurt or killed, even if it meant giving up his life in the process.

These two females were the best things that had ever happened to him. He loved them. Wasn't ashamed of that feeling. He had no idea if Henley would ever return his affection, but he'd work his ass off to show her how important she was to him. Her and Jasna both.

The feel of his hand being engulfed by theirs was everything he hadn't known he'd needed in his life. They weren't a replacement for the love he'd felt for Steel, they were an extension.

His neck had a crick in it, his ass was numb, and his belly growled with hunger, but Tonka didn't even think about moving. No, he was perfectly content to sit there on his couch with Henley under one arm, holding onto both her and Jasna with the other hand.

He didn't fall asleep again, he'd gotten more than enough already. Besides, he wanted to memorize this moment. Wanted to revel in the care and attention these two women were sharing with him. When he'd had Steel, he hadn't been alone. The last few years he'd been so damn isolated. Henley and Jasna had changed him...for the better.

Turning, Tonka kissed Henley's forehead. She smiled in her sleep but didn't wake. Resting his head on the cushion behind him, Tonka did his best to imprint how he felt right this second onto his soul. Whenever he had a tough moment in the future, *this* is what he'd remember.

CHAPTER FOURTEEN

Three days later, in the middle of the afternoon, while Jasna was in cabin three with Jason helping him replace a part in the toilet, Henley gasped as Finn's hips smacked against her ass while he thrust into her from behind.

He'd met her outside the room in the lodge where she'd just finished her last appointment for the day, asking if he could talk to her. Of course, she'd said yes, and he escorted her to his cabin. The second he'd shut the door behind them, he was on her. It was almost a repeat of their first time together when he'd fucked her against the door, but he'd gained control long enough to drag her down the hall to his room and throw her down on his bed.

They'd both stripped in record time, and he'd gone down on her as if he were starving. It had been a week and a half since they'd last made love, and Henley was just as desperate as Finn.

She'd woken up three days ago next to him on the couch, only to find him staring at her with a look she couldn't interpret. He'd seemed different since then. More settled. And the way he looked at her, as if he was two seconds away from tearing off her clothes at all times, had kept Henley in a perpetual state of horniness.

Apparently, today he was done waiting for a more convenient time for them to be together. Henley was more than all right with that.

"Yes! Harder, Finn!"

She and Finn didn't make long, slow, sweet love to each other. Every time they'd come together, they'd been nearly frantic. The sex was hard and fast, aggressive on both their parts. And Henley had never been more satisfied.

One of his hands squeezed her ass cheek hard enough that she knew she'd have a bruise. The other held her hip as he slammed into her soaking-wet pussy.

Suddenly he moved, pulling her up so her back was against his chest. He put one hand around her neck, holding her still but not hurting her in the least. The other hand flew down her body and began to aggressively stroke her clit.

Henley jerked in his grasp, but he held on tightly.

"Finn, please, fuck me," she begged, squirming against him.

The position wasn't great for thrusting, and in fact he simply held still deep inside her body as he pushed her closer and closer to the edge.

"Not until you come on my cock. I wanna feel it. Want to feel you ripple around me," he practically growled.

As if his words were what her body had been waiting for, Henley felt herself crest. He held her tightly as she shook and vibrated in his arms.

"You have no idea how amazing that feels!" he gasped into her ear, seconds before he pushed her down onto the mattress once more. She moaned as he began to pump hard and fast inside her, prolonging her already amazing orgasm.

She heard him grunt as he pushed himself into her with one last punishing thrust, then gripped her hips tightly as he came.

He collapsed over her back, but instead of crushing her, he quickly shifted to the side, taking her with him. Henley went willingly, feeling boneless.

"Holy crap, woman," he said softly. "You almost killed me that time."

She chuckled weakly. "You've got that wrong. Who was the one who dragged me into his cabin to have his wicked way with me?"

"You didn't exactly protest," he told her.

Henley couldn't deny it. She felt him pull out of her, and she immediately turned before he could get up to throw the condom away. She hated losing him, both from inside her body and right after, when he had to get up.

"I need to throw away this condom, baby," he said.

Henley refused to let go of him. She felt him sigh, tie off the condom behind her back, then roll once more until she was lying on top of him.

"I hate them."

"Condoms?" he asked with a frown.

"Yeah. I wish I could feel you inside me without it."

He stilled under her. "What are you saying, exactly?"

"I'm saying I want to go on the pill. Or get an IUD. Or something. I want you bare, Finn. So badly. I want all of you."

"You *have* all of me," he said with a small shake of his head. "Seriously. I've never given any woman so much of

228

myself. And instead of feeling trapped or claustrophobic, I feel freer than I've ever been. You're under my skin, Hen, and I already can't remember a time when you weren't there. Don't want to. That seems crazy, considering it wasn't too long ago when I wouldn't let myself do more than stare at you longingly from across a room, but...it's true."

"Finn," Henley whispered, feeling overwhelmed.

"I know this is fast, and I'm trying not to rush you... but I'm *yours*. For as long as you want me. I'll bend over backward to make you and Jas happy. And safe. I want to go shopping for a bed to put in that second bedroom across the hall, but I also don't want to do anything that might freak you out or make you think I'm moving too fast.

"When I woke up the other night and had you in my arms, with Jasna's hand on mine... I suddenly realized how short life really is. I want to start every day with the two of you. Laughing at my table. Arguing about what Jas should and shouldn't eat. Discussing a cow's digestive system and why it is the way it is. Taking her to school.

"And if you want me bare, you'll get me bare. I can't think of anything better than filling you up with my come, knowing you're mine inside and out. But I can wait. I want you to feel safe, to be protected. I'll use a condom for the rest of our lives if I have to."

"I want to fall asleep with you inside me," Henley admitted a little shyly. "I want to know what it feels like to snuggle with you right after we both come and not have you immediately withdraw because you have to deal with a condom."

"I want that too," Finn admitted.

"Do you think we'll ever make love slowly and tenderly?" she asked with a grin.

She felt Finn's chuckle under her. "No clue. All I know is, the second I get my hands on you, I feel dangerously desperate to get inside you. Like if I *don't* get inside you, I'll simply die."

"Dramatic much?" she teased.

"You gonna tell me you feel differently?" he asked with an arch of a brow. "I seem to remember you were the one who grabbed my cock as soon as I ripped off my underwear and begged me to fuck you already."

Henley grinned. Yeah, she *had* said that. "I like sex," she said with a shrug. "No, that's not true. With you, I *love* sex."

"I'm not a fan of sneaking around, so I have to admit I'm starting to look forward to school starting in the fall. We'll have more time to do things like this without having to worry about being caught. Though I'll miss having her with me, helping in the barn every day."

"Speaking of my daughter...how long does it take to repair a toilet?" Henley asked.

"Not long enough," Finn said with a sigh. Then he palmed the back of her head and held her still as he lifted his lips to hers.

Henley kissed him with all the love she had in her heart. She loved this man, so much it was almost scary. Too scary to admit to him just yet.

"Thank you for being there for me the other evening," he said when he'd torn his lips from hers.

"You're welcome," she returned. "You seem...better."

"I am," he said without hesitation. "Calling Raid was a good decision. And having you there to listen to me talk about Steel forced me to remember the good times, instead of just that awful day. You know...you should be a therapist or something." He grinned to let her know he was teasing.

"I don't want to be your therapist," Henley told him seriously. "I want to be your girlfriend. Your partner."

"You are," Finn said without hesitation. "But you wouldn't be the woman I'm falling for if you weren't so intuitive. You don't have to hide your psychologist side from me. I mean, I don't want you psychoanalyzing every move I make or every word I say, but I'm damn lucky I have you to help pull me out of the pit I fall into sometimes."

His words meant the world to Henley. She was who she was, and she couldn't simply turn off or forget her schooling and training when she was around him.

She felt Finn's cock harden between her legs, and she squirmed over him. She wanted him again.

Right then, both their phones dinged with incoming texts. As much as Henley wanted to block out the world, she couldn't. They both had responsibilities. She leaned over the side of the bed, promptly squealing when Finn's fingers traced up the back of her thigh and probed inside her still soaking folds. She sat up with both their phones that she'd fished out of the pockets of their pants. She handed Finn his phone as she sat astride his lap, reading the text she'd just received.

Alaska: Head's up, Jasna's looking for Tonka. I distracted her by telling her to go look in the barn, but I'm thinking that isn't going to stall her for long.

. . .

"Shit," Finn said with a sigh. "My text was from Jason. Says he finished up with the toilet and Jasna's looking for me."

"Yeah, mine's from Alaska, basically saying the same thing," Henley said with a pout.

Finn sat up suddenly, wrapping his arm around her so she didn't tumble backward off his lap. He held her against him tightly and said, "You didn't comment on me wanting to buy a bed for my guest room. I want you guys to stay here every now and then. We don't have to do anything, but having you sleep in my arms...it's always a dream come true, hon. I want that as often as possible."

"Me too," she told him shyly.

"I'll see about making that happen then," Finn said. Then he scooted to the edge of the bed and stood, with Henley still in his arms.

"Finn? We need to get dressed," she said with a grin.

He sighed and eased his hold on her. Henley's feet dropped to the floor.

"Right. You can use the bathroom in here. I'll use the one in the hall. Meet you in the kitchen?"

She smiled and nodded.

Finn leaned down and kissed her once more. A long, lingering, sweet kiss that made Henley want to attempt that slow lovemaking in the future. Then he leaned over, grabbed his clothes and picked up the used condom lying on the bed, gave her a sly grin, and headed for the door.

It took Henley a second to get herself together before she picked up her own clothes and began to get dressed.

* * *

They ate dinner at the lodge that night, and while Tonka wouldn't ever be the chattiest of the men, he was finding it easier and easier to initiate conversations with the guests and with his friends. Looking across the table, he saw Henley laughing at something Alaska was saying.

"She's really happy," Jasna said from next to him.

"Yeah?" he asked with a small smile.

"Uh-huh. Ever since you guys started going out, she's been more relaxed."

"That's good."

"Yup." Then, more quietly, she asked, "Finn? Are you gonna marry my mom?"

Tonka nearly choked on the corn he'd just put in his mouth. He chewed slowly, trying to figure out what to tell the girl. He finally decided to be as honest as he could be. "I want to, but it'll be up to her."

"She'll say yes. I know she will."

Tonka frowned. Jasna didn't sound all that thrilled with the prospect of her mom marrying him. "You don't want us to marry?"

She shrugged.

This wasn't the time or place for a deep conversation, but since everyone else around them was busy talking amongst themselves, and she'd brought it up, Tonka decided to go for it. "What's concerning you?"

The little girl turned to look up at him. "It's always been just me and her. Two peas in a pod. Best friends." She frowned a little. "I like you, Finn. You've been nice to her, and me too, and I really like being here at The Refuge."

"But?" Tonka prompted when she didn't continue.

"I'm not stupid. I know that step-kids usually get pushed to the side when two people marry. You'll have babies with my mom, and they'll be yours. The two of yours. I'll be moving out and going to college before you know it and things will just change," she finished a little sadly.

Tonka shifted to put one arm on the back of her chair, and with the other, he picked up the hand that was lying in her lap, worrying her napkin. "First of all, if your mom and I ever get married, you won't be my stepdaughter. You'll be my *daughter*. Period. I don't know if your mom and I will have any children or not, but if we do, you will *never* be any less our daughter. And as much as I hate you even talking about growing up and moving away, you'll always be important to me, no matter how old you are and wherever you go. You'll always be your mom's best friend too. I can't take that place, and I don't want to, Jas. You and your mom have a long history together and a special bond. I'd never do anything to mess with that. Yes, things will change...but hopefully for the better."

Jasna nodded, but Tonka wasn't sure she was completely mollified by his words.

"The other night, when I woke up and you were there...it meant something to me," he admitted. "No...it meant *everything*. I love you, Jas. And I don't say those words lightly. You're even hearing them before your mom is, because I'm scared to death she's not *ready* to hear them. Or maybe she won't feel the same. But no matter what happens between the two of us, I'll always love you. Always."

"Really?"

"Really."

"I love you too, Finn."

He inhaled deeply at hearing those words. They shared a tender look.

Then she asked, "Does this mean I'll get double the number of presents at Christmas now? You know, because you love me and all and you're gonna marry my mom?"

Tonka burst out laughing. Leave it to the little minx to break the emotional moment with a joke.

"Definitely," he told her. He already planned on spoiling both her and her mom rotten, as often as he could get away with it. Starting with giving her a room in his cabin any twelve-year-old would die for.

"Cool," she said.

Tonka squeezed her hand, then turned in his seat and faced the table once more. He caught Henley's worried gaze. *"You guys okay?"* she mouthed.

He smiled and nodded at her. Yeah, he and Jasna were more than okay.

* * *

Christian was getting impatient. The summer was almost gone and he hadn't found an opportunity to grab the girl. He'd been practicing his knife techniques on the squirrels, stray cats, and even a couple dogs he'd stolen from a few backyards. But he knew it wouldn't feel the same cutting a person.

He couldn't wait to see her bleed. To hear her cries. To hear her begging for her life.

He could always choose another first victim...

No. It needed to be *her*. Christian wanted the shrink to hurt. She'd turned him away and never looked back. Now she'd regret it.

The next chance he had, Christian was grabbing the kid. He was done waiting. He wanted to get out of this fucking town and get to Albuquerque to perfect his technique. There were millions of people in the city, including plenty no one would miss. Men and women needing a hit would be easiest to lure to a motel, or wherever he found to sleep. Prostitutes would get in his car voluntarily. There would be kids left alone in stores, in parks...even stuck at home while their parents worked.

He wanted the world to know his name.

And he couldn't do that until he got his first kill under his belt.

He looked down and admired the array of knives and weapons he'd lined up on the floor of the abandoned cabin. The carpet smelled funky and there was mouse shit everywhere...but all Christian could see was the girl, naked, spread out in front of him, waiting for him to strike. The blood would run down her white body. It would be like a work of art.

He couldn't decide if he'd use a knife first or the ice pick. Or maybe the screwdriver. He also had a box cutter and a tire iron. He planned on using that last one after all the other instruments. He wanted to see how the blood splattered on the walls and ceiling when he was beating her.

Smiling, Christian stared off into space, picturing the scene in his head. Yeah, he was definitely done waiting. He needed to act. He was ready.

CHAPTER FIFTEEN

"Moooom, I don't want to go to camp!" Jasna whined for what seemed like the hundredth time. "I want to stay here with you and Finn. Alaska said they're having another bonfire and I don't want to miss it! Besides, I love my new room, and we're supposed to get those boxes of books we ordered from that used bookstore out in California that was going out of business."

"No," Henley said, her tone more patient than she felt.

"Why are you so mean?" Jasna exclaimed petulantly.

Henley sighed and did her best to control her temper. She wasn't surprised her sweet kid was finally turning into a hormonal pre-teen, had long been expecting it, but that didn't mean she hadn't hoped it wouldn't happen. She turned from Finn's sink to face her daughter. He'd gone down to the barn to feed the animals, then he'd be back to drive her and Jasna into town. They'd drop her off at camp and he'd take Henley to her office.

"You were excited about going to this particular camp

a couple of months ago, what happened? And Sharyn is going to be there, so it's not like you won't know anyone."

"I know, but I'd rather be *here*. Scarlet Pimpernickel might forget about me, and the kittens are starting to play all the time, and it's so cool to sleep here with Finn and I just don't want to go anymore!"

"It's only four nights," Henley said. "Your calf isn't going to forget about you. And the kittens will still want to play when you get back. There will be other bonfires, and Finn isn't going anywhere."

Jasna sighed dramatically and plopped herself down at Finn's small table.

Henley went over and sat across from her daughter and said gently, "Do you want to tell me what's really bothering you?"

It took a long moment, but Jasna finally said, "I just really like Finn. He's patient and nice, and he treats me like I'm an adult. I mean, he doesn't treat me as if I'm a little kid. He lets me do some hard stuff with the animals and trusts me to do them right. I'm afraid if I'm gone too long, something will happen between you guys and you'll break up and I won't get to spend any more time here."

Henley frowned. She'd moved so fast with Finn, she had some of the same worries as her daughter. That if things didn't work out, Jasna would suffer for it. She'd become attached to him very quickly, and it made Henley sick inside to know that her actions might harm her daughter.

"I don't know what's in store for the future," she said after a moment. "I wish I could sit here and tell you that Finn and I are going to be together forever. That we'll get married and live happily ever after. But I know better than most people that we can't predict the future. What I *can* tell you is that no matter what happens between Finn and I...you will *always* be welcome here at The Refuge. He enjoys spending time with you, and everyone else here does too."

Jasna sighed dramatically.

"I love Finn," Henley blurted. "He makes me happy. But more than that, I love how he makes *you* feel. And you already know I would do almost anything for you. I'd move heaven and earth to make you happy. To give you everything you need to grow up to be a well-adjusted, happy woman who's self-confident and knows her own worth. But as much as I enjoy hanging out with you, and spending all our free time together, you need to be out there having fun and forming relationships with kids your own age, as well. I know you're going to have a great time at camp, and when you get back, you'll see that nothing has changed."

"Whatever," Jasna muttered.

It was Henley's turn to sigh. She'd hoped her little pep talk would snap her daughter out of the funk she was in. "Are you all packed?" she asked.

"Yeah."

"Did you put the sunscreen I gave you into your bag last night?"

"Yes, Mom. Jeez," Jasna said then stood, the chair screeching on the wooden floor as she did. She flounced down the hall toward her room, and Henley winced when her bedroom door slammed a little too hard behind her.

"That was intense," a deep voice said from the direction of the front door.

Spinning in her chair, Henley saw Finn standing just inside the cabin. She'd been so focused on Jasna, she hadn't seen or heard him enter. "How much did you hear?" she asked with a frown, realizing what she'd said there toward the end.

In response, Finn pushed off the doorframe and stalked toward her. Henley remained sitting, trying to read the emotions she saw swirling in his eyes.

When he reached the table, he went down on his knees beside her and swiveled her legs around so he was kneeling between them. He stared at her for a long beat.

Then asked, "You love me?"

Shit, shit, shit. Her mouth dry, Henley desperately licked her lips.

She could play it off, tell Finn she was simply trying to make her daughter feel better. Admit that she knew it was too early in their relationship to be saying things like that. Even make a joke out of it. But she didn't want to do any of that.

So, she simply said, "Yes."

To her surprise—and alarm—tears formed in his eyes.

"Finn?"

"On that boat all those years ago, I thought my life was over. I vowed to never get so attached ever again, to beast or human, so no one could hurt me like that a second time by hurting anyone I loved. I care about the animals here at The Refuge, and it would suck if anything happened to them, but I've managed to keep my emotions locked down inside me. Over the last two years, you've snuck behind my walls. And now?" He tapped his chest, over his heart. "You're in there, Henley. You and your daughter."

She waited for him to say more, but he didn't.

"Does that mean you love me too?"

He chuckled and shut his eyes for a second, then

opened them again. "Figures I'd screw this up. Yes, Henley. I love you. I love you so damn much. And for the record, you *can* sit there and say that we'll be together forever, that we're going to get married and live happily ever after."

"Finn," she whispered, overwhelmed.

"The two of us have been to hell and back, and somehow we found each other and ended up here. I'm not going to let anyone or anything mess with what's between us. I'm in this for the long haul. How many beds for teenagers do you think I've bought in my lifetime?"

Henley smiled. "Um...one?"

"Exactly."

"I'm so happy with you, Finn. But also scared something's gonna happen to make this all seem like a dream."

"It won't. Because we've got each other. We'll weather every storm thrown our way. Are things always going to be easy? No. Jasna's almost a teenager, and I think judging by her outburst just now, we can assume things will be rocky from time to time over the next few years. But we love her, and she loves us...we'll figure it out. You've got your job, and I've got mine. We'll have to work hard to carve out time for the two of us, but I'm willing to do whatever it takes, including take on whoever Brick wants to hire to help out at the barn."

Henley smiled at that. She knew Finn wasn't thrilled about having someone else in "his" domain, but the fact that he was willing to get help so he could spend more time with her was sweet.

"You want me to go check on Jas?" he asked.

"You don't mind?" Henley asked.

"Of course not."

"Then yes. Please. We need to get going in the next twenty minutes or so if we're going to be on time."

"All right. And for the record...when I pick you up later this afternoon, we're going to come straight back here, and neither of us is leaving until the morning."

She grinned. "That sounds perfect." And it did. She and Jasna had been sleeping in Finn's cabin at The Refuge for the last few days, and she loved sleeping in his arms, but she was anxious to do *more* than sleep. They'd been very cautious, since staying at the cabin was so new and the last thing either of them wanted was for Jasna to hear them or—God forbid—catch them making love.

"If someone had asked me even six months ago to tell them one good thing that came out of Steel being killed in front of my eyes, I would've told them 'nothing'. That there wasn't a single good thing that could ever come out of my best friend being murdered. But now? I'm beginning to think Steel led me to you."

Finn stood then, leaning over and kissing Henley so deeply, if she had any doubts about how he felt, she didn't now.

He ran a finger down her cheek, then turned to head down the hall toward Jasna's room.

* * *

Tonka wanted to beat his chest and shout to the world that Henley loved him. He hadn't meant to eavesdrop, but he also hadn't wanted to interrupt her conversation with Jasna. And when he'd heard her say that she loved him, he'd stopped breathing. For a moment, he thought he'd misheard her, that he was simply hearing what he wanted to, but the more she spoke, the more he believed she really did love him.

After Jas had gone to her room, Tonka hadn't been able to stop himself from going to Henley.

She loved him.

It was going to take some time to let that sink in.

His resolve to keep them both safe strengthened. Not that they were in any danger, but he hadn't thought *he'd* been in any danger when he'd stepped on that boat years ago.

When the three of them were finally on their way into town, Tonka made a split-second decision. He'd been thinking a lot about his conversation with Raiden, and figured now was the perfect time for him to share what he wanted to do.

"Jas?" he asked as they drove.

"Yeah?" she replied sullenly.

"I was thinking...maybe this weekend, after you get home from camp, we could go to the shelter and see if there are any dogs who need a good home."

As soon as the words left his mouth, Tonka realized he should've talked about this with Henley before he'd mentioned it to Jasna. But it was too late now.

"*Really?* Oh my God! Yes! Are you serious? Mom? We can really get a dog?" The pre-teen's grumpy attitude had disappeared in an instant.

Tonka could feel Henley's gaze on him, but he resolutely kept his eyes on the road. He heard her sigh slightly before she spoke.

"Yes. But it's going to be your responsibility."

"No problem!" Jasna reassured her.

"I mean it. I'll buy the food, but you'll have to feed it

and walk it. And pick up poop. And when it chews up your shoes and eats your favorite stuffed animal, you can't get mad."

"I know! I will and I won't!" she said.

"Finn has enough on his plate, and you'll have to train it not to spook the animals at the barn. If you don't take care of it, it'll go right back to the shelter."

"Mom! I *said* I'll be responsible for him or her. I wonder what kind of dogs they have?" she asked, more to herself than to either Tonka or her mom.

He risked glancing over at Henley. She raised a brow when she saw him looking at her, and he did his best to give her an apologetic look. He was sure she'd have plenty to say to him after they saw her daughter off.

Jasna talked nonstop the rest of the trip to the outdoor camp on the outskirts of Los Alamos. The cabins were surrounded by trees, much like those at The Refuge. But there was also a manmade lake nearby where the kids could swim, tube, and kayak. Henley had done a lot of research on the place. Their safety rating was excellent and the reviews had mostly been positive.

Jasna was still chattering about what kind of dog she was going to get and how it would sleep with her and follow her everywhere. The second she saw Sharyn, she gave her mom a quick distracted hug, waved at Tonka, then rushed off to tell her friend the good news about her upcoming dog adoption.

"I'm sorry," Tonka said the second Jas was out of earshot. "It just kind of popped out. I hated seeing her so grumpy."

"You're going to spoil her. And you *know* we're going to end up taking care of the mutt, right?"

"Yup," he said with a smile.

Henley gave him some side-eye. "Which is what you really want, isn't it?"

Tonka shrugged. "I've thought a lot about my talk with Raid. He has a bloodhound, said it's helped his recovery. And I...I wouldn't mind having a dog around again. But not a working dog. A pet. I want one that will be playful, but also protective of you and Jas. I'm hoping they have a couple of pitties we can choose from. They're generally very loving dogs, but the sight of one alone would make people think twice about messing with you or Jasna."

Henley smiled slightly and rolled her eyes. She didn't seem mad, which was a relief.

"Come on, the faster I get you to work, the quicker I'll be able to pick you up and the sooner I'll have you to myself," Tonka said as he took her elbow in his hand and turned her back to his truck.

As they pulled out of the parking lot, neither Tonka nor Henley noticed the nondescript older-model sedan sitting in the back of the lot, with a teenager wearing sunglasses sitting behind the wheel.

CHAPTER SIXTEEN

The week had gone by way too fast for Henley. Usually she was happy to have time go by quickly, especially when Jasna was away from home. But this week had been one of the best of her life. She worked in the mornings and had a few sessions at The Refuge each afternoon, then she and Finn spent every night alone in his cabin.

She'd finally gotten her slow, tender lovemaking, and it had been more than worth the waiting.

An impatient and lustful Finn was a dream come true, but a loving and patient Finn blew her mind as he leisurely tortured her with pleasure. She'd ended up begging him to let her come. To get inside her. To fuck her. But even when he relented, he'd somehow found the control to keep his thrusts slow and steady, driving her to the edge of her orgasm time and time again before backing off.

By the time his control broke, she'd threatened all sorts of things she'd never carry through with...the least of which was never having sex with him again.

Then he ran a hot bath for her and carried her into the

bathroom. Since they wouldn't both fit, he'd sat next to her as she soaked and told her more about his time when he was in the Coast Guard. Slowly but surely, he was opening up, telling her things about himself and his past that he admitted he'd never shared with anyone else.

If she hadn't been head over heels in love with this man before, she was now.

But what made her feel truly secure that their relationship might stand the test of time was that Finn wasn't perfect. If he was, she probably would've been waiting for the other shoe to fall. She didn't need a Stepford boyfriend. She wanted to be with someone who felt safe enough to be moody, yet not take it out on her. Who got irritated with work, but didn't just bitch about it ad nauseum without finding ways to ease his stress. He complained about her dropping dirty clothes on the floor, but not in a way that made her feel like shit about the habit.

They argued about the best way to make pasta, disagreed about what they liked to watch on TV, and had different thoughts about what was going on in the country politically, but she adored that they could have such differing opinions and thoughts, yet still love each other as much as they did.

Today was Thursday, and they had this last night alone before Jasna came home from camp. Henley had received numerous texts from her daughter when they were allowed to use their phones in the evenings, and she'd been relieved to see her daughter's excitement about all the things she'd been doing. She may have been reticent to go to camp, but now that she was there, it was obvious she was having a wonderful time.

She was still over-the-top excited about going to the shelter on Saturday, telling Henley that she'd already looked at the website to see what dogs were available. Henley had a feeling if they weren't careful, they'd come home with more than one new member of the family.

"What are you thinking about so hard?" Finn asked as he came up behind her and wrapped his arms around her waist, resting his chin on her shoulder. She'd been standing on the back porch of Finn's cabin, staring into the trees as she sipped her coffee.

She didn't turn, leaning back into Finn, giving him some of her weight. "Just that I'm happy. This week has gone by fast, but it's been really really *really* good."

He nuzzled her neck under her ear. "Yeah, I kind of got the feeling you felt that way last night when you grabbed my hair and wouldn't let me come up for air when I was between your thighs."

Henley chuckled and finally turned in his arms, being careful not to spill her coffee, then smacked his chest. "I didn't hear you complaining," she retorted.

"You wouldn't have been able to hear me if I did, since my mouth was otherwise occupied."

Henley laughed long and hard. When she had herself under control, she said in a serious tone of voice, "You know, I used to think I knew what good sex was. But I was so wrong. I had no clue. You, Finn Matlick, make me feel things I've never felt before."

"When you're with someone you love, everything's better. Even standing on the porch, watching the world come to life in the morning," he said solemnly.

"I love you," she said.

"You've given me back my love of being alive," he returned.

She smiled. "We're being sappy this morning."

"Yup," he said with a small shrug.

"We're gonna need to figure something out," Henley told him.

"Figure what out?" he asked.

"How to make love with Jasna in the house."

He grinned. "You think you can be quiet?"

"Um...maybe?"

Finn burst out laughing.

Henley mock-scowled at him. "That's exactly what I mean! We have to figure something out. Because I like being with you, Finn. I like having you inside me."

He sobered. "We will. We might end up being daytime lovemakers instead of nighttime, but I'm okay with that if you are."

Henley thought about it for a moment, then nodded. "I can work with that. Jasna goes back to school soon."

"Exactly," Finn agreed.

She smiled up at him. "Although there's something to be said for lying in your arms and not having sex too."

"Never done it before you, and I'd have to say I agree."

"You haven't?"

"Nope. Before you, I was a love-'em-and-get-out-of-Dodge kind of man. Didn't see the point in staying when I didn't want to lead anyone into thinking we might have more than we did," Finn said with a shrug.

Henley wrinkled her nose.

"What?" Finn asked.

"I'm jealous," she admitted. "I don't like to think of you with anyone else."

"Same," he agreed. "So how about we make a pact from here on out to never talk about past partners again."

"Done."

"Good. You're going out with the girls today, right?" he asked.

Henley nodded. "Yeah, Alaska, Ryan, Luna, and I are all going to lunch, then we're taking Luna to that shop that sells all the British stuff because she wants to get some of that chocolate we bought last time."

"Cool."

"You want me to pick up something from town for dinner?" she asked.

"If you'd like."

"What do you want?"

"Don't care. As long as I get to be with you on our last night alone for a while, I don't give a shit what we're eating."

Henley couldn't help but smirk.

Finn rolled his eyes. "You have such a dirty mind."

"I can't help it!" she protested. "Especially after what you were just talking about."

"How about this—I don't care what you bring home for dinner, because I'm gonna eat my fill *afterward*."

Henley chuckled. She loved this man. So damn much. "What are you doing today?"

"Chores, as usual. The vet's coming by to check out that scratch on Melba's side that she got in the paddock the other day...which will be a pain in the ass, because you know how much she hates being examined. Then I thought I'd swing by the shelter to check out the available dogs. I want to check out the temperament of the one pittie they have, as well as the hound mix. The last thing I want is Jas falling in love with one of them, only to have them end up being aggressive or untrainable."

His concern for her daughter made Henley's insides melt.

"I love you," she whispered.

He smiled at her. "I love you more. Now, we need to get moving so you aren't late for work. Are you sure you're all right with Ryan picking you up?"

"Why wouldn't I be? She's going to come straight from here, after she finishes up the rooms on her schedule and after Luna's done helping her dad with lunch. She can drop all three of us off after we shop. It's fine."

"I was just making sure. And since you won't be driving, don't worry about dinner. We can make something here, or I'll grab something from Robert."

"All right. My poor car isn't getting much use just sitting here, since you drive Jasna and me around all the time," she said.

Finn shrugged. "It's my pleasure to take you both wherever you need to go."

"You're kind of a control freak," she teased.

"Yup. And you love me anyway."

"I do," she agreed.

Finn took the coffee cup out of her hand and brought it to his lips and downed the rest of the drink.

"Hey!" Henley complained. "I wasn't done with that."

"Now you are," he said with a grin. "And you still need to get in the shower. Oh, wait, so do I. I know—we can shower together to save time and water."

"You think we'll save either of those things if we get naked together in the shower?" Henley quipped as Finn led her back inside the cabin.

He didn't answer, simply smirked as he led them toward the bedroom.

Henley chuckled. Did they have time for a quickie? Not really. But her first appointment wasn't for an hour and a half, and Mike never expected her to be in the office at a specific time. She didn't protest as Finn dragged her into the bathroom and grabbed the hem of her shirt, lifting it up and over her head.

"You owe me a coffee," she teased as she stepped into the warm shower.

"We'll stop at that coffee place you love," he said absently as he pulled her against his warm, naked, wet body. His cock was hard between them, and Henley could only smile.

This was what she'd dreamed about when she was in her early twenties. *This* was what she'd always wanted with a partner. Someone to laugh with, who wanted her as much as she wanted him, and someone to share her life with.

Then he was kissing her, and Henley couldn't think any more.

* * *

Hours later, when she was sitting at lunch with her friends, Henley could still feel Finn between her legs. He'd made love to her hard, fast, and passionately in the shower. And even though they'd been spontaneous and were in the freaking shower, he hadn't forgotten a condom.

Not once had he gone back on his word to always protect her.

But as she'd told him before, she was ready to be done

with them. She had an appointment for the next week with her OBGYN to discuss birth control options.

"So...I'm guessing that grin means you've had a good week?" Alaska teased.

Luna shook her head. "I still can't believe you and Tonka are a thing."

"Why not?" Ryan asked. "I think they're adorable together."

"Oh, they are," Luna agreed. "But it's *Tonka*. He's like, the antisocial one. My dad told me he didn't even *meet* Tonka until he'd been there a month."

"You know what they say," Alaska teased. "The quiet ones make the best lovers."

Everyone chuckled.

"Right, Henley?" Alaska probed, leaning over the table.

"Yes," Henley confirmed without any embarrassment whatsoever.

The other three cheered, making everyone in the small café look at them with curiosity.

"Shush, you guys, jeez." Henley giggled.

"But seriously, it's still going well?" Alaska asked.

"Yeah. Really good," Henley said with a nod.

"I heard you're getting a dog," Luna added. "Is that right?"

Henley snorted. "Yup. Finn totally bribed Jasna out of her bad mood when we were on the way to drop her off at camp. Asked if she would be *interested* in getting a dog." She rolled her eyes. "As if she was going to say no."

"So are you going on your way home from camp tomorrow?" Ryan asked.

"My daughter wishes. No, we're going Saturday."

Everyone laughed again.

Henley sobered. "This really is a big step for Finn, though. He lost his canine partner right before he got out of the Coast Guard. And it was traumatic and violent. I honestly wasn't sure he'd want to get another dog ever again."

"I'm sorry," Alaska said, reaching over and putting her hand on Henley's.

"Yeah, that sucks," Ryan agreed.

She nodded. "I think it'll be good for him. He talked to his ex-partner recently—the partner who'd been with him that day—and after he heard he had a bloodhound...I think it shook something loose for him. Like, if his friend could move on and do it, maybe he could too."

"He's amazing with the critters around The Refuge," Luna said with a nod. "He's gonna be fine."

"I think so too," Henley agreed. "He's going overboard though, just like he does with most things that involve me or Jasna. He said he was going to go to the shelter today to 'check out the dogs' to make sure they were suitable for being around someone Jasna's age."

"I don't know, I think that's smart," Alaska said.

"Have you checked out the website? To see what dogs are available?" Ryan asked.

"Of course I have. Finn and I had a discussion about them the other night. He said we were only allowed to look at the big dogs, but I thought the little yorkie was adorable."

"Let me guess, he wants a big bad dog that can protect you and Jas, right?" Luna asked with a laugh.

"Yup."

"Well, the smaller ones do tend to be yappy," Ryan

pointed out. "And I'm assuming the guys at The Refuge don't want a yapper around, disrupting the guests."

"True," Henley agreed a little reluctantly. "But I'm guessing Finn would be able to train any dog we get *not* to be an obnoxious barker. He's kind of amazing like that."

Alaska squeezed Henley's hand, which she hadn't let go of yet. "Please tell me you guys are madly in love and you're going to marry Tonka and move to The Refuge, so I won't be the only woman living there full time."

Henley felt herself blushing. She gave her friend a small smile and shrugged. "I do love him, and he says he loves me too. But we aren't anywhere near the getting-married stage. We'll just have to see what happens."

Alaska squealed in delight and sat back in her chair. She picked up a fork and speared a French fry, dunking it into a container of ranch dressing before looking up at Henley with a huge smile. "You guys are *so* getting married. If you think Tonka's stupid enough to wait long to put a ring on your finger, you don't know these guys very well."

"I don't see a ring on *your* finger," Ryan said reasonably.

Alaska stuffed the French fry into her mouth and grinned again as she chewed. As soon as she swallowed, she said, "Oh, Drake's got a ring, but I'm not quite ready to take that last step yet."

All three women spoke at once.

"What?"

"He does?"

"Holy crap, really?"

Alaska nodded. "I love him. I've always loved Drake. But I don't know...something inside me, that little niggling of a doubt, wonders if we moved too fast. If he only started having feelings for me because of what happened. You know, the whole damsel-in-distress thing and all that."

"Please, woman. Brick can't keep his eyes off you. Or his hands, for that matter," Luna told her. "I swear, the other night I thought he was going to jump your bones right there at the front desk after you handled that obnoxious guest who was complaining about every little thing. You had him eating out of your hand by the time he left, and he even promised to make a donation for the POW cabin. And Brick was in awe, watching it all go down. You two are perfect for each other. Marry the man and put him out of his misery already."

Henley nodded, along with Ryan.

"I'm getting there," Alaska assured them.

Henley was relieved when the talk turned to more mundane things, like the menu for next week, and how the guys were thinking about ordering all new softer towels.

"I don't know about you guys, but I'm stuffed," Alaska said after they'd each ordered a brownie ice cream sundae and devoured every crumb.

"Same," Ryan said, patting her stomach.

Henley felt as if she wouldn't have to eat for a week. The food had been that good and that filling.

"So, what's the plan for the rest of the day?" Luna asked.

"I thought maybe, if you guys didn't mind, we could stop at that consignment shop again. It's so fun to look for treasures among the trash," Alaska said. "Then we can stop at Bliss for Luna before heading back. I'm guessing Henley wouldn't mind returning a little early, so she can spend the last night before Jas comes home with Tonka."

Henley wasn't even embarrassed when she nodded

eagerly. She didn't care if her friends knew how anxious she was to spend more time with her man. She didn't care who knew that she loved him.

They all pushed back from the table, and when they argued over who was going to leave the tip, they decided to all leave some money for the college kid who'd been their waiter. They climbed into Ryan's Explorer, and Henley couldn't remember a time when she'd been more content.

Her daughter was healthy and happy, she had a job she loved, she had Finn, and now she had a circle of friends she could laugh and hang out with.

They'd visited the consignment shop—the back of the SUV was now full of bags—and were on their way to get Luna some British candy when Henley's phone rang. Smiling, thinking it was Finn, she barely glanced at the screen before bringing it up to her ear.

"Hello?"

"Henley McClure?"

"Speaking," she said with a small frown when she didn't recognize the voice, wondering who was calling...and sounding so serious.

"This is Samantha White, from Horseshoe Bend Outdoor Camp. Have you heard from Jasna this afternoon?"

All the blood drained from Henley's face. "What? No. Why? What's wrong?!"

"She's missing. We've looked everywhere and can't find her. There was a group hike this afternoon and when we did a head count after arriving back at camp, she wasn't there. We have counselors out searching now, but I wanted to make you aware of what's happening."

Henley couldn't breathe. This was literally her worst nightmare.

"And I hate to have to ask this, but I know the police will want to know as well. We've already called them and they're on their way. Is there any reason why she might not want to come home? Did the two of you get in any arguments before she arrived at camp or since she's been here? Kids her age are notorious for getting in a snit and running away for one reason or another."

The other women in the car were looking at Henley worriedly, but she couldn't do anything but stare at the headrest in front of her blankly.

"What? No! Jasna would never run away. Yes, we had some words before camp, but everything was resolved before we dropped her off. She's excited to get home because we're getting a dog this weekend. Does she have her phone with her? Did someone...did someone *take* her?" She was practically whispering by the time she got to that last question.

"We don't allow the campers to have their phones during the day, they have to leave them in the cabins. And I'm sure she's okay. She probably wandered off to use the bathroom and got turned around. We're going to find her, I'm certain of it. But due to our protocols, I needed to let you know."

Henley wanted to scream. *Of course* they should tell her that her child was freaking *missing*! The only thing she wanted to do was call Finn. He'd know what to do. He'd find Jasna. "Call me if you find her," she said shortly, then quickly hung up.

"What's going on? Jasna's missing?" Alaska asked urgently.

Taking a deep breath, Henley refused to let herself cry. "Yeah. I guess everyone went on a hike, and she wasn't with them when they all got back to camp."

"So she's probably just lost in the woods then," Luna said, her voice shaking a bit. "I mean, it's not like anyone's out to get her. She's only twelve."

At her friend's words, Henley's blood ran cold.

She instantly thought about her conversation with Mike at the beginning of summer. How Christian Dekker had a hit list. She hadn't given it much thought since that day. It had been years since she'd had any contact with the troubled boy.

But now she couldn't stop thinking about him.

"What? What are you thinking?" Alaska asked from next to her in the back seat.

"Christian Dekker," Henley whispered, almost afraid to say the boy's name out loud.

"What? Who's that?" Ryan asked.

"He's a kid I counseled a few years ago when he was twelve. He was...not right," Henley told them. "He was truly evil—and I don't say that lightly. My boss took over his sessions. I haven't seen him in years, but at the beginning of the summer, Mike told me his parents had called. Told him they'd found a notebook with a list of names of people he wanted to kill."

"*Jasna* was on that list?" Luna asked, horrified.

"Well, no. But I was. And Mike, and around two dozen other people. I didn't think much about it at the time, but now...what if he went after her?" Henley asked, her eyes filling with tears.

"No, don't think the worst," Luna said firmly. "Don't borrow trouble. They're looking for her, right?"

Henley nodded.

"And the police are going out there?"

Henley nodded again.

"Okay, so they'll find her," Luna continued, obviously trying to stay positive.

"Ryan, we need to get back to The Refuge," Alaska said urgently. "The guys will know what to do."

Without a word, Ryan pulled a U-turn in the middle of the street. She ignored the people honking their horns and flipping her off as she sped back toward The Refuge.

"I need to call Finn."

Alaska put her hand over Henley's before she could lift the phone. "We're going to be there in five minutes," she said firmly. "You can tell him in person. He isn't going to take this well, and you shouldn't tell him over the phone."

Henley wanted to shake her friend off. Tell her she was wrong. That she needed Finn's support *right this second*. But after considering Alaska's words, she nodded.

Finn was definitely going to lose his mind, and the last thing she wanted was for him to do something impulsive and rash. If she told him in person, they could figure out what to do together, and maybe she and his friends could keep Finn from going off half-cocked.

She nodded and took a deep breath. She wanted to believe that Jasna had simply wandered off and gotten lost. That she'd reappear from the forest, maybe a little scared but embarrassed over the worry she'd caused.

Deep down, she knew better.

Jasna was a responsible kid. She wouldn't wander off, at least not without telling someone what she was doing.

She had no proof Christian had taken her daughter, but despite that...she just knew.

Evil had found her again—and this time, it was going after the most precious person in her life. It wasn't enough that she'd had to listen to her mother being assaulted and stabbed, and then lost her father in a knife fight. Now she had to deal with Jasna being missing.

It wasn't fair.

"Hold on, Hen," Alaska said as she held her hand tightly. "We're almost there. We're getting you to Tonka."

Closing her eyes, Henley couldn't think. She couldn't even cry. She needed Finn. Now. He'd know what to do. He'd find her daughter.

The alternative was unthinkable.

CHAPTER SEVENTEEN

"Finnnnn!"

Tonka's head whipped up at hearing Henley scream his name. He immediately dropped the pitchfork where he'd been moving hay, the fear and pain in her voice making his adrenaline spike. He had no idea what was wrong—but there was definitely something.

He'd gotten a text from her not even an hour ago, saying that they were having fun and she should be back at The Refuge before dinnertime.

It was too soon for her to be back already.

Tonka was running without even realizing it. He saw Ryan's Explorer parked haphazardly in the lot and Henley was racing toward him.

She threw herself at him and was talking so fast and with so much emotion, he couldn't understand anything she was saying.

"Take a breath, love. What's wrong?"

He watched her inhale deeply before blurting, "Jasna's missing! Her camp called and they can't find her!"

Tonka was certain his heart stopped. "What? *How?*"

"I don't know!" Henley practically wailed. "They said they were on a hike and when they got back, she wasn't there! They're looking for her, but, Finn...what if they can't find her?"

"They will. *We* will," he said resolutely. Adrenaline flooded him and he wanted to panic. Couldn't help but think about how scared Jas had to be.

"It's Christian!"

"What?" Tonka asked, doing his best to concentrate. He'd already turned Henley and was leading her quickly toward the lodge. He needed help.

"Christian Dekker. I told you about him. That boy I was counseling and couldn't help? The evil one." She whispered the last part.

Tonka shook his head. "You don't know that."

Henley was shaking so much against him, she was having trouble walking. "I *do*," she insisted as she held on to Tonka with an iron grip.

He steered her toward the lodge, noting absently that Luna and Alaska were on their heels. He wasn't sure where Ryan had gone, but at the moment, all he cared about was the woman in his arms and getting information so he could find Jasna.

Alaska must've sent a text to Brick, because he burst through the back door with Spike and Pipe right behind him.

"I've notified the others. They're on their way," Pipe said in a hard voice.

"What info do we have? Where was Jas last seen?" Spike asked.

"Have the police been called? We need to get an Amber Alert out," Brick added.

Tonka ignored his friends. All his attention was on Henley. He hauled her inside and sat them on one of the couches in the lobby, then gathered her in his arms. "Start from the beginning. Tell us everything," he ordered gently.

They all listened as Henley repeated the conversation she'd had with the lady who'd called from Horseshoe Bend. After she'd told them what she knew, which wasn't a hell of a lot, Henley said, "Mike took me aside at the beginning of the summer and said Christian's parents had found a hit list or something that he'd written, of people he wanted to die. Or kill. Mike and I were on the list, but so were like twenty other people. I didn't think much about it afterward—but now I can't stop."

"Shit," Brick muttered.

"I'm going to alert the guests," Spike said.

"Was Jasna on that list?" Tonka asked Henley.

"Not that I know of, but what if he decided to go after her because she's a kid? An easier target?"

That was exactly what he was worried about.

"I think before we do anything, we need to talk to Mike. And the police. Let them know about Henley's concerns. Maybe even talk to this Christian kid's parents. Hold old is he now?" Tonka asked.

"Sixteen, I think," Henley said.

She was still shaking, but Tonka wasn't sure she even realized it. Her hands were freezing and he suspected she was going into shock. By now, Owl, Stone, and Tiny had arrived. Tonka looked up at Owl. "Will you grab a blanket for Henley?"

Without a word, the other man nodded and spun

around to grab one of the throw blankets the lodge always kept handy in case a guest got cold.

He returned in a few seconds, and Tonka wrapped it around Henley. His mind was going a million miles an hour.

"Are we going to the camp to help look?" Stone asked the others.

Tonka pressed his lips together hard as his friends discussed what to do next. He wanted to be doing something. Needed to be out searching for the little girl who'd become as important to him as her mom. But who would comfort Henley?

He was torn—and it was *agonizing*. He'd sworn never to sit around and do nothing if there was even the slightest chance he could prevent someone he loved from getting hurt. Letting Garcia torture Steel had left a huge scar on his heart and psyche, and he couldn't go through that again, even if it meant Tonka himself was hurt in the process.

But how could he leave Henley when she needed him most?

"Tonka?" Tiny asked. "Are you coming with us?"

After a pause, he shook his head, even as he clenched his teeth together so hard, it felt as if he'd crack a tooth. "I'll stay here with Henley."

"No."

Ignoring the surprised looks on his friends' faces at Henley's declaration, Tonka turned to the woman he loved.

"You need to go."

"I need to take care of *you*," he countered.

She stubbornly shook her head. "No. Jasna needs you. I

know you want to be out there helping. And when you do find her, and she's scared, it'll be best that you're there to comfort her."

This sucked. Tonka felt immense guilt at how relieved he felt that he could help look for Jas, despite wanting to comfort Henley.

"We'll be right here with her," Alaska said. "We won't leave her alone for a second."

"Owl and I will stay with her as well," Stone said.

"Me too," Pipe said. "I'll make sure the guests know what's going on, and they stay aware in case this Christian kid decides to come here for any reason."

"Taking Jas might be a diversion so he can get to Henley," Owl pointed out.

Shit, Tonka hadn't even thought about that. "Then I *should* stay," he said.

"No!" Henley said almost frantically. "Please, Finn! I'll feel better if you're out there looking for her. I trust you."

This woman slayed him. He took her face in his hands and leaned down so his forehead rested against hers. She grabbed his wrists and hung on so tightly, Tonka knew she was leaving marks on his skin.

"I swear I'm going to bring her home to you."

"Okay."

"I am," he insisted.

Henley took a deep breath, and he mentally cursed at the tears that fell from her eyes and down her cheeks. "You can't promise that. I know better than anyone that sometimes bad things happen to good people. But I know that you'll do whatever you can to bring her home safe and sound if it's at all possible."

Tonka hated that she was right. He shouldn't promise anything, yet he couldn't help it. "I will," he vowed.

She nodded. "Go, Finn. Please find my baby."

He kissed her then, and took precious seconds to wipe the tears from her cheeks. Then he turned to Owl, Stone, and Pipe without taking his hands from her face. "Take care of her," he ordered gruffly.

All three nodded immediately.

"We won't let her out of our sight," Stone promised.

"Thank you," Tonka told his friends. Then he turned to Henley and repeated those two words. She'd know what he was thanking her for.

For letting him do what he needed to do.

She lifted her chin and kissed him briefly before letting go and giving him a little push.

Tonka stood and turned to Brick, Spike, and Tiny. "Let's go."

"I'm driving," Brick said firmly.

Tonka nodded, because honestly, it was better if he wasn't behind a wheel right now. The four men stalked out of the lodge, intent on getting to Jasna's camp and finding out what the hell was going on.

By the time they arrived, the place was crawling with police officers. The kids had all been herded into one of the many buildings, to keep them safe and out of the way.

Tonka went up to the first cop he saw and said, "I'm Jasna's family. Has there been any clues about where she might be?"

The woman gave him a compassionate look and shook her head. "No, but we've got people all over these woods. They've got whistles and if she's here, they'll find her and notify us."

It was the "if she's here" that worried Tonka.

"We're from The Refuge," Brick told the woman. "We can help. Tiny and I are former SEALs, Spike was Delta Force, and Tonka was a member of the Coast Guard. We've got training to assist in a way most volunteers don't."

When he first said they wanted to help, the woman looked like she was on the verge of declining politely, but when he explained who they were, and their backgrounds, she seemed to change her mind. Lifting a radio to her lips, she informed whoever was on the other end that additional help had arrived.

Within minutes, four men strode toward them. They all had police radios but were dressed for hiking. Cargo pants, T-shirts, backpacks, and boots.

"These guys are from The Refuge. This one is a relative of the missing girl," the officer said to the newcomers. Then she turned to Tonka and his friends. "Each of you go with one of our off-duty officers. Do what they say, when they say it. Don't make me regret letting you help."

Tonka understood. Allowing civilians, even ones with military backgrounds, was risky in searches like this. The last thing they needed was to deal with someone getting lost or doing something that might distract the searchers from their goal—finding Jasna.

They all nodded.

Brick turned to Tonka. "Stay in touch. We'll meet back here if something happens. Do *not* go off on your own. Understand?"

Tonka nodded. He appreciated Brick's professionalism more than he could say. It helped keep his mind on the task at hand, instead of worrying about what Jasna was feeling or going through.

Brick clasped Tonka's shoulder tightly, nodded, then the four of them followed behind their escorts as they entered the woods in different directions.

"I'm Tonka," he said, introducing himself to the man he was paired with.

"Bret. I'm a forest ranger stationed here in Los Alamos."

Tonka nodded. Frankly, he didn't care if the man was President of the United States. As long as he knew what he was doing and could communicate with the other searchers, he'd be satisfied. "Where have you looked so far?"

As Bret explained how the search was being conducted and where they were headed, Tonka swallowed hard. The weather was fairly decent. Not too hot or cold. It wasn't raining and the night was supposed to be warmer than usual. All things that should've made him happy. But they didn't. Because thinking about Jasna having to spend the night in the forest scared the crap out of him. She was a smart girl. But did she know it was best to stay put if she ever got lost?

Tonka kicked himself for not making sure she knew the basics of outdoor survival. No, he hadn't thought she'd ever need them, but did *anyone* ever think they would get lost in the woods? The Refuge was smack dab in the middle of some of the sparest populated land in the state. He should've at least had a talk with her about how to use a compass, what to do if she ever found herself lost on the property.

They'd been walking and calling Jasna's name for about

twenty minutes when Tonka's phone rang. Looking down, he saw it was Tiny calling.

"Did you find her?" he asked as he answered.

"No. But I wanted to let you know that Christian Dekker's parents showed up at the police station. The Amber Alert went out about Jasna's disappearance and they're scared to death."

"Why?"

"They think they might be next. That their son might be working on that hit list he wrote. They went in to talk to the detectives and tell them everything they could about Christian. There's no proof he's behind Jasna's disappearance, but they didn't want to take that chance when they recognized Henley's last name. As soon as they're done at the station, they're leaving town."

"Shit. What did they say?"

"I don't have all the details, just what I overheard on the radio of the officer I'm with. But I guess he's been coming and going from their home as he wants all summer. He dropped out of school in the spring. He doesn't say much to them, kind of pretends they're not even there. They said he's been acting creepy.

"The bad news is that no one's seen the kid. No one around the camp remembers him being there, his parents haven't seen him in days. There's no proof he's got anything to do with Jasna being gone. At the moment, the officers are still acting under the assumption that she wandered off and got lost."

Tonka's gut churned. He remembered the fear in Henley's voice when she told him about the client she believed had literally been born evil. Before going through what he had with Steel, he probably wouldn't believe that some people were born bad. But after experiencing Pablo Garcia's utter lack of humanity, he'd changed his mind.

If Henley thought Christian Dekker was capable of hurting those around him without remorse, he believed her.

"Are the cops even looking for Dekker?" he asked.

"Unofficially, yes," Tiny told him.

That was at least something. "Okay. Does he have a phone? Can they trace it?"

"Not without a search warrant."

Shit. There was no telling how long a court order would take to obtain. Especially without any evidence, only his parents' fears and Henley's suspicions.

If Christian Dekker had grabbed her, Jasna could literally be anywhere. They could be halfway to Albuquerque by now. The Amber Alert was good, it would hopefully encourage people to be on the lookout for her. But without a person of interest's name or car description attached to the alert...it was like looking for a needle in a haystack. If Jas was in the trunk of a car or hidden some other way, no one would even have a chance to see or identify her.

Tonka knew the statistics. Children who went missing had a very small window to be found before the chance of them being found alive plummeted. He couldn't imagine Jasna being abused or hurt...or killed. Her death would break Henley.

She'd survived her mother's assault and murder. He wasn't sure she'd be able to handle her daughter becoming the victim of a violent death, as well.

"Thanks for calling," he told Tiny in a ravaged tone.

"I'm sorry, Tonka."

"I know. We just have to hope she's out here. Somewhere."

"I'll let you know if I hear anything else."

Tonka nodded, even though his friend couldn't see him. "Okay."

"Later."

He clicked off the phone, grateful that his friend hadn't given him empty platitudes. Taking a deep breath, he turned to Bret. "How fast can you walk?"

"Fast," Bret said with a determined look on his face.

"Good. Because if I have to search every inch of this damn forest, that's what I'm going to do," Tonka told him.

Bret nodded and they both set off again, at a much quicker pace than they had before. If Jasna was out here, someone was going to find her. They had to.

CHAPTER EIGHTEEN

Christian Dekker watched the girl he'd handcuffed to a stake he'd pounded into the floor of the dilapidated cabin —and frowned.

It was even easier to grab her than he'd envisioned. Almost anticlimactic.

When he'd followed the shrink, only to find her dropping the brat off at an overnight camp, he'd been delighted. While there were lots of kids and counselors around, they were hardly former military, like the owners of The Refuge. He knew it would be easy to get the girl.

And he'd been right.

He stayed hidden in the forest for days, right under everyone's noses. He was good at blending in, having been hunting since he was a boy. And when the girl fell behind the other kids during a hike, Christian had simply stepped out of hiding, grabbed her with a hand over her mouth, and dragged her back into the trees.

Her eyes had been huge in her face and she was so

shocked, she'd barely struggled. He'd held out a bottle of orange juice and vodka—which he'd drugged—and ordered her to drink. When she didn't want to, all it had taken was a threat to kill all her little friends at the camp.

She'd docilely done his bidding.

The power he'd felt in that moment had been overwhelming. This was what he'd craved his entire life. People doing *what* he wanted, *when* he wanted.

She became groggy immediately, and he'd had to throw her over his shoulder when she couldn't walk anymore. He'd been out of breath by the time he'd arrived at his car, hidden along a dirt road nearby. He'd have to adjust that technique in the future. But otherwise, the kidnapping had gone flawlessly.

He'd driven the unconscious girl to this cabin before anyone even realized she was gone. His cell phone had let out an obnoxious clanging noise about an hour after he'd arrived, with an Amber Alert for the girl now lying on the floor in front of him.

Christian had laughed. Hard.

But the longer he sat there, waiting for her to wake up, the more bored he became. The girl was *still* completely out of it. No matter what he did to rouse her, nothing worked. He'd dumped water on her face. Nothing. He'd used his knife to cut the bottom of her foot, where he knew she'd be extra sensitive. Nothing.

He'd fucked up and used too much of the Rohypnol. He hadn't been sure of the right amount without knowing her weight, and he'd obviously put too much into the drink. From what he'd read, the alcohol would make her more compliant and the drugs more effective, but apparently he'd miscalculated. Another thing he'd have to fine-tune later. He'd wanted to quickly subdue her and ensure she didn't fight. His plan would've gone to shit if she'd screamed and alerted everyone to what was happening.

Now time was ticking, and he wanted to get on with his fun.

But torturing an unconscious victim wasn't fun at all. He wanted to hear her scream. Wanted to mess with her head by slowly cutting her clothes off, telling her he wasn't going to kill her, then make her cry with every stick of his knife or hit from one of the many blunt objects he had all lined up and ready to go.

He hated waiting. Especially when he was *so close* to his first real kill. He'd dreamed about this day for so long and it was finally here. Except the stupid bitch was still asleep!

Sighing, Christian paced.

Back and forth.

Back and forth.

He checked the girl...still no response to him jabbing her with his knife.

More pacing.

The more time that went by, the more irritated he got. He should've given her just a little of the drink to start, gauged her reaction. Instead, he'd insisted she chug the entire bottle. Next time, he'd know better. He'd improve with each kill, of course. But that didn't help him right now.

Sighing, he stood above the girl and stared down in frustration.

His stomach growled.

Putting a hand on his belly, Christian scowled. He was

starving. And he planned on being very busy for the next eight hours or so...at least once the girl finally woke up. He didn't want to be distracted by hunger pains while he was busy torturing her.

He looked at his watch. Five-thirty. He could run into town, grab a hamburger and fries, then come back and get to work. Even if the girl woke up while he was gone, it wasn't as if she could go anywhere. Not while cuffed to the floor. It would probably scare her even more to wake up alone, having no idea where she was or what was happening.

Christian grinned. Yeah, he'd go and grab some dinner then come back. Maybe he'd tease her by letting her eat too. Make her lower her defenses. It would make the moment she realized he wasn't going to let her go all the more sweet.

He could almost taste her fear. Her terror. *Fuck*, he couldn't wait!

His decision made, Christian squatted next to the girl and patted her cheek none too gently. "Be good, you hear?" he said, laughing at himself. "Don't go anywhere. I'll be back. Then we'll *really* have some fun."

His stomach growled once more, and Christian stood. He headed for the back door and his car, which he'd hidden behind the building. He'd assuage his hunger, then come back and get to work.

Today was the first day of the rest of his life. Soon, everyone would know his name. No one would underestimate him ever again. He'd go down in history as the most notorious and successful serial killer of all time. He had no intention of being caught until he'd killed hundreds, maybe even a thousand people. Blood would run like rivers, and he'd bathe in it gleefully.

With a huge smile on his face, Christian started his car and headed for Los Alamos.

CHAPTER NINETEEN

Nothing.

No one had found even one scrap of evidence that Jasna had been anywhere in the surrounding woods. It was as if she'd literally disappeared out of thin air. But every single one of the searchers knew that was impossible.

Tonka was back at the main camp with the rest of his friends. Everyone was standing around, waiting for more directions. Everyone but him. He was pacing furiously. Impatience swam in his veins. It would be dark soon, and the thought of Jasna being somewhere out there, scared to death, in the dark, made him want to scream.

They'd been in the woods for a couple of hours, and every time Tonka had to answer a text from Henley, telling her they hadn't had any luck yet, a piece of him died inside. She had to be completely undone—and he wasn't there for her. And yet, he wasn't there for Jasna either. Was he doing the right thing, being away from Henley right now? Maybe he should go back to The Refuge and let his friends take the lead on finding Jas.

Just when he was about to go over and tell Brick to take him back to Henley, the radios on all of the officers' belts began squawking. Everyone could hear the report that was being broadcast.

"Message received on the Crime Stoppers tip line… person of interest, Christian Dekker, was last seen pulling out of Sonic and heading west. Address of where he may be headed is as follows…"

An address was rattled off, and Tonka didn't recognize it, but as the officers all headed to their cars, so did Tonka, Brick, Tiny, and Spike. They all piled into Brick's Jeep and held on as he did his best to keep up with the line of cars leaving the overnight camp.

"How did anyone know he was even a person of interest?" Tiny asked as Brick drove through town.

"And how would the person who called in the tip know where he was going? Also, his house is north of town, right?" Spike added.

Tonka didn't give a shit *how* someone had the info on Dekker, he was simply relieved they were finally doing something other than searching blindly. If Henley was right, and Dekker had taken Jasna, they might just be on the verge of getting her back.

The road the line of cars eventually pulled down was nothing more than a rutted, hole-filled dirt path that led into the woods. It was obvious it had been years since any maintenance was done on the road, and there was no telling what was at the end of it.

The cars stopped before reaching any kind of dwelling and officers spilled out, some fanning to the left and right, all of them silently making their way forward, following the dirt path with their weapons drawn.

Tonka and his friends had no guns, but they weren't about to be left behind. No fucking way. If Jasna was being held captive somewhere at the end of this road, Tonka had to be there when she was found. He was glad for the police presence, but a hostage situation would *not* be good. And it would scare Jasna half to death. She was a tough kid, but that would be too much for almost anyone.

Finally, he could see a small, dilapidated cabin at the end of the road. What had probably once been someone's pride and joy was one strong storm from being blown over. The shutters were hanging off their hinges, there was no glass in any of the windows, and moss grew over the wooden walls.

A few officers prevented Tonka and the others from getting any closer.

"Christian Dekker!" one of the police officers said loudly and firmly through a bullhorn, once the cabin had been surrounded and there was no chance of anyone being able to slip out unseen. "You are surrounded. You need to come outside with your hands up!"

Silence met the officer's order.

Tonka shifted uneasily.

"Fuck. They should've just gone in," Tiny muttered.

"Right?" Spike agreed. "Now they've given him notice that we're here. He could retaliate. Or create a hostage situation."

Exactly what Tonka had already been thinking. He stepped away from his friends, itching to race up to the door and burst inside himself. But he knew he wouldn't get halfway there before one of the officers stopped him.

This was just as bad as being on that boat, watching

Garcia hurt Steel and Dagger. Dekker could be inside right this second, plunging a knife into Jasna, just as Garcia—

He cut off that line of thinking abruptly. He couldn't go there. Not now.

There was no evidence that Jasna was in that cabin. Hell, did they even know for sure that *Dekker* was inside? He couldn't see a vehicle of any kind.

The more seconds that ticked by, the more tense the atmosphere became. Something big was about to happen. Tonka could feel it. And all they could do was brace.

* * *

Christian paced anxiously. He'd gone to Sonic and eaten his hamburger and fries. He'd sat there at the restaurant, fantasizing about killing the woman and little boy in the car parked next to his. He thought about grabbing the asshole who'd brought him his food, yanking him into the car and slitting his throat. Everywhere he looked, Christian saw people he could kill. People who were oblivious to the constant danger they were in. They only lived because he allowed them to.

He'd been in an excellent mood when he'd pulled behind the cabin and entered. He was ready to get started.

To his utter shock, the girl was gone.

The cuff was still there, as was the stake he'd pounded into the floor. But the girl was nowhere to be seen.

His mouth hanging open, Christian had searched the tiny house. There weren't too many places to hide since it was mostly empty. But he'd checked inside all the cabinets in the kitchen and in every closet.

He couldn't understand it. She was simply *gone*! How

could that happen? He hadn't been away from the house very long. Had the cops found her?

No, if they had, they would've been waiting for him. It was as if the bitch simply up and disappeared.

Of course, she couldn't have. Someone had found her and stolen her from him.

Anger raged inside Christian. *No one* took what was his! *No one!* He'd find whoever it was and kill them too! Slowly and painfully.

As he paced, Christian tried to figure out where he'd gone wrong. He'd done everything almost perfectly. The girl hadn't made any noise when he'd grabbed her. He hadn't left any clues in the forest. As far as he knew, no one had seen him or his car as he drove away.

His phone vibrated in his back pocket—and Christian froze. He didn't bother to take the stupid thing out.

Fuck. The phone.

He'd been traced. Someone had figured out he'd taken the girl and tracked him by his phone. That had to be it. But...he should've had more time! He'd watched enough crime shows to know the cops had to get a court order to track his fucking phone.

He'd planned on torching the cabin when he was done to make sure none of his DNA was left behind. He was going to take the girl and dump her body parts one by one in dumpsters along the way to Albuquerque. They'd never find her once she got to the various landfills. *He'd had it all planned!*

And yet, someone had stolen his prize right out from under his nose.

"Fuck!" he yelled, regretting going to town for food. If

only he'd eaten before the kidnapping. If only he'd ignored his growling belly. If only, if only, if only...

Just as he turned to head out to his car and get the fuck out of town, something through a broken board covering a window caught his attention.

He froze yet again, ice filling his entire body.

No! No, no, no, no, no!

The cops were here.

He was too late.

Not only would he not get to experience the thrill of his first kill, he wasn't going to be able to escape the number of cops he just *knew* were surrounding the cabin even as he stood there, dumbfounded.

Fuck going to prison.

No one told Christian Dekker what to do. Not his parents, not the fucking shrinks, not the damn cops.

Ignoring the bottles of gasoline he'd stacked against the wall, the instruments of death and torture he'd planned to use, and the empty cuff lying forlornly on the floor, Christian picked up the shotgun he'd brought along as another way to scare the shit out of his victim.

Taking a deep breath, he lifted a foot and slammed it against the front door of the cabin.

If he was going out—he'd go out on his terms.

* * *

Tonka jerked in surprise when the door to the cabin was kicked open from the inside. Because the hinges were probably rusted and weak, the entire door flew off, landing on the dirt and grass down the two steps leading up into the structure.

"Where is she?" the boy Tonka assumed was Dekker screamed as he stood in the doorway with his feet braced apart, a shotgun in his arms. He aimed it at the officers standing nearest the cabin with their weapons drawn. "Did you take her?"

"Put down the gun and let's talk!" the officer with the bullhorn yelled.

Tonka could tell Dekker had no intention of doing any such thing.

"Fuck you!" the boy yelled back.

Studying him, Tonka never would've guessed he was only sixteen, solely by his size. This was a man hell-bent on dying. Not only that, but he was going to take as many people with him as he could.

His heart in his throat, Tonka grabbed Brick's arm and pulled him backward as his friend stepped off the dirt driveway toward a large tree. But he didn't have to warn Brick. Or Tiny and Spike. They read the same intent in Dekker's eyes and tone.

The four of them took cover behind the trees as best they could.

Tonka held his breath. He prayed if Jasna was in the house behind the kid, that she was on the floor. Because any second now there was going to be a huge fucking shootout—and if she got caught in the crossfire, he was going to lose it.

Then Dekker's words upon busting through the door sank in.

Tonka had just a second to wonder what the boy meant when he'd asked "where is she" and "did you take her" before the sound of gunfire rang out in the previously quiet evening.

Dekker opened fire on the police officers. Not one of them hesitated to shoot back, their only thought to disable the threat.

Tonka wanted to scream at them to stop. Jasna could be inside that cabin! They could hit her!

By the time the officer in charge yelled "cease fire!" above the sound of the firefight, Dekker was lying in a bloodied heap in the doorway to the cabin...which looked even more eerie with hundreds of bullet holes in the walls.

Tonka was moving before he even thought about what he was doing.

He didn't get far. Brick and Tiny grabbed his arms and held him back.

"Let go of me! I need to get to Jas!" Tonka shouted as he struggled.

"You run into the middle of that clusterfuck, they'll shoot your ass too!" Spike told him. "Calm down and let them do their job. If Jas is there, they'll get her out and you can go to her."

Tonka knew his friend was right, but he still fought. It went against everything in him to stand there and do nothing—yet again.

He watched as one officer checked Dekker for a pulse and others walked over and around him to enter the house. His friends now had him in a tight lock. He held his breath, waiting for confirmation that Jasna was inside and still alive.

Ten seconds went by. Twenty.

Tonka's heart was beating a thousand miles an hour. His adrenaline was sky high. He was jittery and desperate to see Jas. To make sure she was all right. For himself, for Henley.

To his confusion and horror, the police officers began to file back out of the house, holstering their weapons as they went.

"What's happening?" Tonka whispered. As eager as he'd been to rush into the house a moment ago, now his feet felt as if they were encased in lead. He couldn't move. Were the officers coming out because she was wasn't there? Because she was *dead?*

No. Neither option was acceptable.

Brick and Tiny remained right by his side, both with a hand on his arm but neither holding him back anymore. They were holding him up.

"Don't panic," Tiny ordered. "I'll be right back."

He jogged over to the nearest officer and spoke to him briefly before walking back to where Tonka was waiting.

He could read by the look on his friend's face that whatever was happening, it wasn't good. Feeling faint, Tonka locked his knees.

"She's not inside," Tiny said, not dragging out the news.

A part of Tonka was relieved, had expected that answer after what Dekker had said, but another part was even more horrified. If she wasn't in that cabin, where the hell was she?

"*Fuck*," Brick swore. "Where is she?"

Hearing his own thoughts echoed by his friend was both painful and a relief.

Tonka's phone vibrated in his pocket, and as much as he dreaded having to tell Henley *again* that they hadn't had any luck finding Jasna, he refused to ignore her messages.

He reached for his cell, and his friends let go of him reluctantly. Tonka could feel three pairs of eyes on him, but he ignored them as he looked down at the screen on his phone.

Instead of seeing Henley's name, there was a text from an unknown number.

He unlocked his phone and clicked on the text that had just arrived.

Unknown: Jasna is in cabin 103. She's unhurt.

Tonka read the text again.

Then a third time.

He turned without a word and starting running back to Brick's vehicle. Thank God they'd been the last car to turn down the dirt driveway. They'd be able to get out quickly.

"Tonka? Who was that? Henley? What's wrong?" Brick asked as he ran to catch up to him.

In response, Tonka handed the phone to his friend but didn't slow his pace.

"*What the fuck?*" Brick exclaimed as he handed the phone to Tiny, who read the message to Spike.

Tonka had so many questions, but at the moment, all he cared about was getting to Jas.

"Who's this from? And how the fuck do they know about the bunkers?" Spike growled as they reached Brick's Jeep.

"I just tried to respond to the text," Tiny said. "Came back as undeliverable."

"You think Pipe, Owl, or Stone somehow found her and stashed her there?" Spike asked with a frown, clearly grasping at straws as Brick started the car.

"No," Tiny said with a shake of his head. "There's no way they would've done that without calling Tonka. And they'd take her to the lodge, or to the hospital if necessary. They certainly wouldn't stash her in a bunker."

"103 is the closest to a road on that end of the property," Brick mused as he backed up quickly, nearly clipping a police car. Then he pulled forward, almost taking out a tree, before backing up again and heading for Route 4, which led to The Refuge.

"Why wouldn't they just pull down our drive and bring her to her mom? Even if they didn't know Henley was at the lodge, they had to know *someone* would be there," Tiny asked.

"Even better, why didn't they go to the police station? If they found her wandering along the road or in the woods, they had to have seen the Amber Alert on their phone," Spike added.

Tonka didn't say a word. He couldn't. If he opened his mouth, he'd scream with the amount of tension bottled up inside. He had all the same questions as his friends, but at the moment, all he cared about was getting to the bunker and seeing if Jasna was truly inside. If she wasn't...if someone was fucking with them...he didn't know what he'd do.

For the second time since he'd heard that Jasna was missing, he thought about Pablo Garcia. Could this be him?

No. As far as he knew, the man was still in prison. He would've been contacted if he'd been released. And it would be many, *many* years before that happened. Dekker had obviously been the one behind Jasna's disappearance, but how the hell did she get out of that cabin and into one of their bunkers? Their *secret* bunkers that literally only eight people in the world should know about?

"Could Alaska have let something slip about the bunkers?" Spike asked, as if he could read Tonka's mind.

"No," Brick said resolutely.

"She could've said something in passing, to someone she thought she could trust, not thinking. Or maybe someone overheard her?" Tiny suggested.

"I said no," Brick repeated brusquely. "She knows how important it is to keep those bunkers on the down-low. She would never tell anyone anything without asking me if it was okay first. I trust her one hundred percent. It wasn't her."

"Okay, then how the hell did some anonymous person know about them?" Spike asked.

No one had an answer.

"Tonka? How're you holding up?" Brick asked as he sped down the road.

Tonka appreciated him driving like a bat out of hell. "Not good," he said between clenched teeth.

He was glad when no one tried to reassure him.

There was no telling what they'd find when they got to bunker 103. It was at the three o'clock position relative to the lodge. There were seven bunkers in total, deep in the woods of their property at the nine, ten, eleven, twelve, one, two and three o'clock positions. Brick stashed Alaska in bunker 111 when he went to hunt down the psychopath that was after her. 103 was about five miles from the one he'd used to stash Alaska.

And as Brick had already mentioned, it was the closest bunker to a main road. There no cameras on the road, so if someone had stopped alongside Route 4 to take

Jasna to the bunker, they'd had the privacy to do so unseen.

"I'm fucking setting up cameras," Brick mumbled, yet again reading Tonka's mind as he executed a U-turn in the middle of the road and pulled over.

All four men climbed out and immediately set off through the woods with Tonka in the lead. None of them needed a GPS to tell them where to go. They'd all memorized the locations of the bunkers in case of an emergency. When they'd first arrived at The Refuge, they'd all still been a little messed up in the head because of the traumas they'd gone through. Having the bunkers felt like a necessary fail-safe. Places where they could go if the shit ever hit the fan, or if they just needed to hide themselves away for a mental break. They informally referred to them as "cabins," but they definitely weren't. They were underground boxes of varying sizes.

They hadn't been used in years, until Brick used one to hide Alaska, but they'd always been kept stocked, just in case.

Tonka felt as if he was going to throw up as they approached the area where the bunker was hidden. Stopping, he looked around, searching for something, *anything* that would indicate someone had been there. But all he saw were trees, grass, and rocks. As usual.

"Let me," Tiny suggested as he started to push past Tonka.

His arm whipped out and he blocked his friend. "No."

He didn't need to say any more. Tiny nodded and stepped back. Tonka took a deep breath as he headed for the entrance. It was well hidden. No one simply walking by would even notice the circular ring buried in the debris on the forest floor. Tonka unerringly took hold of the ring and pulled upward. It didn't take a lot of strength; they'd built the doors so they could be lifted with minimal effort, just in case one of them was wounded when in need of a bunker.

Looking through the round opening, Tonka couldn't see anything. It was pitch black, and his stomach clenched in fear. This particular bunker was longer than it was tall, so he sat on the edge and jumped down easily. He got down on one knee and used his hand to brace himself as he stared into the darkness of the bunker, praying harder than he'd ever prayed before. Even on that awful day on the ocean.

"Here," Spike said, holding his phone down toward Tonka. He'd turned on the flashlight function already, and even though the light wasn't terribly bright, nothing like the flashlights they carried on their belts when they went out into the forest with guests, it would be enough. Tonka hadn't even thought about using his own phone's light. He was grateful his friend had been ready.

With shaking hands, he lifted the phone and pointed it toward the opposite end of the bunker, every muscle in his body tensed.

"Is she there?" Brick asked urgently.

"I...I think so," Tonka croaked. "Hang on."

He shuffled forward on his knees toward the dark lump at the end of the bunker. As he got closer, he could see wisps of dark blonde hair spread across the narrow cot. There was a warm blanket over the lump, and Tonka held his breath as he reached out to pull it back.

He let out his first shaky breath as he gazed down at Jasna. But his fear hadn't abated.

His hand trembling so hard he wasn't sure he'd be able to tell if she had a pulse or not, Tonka placed his fingers on her carotid artery. For a fleeting moment, he panicked. But then he felt it. The reassuring *thump, thump, thump* of her blood coursing through her body.

She was also warm to the touch, another indicator she was alive.

"She's...she's here. And she seems to be okay," Tonka said. He meant to call out the news, but his voice was no louder than a whisper.

"You need help getting her out?" Tiny asked through the hole.

Taking a moment to look her over and make sure she wasn't visibly hurt, Tonka almost cried when he didn't see any sign of blood or an injury.

"No. I got her," he said, answering Tiny's question. He pocketed Spike's phone, not needing the light anymore, now that he knew Jas was all right. He picked her up and shuffled backward on his knees. He barely felt her weight, his mind nearly blank, he was so thankful they'd found her.

When he got to the hole, he carefully stood, letting Tiny take her from him so he could jump out, then immediately taking Jas back in his arms as they headed for Brick's Jeep.

"You want me to text Henley?" Brick asked.

Tonka shook his head. "I'll call her from the car on the way to the hospital."

The others nodded.

"I'll tell Pipe to drive her and Alaska there," Tiny said.

It worried Tonka that Jasna hadn't stirred at all—but just as he had that very thought, she shifted in his grip, slowly winding her arm around his neck. "Finn...?"

His knees almost buckled with relief. "Yeah, baby girl. It's me."

She buried her nose into the side of his neck and said, "You smell good."

Tonka almost laughed—until she went limp once more. She shouldn't be this out of it if Dekker had just knocked her over the head or something. He immediately suspected she'd been drugged. Despite that scary thought, even her brief moment of lucidity made him feel a little better. The sooner he got her to a doctor and they did a full blood workup and made sure she was all right, the better.

CHAPTER TWENTY

Henley sat next to Jasna's bed at the hospital with one hand gripping her daughter's and the other grasping Finn's. The last few hours had been the worst of her life. Even worse than what she'd gone through when she was ten. Losing her mom so violently, having to listen to the attack, was devastating...but not knowing where Jasna was, if she was being hurt, if she was even alive, was *excruciating*.

Every time she'd gotten a text from Finn saying they hadn't found her yet, it was like dying.

When he'd called her to say he'd found Jasna, and was on the way to the hospital, the relief was overwhelming. Pipe had driven her and Alaska to Los Alamos, and she'd been able to see her daughter briefly before Jas was brought into one of the examination rooms. Got to see for herself that she was whole, that she seemed to be okay.

When she and Finn were finally allowed to sit with Jasna, she'd still been sleeping. The doctor had bandaged a cut on her foot, done a thorough exam and confirmed she hadn't been raped—which had been a massive relief to everyone—and run a blood panel, finding both alcohol and Rohypnol in her system. Knowing that her baby had been drugged was a blow, but it explained why Jasna hadn't fully regained consciousness.

She'd been in and out of it since then, waking up enough to recognize her mother and know she was safe before falling back to sleep. The doctor said she could be out of it for up to twelve hours, and it was likely she wouldn't remember much of what happened to her, if she remembered anything at all.

As far as Henley was concerned, that was a blessing.

The doctors had inserted an IV to make sure she was hydrated and wanted to keep her overnight for observation, just to make sure there were no lasting effects of the drug or from her ordeal.

Finn had told her about how they'd had no luck finding any trace of what had happened at the camp, and how someone had called in a tip to the police officers about where to find Christian. She hadn't yet heard the story about how Finn himself had ended up finding Jasna, but they hadn't had much time to talk.

Now it was after midnight, and Henley was alone in Jasna's room with Finn. She sighed and leaned against him, not letting go of either his or her daughter's hands.

"Can you tell me the rest of the story about what happened tonight, and where Jasna was?" she asked quietly.

"We went to the cabin the tipster said Dekker would be at, and he was. He came outside with a shotgun and shot at one of the officers."

"He was killed?" Henley asked.

"Yes."

"You're sure?"

Finn hugged her tightly, as if he knew what she was thinking. "Yes. He's dead. He can't hurt anyone again."

Henley nodded. She should feel bad. Christian was only sixteen. He'd had his entire life ahead of him. But what kind of life would it have been? There was something seriously wrong with the boy. Had been since he was a child, maybe even since he was born. It wasn't a sickness. Wasn't a mental illness. He was just...wired wrong.

Finn went on. "One of the detectives spoke to me in the waiting room, while the doctor was with Jas, and he told me what they'd found inside the cabin. From all indications, he'd planned on...hurting her. There were handcuffs, and he had various items laid out. They're assuming he was waiting for her to wake up. He also had gasoline, probably to burn the cabin down. The cops found a notebook filled with ramblings about how many people he wanted to kill, which neighborhoods in Albuquerque were most likely to have homeless and prostitutes. The assumption is that he was going to leave here after burning the cabin and head to the city, where he'd find others to kidnap and murder."

Henley's entire body shook. She closed her eyes. God, Jasna'd had such a close call. She'd been in the hands of pure evil, and somehow she was still here. Nearly unscathed. It was literally a miracle.

"How?" she whispered, turning to look at Finn.

"How did she escape?" he asked.

Henley nodded.

He shook his head slightly. "I don't know."

She frowned at him. "You can tell me. I'm not going to freak out."

"Honey, I honestly don't know," Finn repeated. "The only thing Dekker said when he came outside with that shotgun was, 'Where is she?' and 'Did you take her?' I didn't think much about it at the time, as I was more worried about the weapon in his hands and whether Jasna was going to get caught in the crossfire of the inevitable shootout. But if Dekker was talking about Jas...then he had no idea where she was at that point either."

"I'm so confused. How did *you* find her then?"

"I got a text. It was after the police realized Jas wasn't in the house. I was seriously losing it, Brick and Tiny were literally holding me up...when my phone vibrated with a text. It was from an unknown number. Whoever it was, they let me know where Jas was located."

Henley waited, but Finn didn't say anything more. "*And?* Where was she?" she asked with a tilt of her head.

Finn sighed. He looked around the room as if someone might be lurking nearby, listening. Then he looked her in the eyes. "What I'm about to tell you, only eight people in the world know. Shit, well...maybe nine. You'd be the tenth. And it's really important that you never tell anyone."

He looked so serious, Henley got slightly worried. "I promise."

Finn nodded. "There are seven hidden bunkers on The Refuge property. They're underground and were put in when we were building the retreat. None of us were in the best frame of mind, and we needed the security those bunkers provided. When that man was here, looking for Alaska? Brick hid her in one of the bunkers while he went to track down the asshole."

Henley could certainly understand that. She nodded.

"The text I got said Jas was in one of them. It wasn't from any of our friends. We have no idea *who* it was from —or how the person knows about the bunkers."

Henley was still confused. "So, this mysterious person somehow found Jasna, got her away from a serial killer, brought her to one of the bunkers, and left her there? Then texted you so you could go get her?"

"Yes."

The implications were disturbing. "Can you trace the text or something to see who sent it?"

"We've got a friend of ours working on that. He's a genius when it comes to techie stuff. He'll let us know when he has a name," Finn said.

"So there's someone out there who knows about the top-secret bunkers and...what? Were they in on Jasna's kidnapping? Maybe working with Christian?"

"Breathe, Hen. I've talked about this a little with Brick, and we don't think that's the case."

"Then how...what... I don't understand, Finn!"

"We're baffled ourselves," he admitted. "But whoever texted me...if they wanted to do Jas harm, they had plenty of time to do so. They could've taken her far away and we never would've found her."

Henley winced. His words were a little harsh, but he was absolutely right. "So what now?"

"We take Jas home and get on with our lives," Finn said firmly.

"But...what about the person who knows about the bunkers? They might be watching The Refuge."

"Tex will figure out who it was, but in the meantime, we continue living. Maybe we're a little more careful, but again, I don't think we're in any danger from whoever led me to Jas."

Henley turned and looked at her sleeping daughter. It was an absolute miracle she was here. The statistics of missing children were heartbreaking and depressing. Most kidnapping victims were killed within two hours of going missing. But Jas had beat the odds. She'd been in the hands of someone who could've become the most prolific serial killer the country had ever known. And yet...here she was. Smiling in her sleep and completely oblivious as to what had happened.

She spared a moment to actually be *thankful* that Christian had used Rohypnol on Jasna. That she wouldn't remember being in his clutches. At least, Henley hoped she wouldn't.

She turned back to Finn. "How are you doing?" she asked.

"I'm good."

"No, Finn. Seriously. How are you doing? I know nothing about what happened was easy for you. I wanted you to stay with me, but I knew you needed to go and help look for Jasna. Where's your head at right now?"

Finn gave her a small smile and squeezed her hand. "Are you pulling out the shrink on me?"

"Yes," Henley said without an ounce of hesitation or remorse. She needed the two people she loved most in this world to be okay. And now that she knew her daughter was fine, or would be, she had to figure out where Finn stood.

"I'm honestly okay," he said softly. "You're right, I did need to be out there looking for Jas. I couldn't sit back and simply watch what was happening, like I did with Steel."

Henley opened her mouth to object. To again tell him

that if he'd done anything differently back then, he might not be here today, but he held up his free hand, stopping her.

"I know what you're going to say—and you're right about that too. But it doesn't change how I feel. I won't lie. Tonight scared me. I fought with my demons and there were a few moments when I thought they were going to win. But here we are. I'm going to miss Steel the rest of my life. I'll never forget what happened, but the pain I felt that day, and every day since, is fading. You know why?"

"Why?" Henley asked gently.

"Because of you. And Jas. And Melba, Scarlet, and Chuck. Because of Brick, Spike, Pipe, and all my other friends. Because of Raid, and hearing how he's been able to bond with his bloodhound. I'll always be overprotective. I can't help it. I'll never be voted Mr. Congeniality, but I'm ready to embrace my future. Being around Jas all summer has made me see the joys of living again. In many ways, she reminds me of Steel. She's friendly and loyal and excited by the smallest thing. She embraces new experiences and isn't afraid of anything. That's how my boy was. He loved life, and I loved seeing the world through his eyes. Now I want to see the world through Jas's eyes. And yours. And through the eyes of our new dogs. And our children, if we're blessed with them."

"Finn," Henley said, her eyes filling with tears.

He pulled her into him, and Henley let go of his hand long enough to wrap her arm around him as she buried her face in his chest. The position was awkward, as they were sitting in separate chairs next to Jasna's hospital bed, but it didn't seem to faze either of them.

"I can't promise not to have my bad days in the future,

but I feel as if I'm finally coming up for air after being stuck underwater for years. I *need* you, Hen. And Jas. Without you both, I'm afraid I'll get sucked back under, and I won't be able to surface a second time."

"You have us. But you're wrong. You don't *need* us. You never have. You're the strongest man I've ever met. And we don't need you to be anyone but who are you. We don't care if you have bad days. I'm guessing we're going to see quite a few of those from our hormonal teenager in the years to come. We just need you to be here. To laugh with us, to watch over us. To be you."

"I love you," Finn said, his voice breaking.

Henley looked up from his chest. "I love you too. Can I ask a question?"

"You just did," he said with a small grin.

She rolled her eyes. "Are we still going to the shelter this weekend?"

"Yes," Finn said firmly. "The sooner I get a hundred-pound mean-looking pit bull to follow Jasna around and look as if he'd eat anyone who stepped a toe out of line, the better."

Henley chuckled. "You know that wouldn't have stopped what happened, right? It's not like she can bring her dog to camp."

"She can if it's her therapy dog."

"Not happening. We aren't lying about something like that. It's not cool," Henley said a little huffily.

"Relax, Hen. I know," he sighed. "But if I could give Jas a bodyguard that would glare at anyone who dared to look at her wrong, I would."

"You'll just have to teach her to do the glaring. And the kung fu fighting."

"Oh, that's definitely happening," Finn said.

"You're going to be an awesome dad," Henley declared.

He stared down at her with a worried look. "I don't know."

"I do," she told him firmly.

"Babies are even more helpless than dogs," he mused. "I couldn't protect Steel. What makes me think I can protect a kid?"

Taking a deep breath, Henley let go of her daughter's hand and stood. She climbed onto Finn's lap, straddling his waist, and he grabbed her hips, holding her steady. She took his face in her hands and leaned in close. "What happened to Steel wasn't your fault. It was *all* that asshole's doing. Besides, you'll have help from me. And everyone else at The Refuge. *And* the dog we're gonna adopt, and every single guest who comes to stay at the retreat.

"Raising Jasna alone was hard. Really hard. And if I had to be a single parent again, even with how much I love my daughter, I wouldn't want to try. But knowing, if we're blessed with kids, that I won't be alone? It makes me excited about the prospect. You don't have to protect me, Jasna, or our children by yourself, Finn. It takes a village. And our Refuge village will step up, I have no doubt."

"I love you," Finn whispered.

"I don't think I'll ever get tired of hearing that," Henley said.

"Good, because I'm not going to get tired of saying it. Now, I'm thinking you need to crash for a few hours." He looked behind them at the cot that had been brought in a while ago. "And before you say no, I'll stay up and watch over Jas. If she wakes, I'll let you know. Promise."

"I am tired," Henley admitted. "But you have to be exhausted too."

"I'm more wired than anything. I'll crash later. For now, I just want to watch over my girls."

His girls. Henley liked that. No, she freaking *loved* that.

"Okay. Finn...thank you for being there for me and Jasna today."

"I'll always be here for you both." Then he stood with her in his arms, and she lowered her feet to the floor. He led her to the cot, and when she lay down and got situated, Finn leaned over and kissed her forehead. "Sleep, love."

Henley wasn't sure she'd be able to fall asleep with the hustle and bustle of the hospital. But before she knew it, her eyes closed. The last thing she heard before giving in to the temptation of rest was Finn's low voice, murmuring to Jasna how much he loved her.

CHAPTER TWENTY-ONE

Tonka looked at the stall next to the one he was in and smiled. He was brushing down one of the horses, and Jasna was sitting in the hay in the next stall, petting Scarlet Pimpernickel and telling her how sweet and beautiful she was.

Two and a half weeks had passed since her kidnapping, and Tonka was thankful each day that she didn't remember *anything*. The last thing she had a clear memory of was eating lunch before heading out on the group hike at camp. It was a blessing for sure, but Tonka could admit it was a little frustrating as well. He and the rest of his friends had hoped she'd be able to tell them who had brought her to the bunker. But she didn't remember anything except waking up in the hospital and seeing him and Henley, hovering around her.

He thought of the phone call he and the others had with Tex the day before. The former SEAL had attempted to track the number from the text Tonka had received.

His exact words were, "Whoever this is, they're better than me."

They'd all been shocked to the core. Tex not being able to track a phone number seemed impossible. He prided himself on being able to hack anything, find anyone. But in this case, whoever it was had used a burner phone and had not only somehow bounced their signal off several different towers—or at least made it *look* like they had— they'd also apparently used satellites just for fun. So far, it had been impossible to backtrack through the spiderweb of bread crumbs to find who'd sent the text.

They were no closer to figuring out how the hell Jasna had gotten from that cabin where Dekker had stashed her, to the bunker on The Refuge property. And it was still a mystery how their anonymous savior had learned about the bunkers in the first place.

Tex had hypothesized that if the person was as good as they appeared to be at covering their tracks electronically, it was probably fairly easy for them to find out about the bunkers.

None of the guys were that thrilled to know someone was out there possibly keeping track of them and following their every move, but since whoever it was had rescued Jasna, they were doing their best to get on with their normal lives—albeit more cautiously.

Jasna herself had no lingering effects from what had happened. She'd been a little worried and had wanted to know every detail about that day, but generally she was the same kid she'd been before the incident.

It was *Henley* who'd been struggling. She had night-mares that tore Tonka's heart out every time he woke up to her whimpering and thrashing. All he could do was hold her and tell her she was safe. That Jasna was safe. That it was over. Everyone at The Refuge was keeping a close eye on her. Making sure she knew she had their support.

Dekker's family had moved out of state. They'd sent a letter to Henley's boss, apologizing unnecessarily for their son's actions. They were relieved they didn't have to look over their shoulders anymore, but were understandably sad things had turned out the way they did.

One afternoon, Tonka and the rest of the guys had gone to the cabin where Dekker had planned to torture and kill Jasna, tearing it down to the foundation. It was cathartic, removing a building where so many evil things had been planned and almost carried out.

"Finn?" Jasna called out.

More than happy to take a break from brushing the horse's coat, Tonka wandered over to the next stall. "Yeah, Jas?"

"Do you think Scarlet likes her bow?"

Tonka did his best not to laugh. The calf was growing quickly, and was no longer the cute and cuddly little gal who'd first arrived. She was also spoiled rotten, but Tonka couldn't care less. She loved sitting with her head in Jasna's lap and having her ears scratched.

Jasna had brought a huge neon-pink bow into the barn earlier and told Scarlet that it was a present. Tonka had no doubt by tomorrow, the pretty pink bow would be dirty and probably untied and smashed into the mud outside, but seeing the grin on Jasna's face right now was priceless.

"I think she loves it," he finally said.

"Of course she does," Jasna agreed with the confidence of a child. Then she looked up at Tonka a little more somberly. "How's Mom?"

Ever since her kidnapping, Jasna had been obsessed with Henley's mental state. Tonka assumed it came from her knowing about what happened to her mom when she was a kid, and how she hadn't spoken for years afterward. While Jas wasn't affected by what happened simply because she couldn't remember it, she *was* concerned for her mom.

"She's good," Tonka said. "What brought that up? Did anything happen?"

"Not really. But I start school tomorrow, and I'm worried about her. You know, that she might think I'll be taken again. I've told her that I'll be more careful, but I'm not sure that made her feel any better."

"I'll tell you a secret, Jas. Are you listening?" Tonka asked as he crouched down beside her.

"Yeah."

"Moms will always worry about their kids. No matter how old you are, Henley's gonna fret. All you can do is just what you said...be aware of your surroundings and be as careful as you can. But you need to live your life. Don't let fear hold you back."

Jasna thought about his words for a moment before nodding.

Tonka hadn't planned on doing this right now, but he figured it was as good a time as any. "I might have something that will take your mom's mind off of worrying about you a little."

"What's that?"

"I want to ask her something...but I want to make sure you're okay with it first."

To his surprise, Jasna wiggled her way out from under Scarlet's huge, heavy head and scooted over to him. Her amber eyes sparkled, once again reminding him of how Steel would gaze at him when Tonka held the ball Steel wanted to chase. With a mixture of anticipation and excitement.

"Please please *please* tell me you want to ask her to marry you!"

Tonka blinked in honest-to-goodness surprise. "Well... yeah. How'd you know?"

Jasna laughed. "Finn, you guys are ridiculously gushy together. You're always saying how much you love each another and sneaking off to kiss when you think I don't know. Of *course* you want to marry her."

Her astuteness was surprising, while at the same time a little disconcerting. Tonka wasn't sure he was ready for her to grow up. It felt as if he'd known the girl forever, when it had only been a few months.

"I do love your mom," he said. "But I don't want you to think I'm butting into your relationship or anything. You two will always have a close bond."

"I know," Jasna said. "Are you guys going to have babies? Will I get a brother or sister?"

It was Tonka's turn to chuckle now. "I don't know."

"But you want a baby?"

"Honestly? I think so, yes."

"Cool. Me too. Although I'm gonna be old by the time he or she is big enough to play, but that just means I'll have to come home lots and lots so I'm not forgotten. When are you going to ask her?"

This talk was going nothing like he'd thought it would. Tonka shrugged. "I'm not sure."

"Tonight," Jasna said firmly. "I'll see if Alaska will watch a movie with me at the lodge. That way you guys can be alone. You can have a romantic dinner or something, do some smooching, then you can ask her. And when she says yes, text me and I'll come home and we can celebrate."

Tonka grinned and stood, holding out his hand for Jasna. She took it, and he pulled her to her feet. "Sounds like a plan."

She threw herself against him and hugged him hard. "I'm glad you came into our lives, Finn."

Tonka squeezed her back, trying to control his emotions.

Fortunately, a bark sounded from the door of the barn.

"Wally!" Jasna said excitedly, letting go of him to go greet her dog.

They'd gone to the shelter the Monday after she'd gotten out of the hospital, and to his delight, Jasna had fallen in love with the large black pit bull mix the second she saw him. He was a little too prone to licking people's faces for Tonka's liking, and he had a penchant for jumping into the water trough in the corral, but he was a big goof, and he made Jasna happy, so Tonka didn't really care.

Then, when they'd been on their way out of the shelter, walking down the row of kennels, Tonka had seen the most pathetic dog he'd ever lain eyes on. Some kind of terrier mix, and she was cowering in the back corner of her cage, trembling. She couldn't have weighed more than ten pounds...and the second he saw her, Tonka knew she was meant to be his.

He couldn't explain the feeling, and he certainly never would've picked such a small dog. He liked big dogs. Ones he could roughhouse with and not worry about hurting.

Dogs like Steel and Dagger. And the pit bull mix Jasna had picked out moments before.

There was just something about the little dog that called to him.

He'd asked the shelter employee if he could see the little dog, and she gave him a small smile. "Sure. But don't be offended if she doesn't take to you. She's really shy." Then she frowned. "And to be honest...she's on the list for this afternoon."

Tonka knew what that meant. On the list for euthanasia.

To his surprise, and the employee's, the little dog crawled toward him the second her kennel door was open. She smelled funky, needed a haircut badly, but when Tonka picked her up, it was love at first sight. For him *and* the little dog. All he got out was, "I'll take her."

Henley had simply smiled when he'd informed her they were taking two dogs home. Brick and the others had laughed their fool heads off when they'd seen the pathetic little dog nestled trustingly in his arms. Tonka didn't care. He named her Beauty, because it made Jasna laugh...and he hoped the name would give the little thing some confidence.

It was ridiculous, he knew it, but he didn't care. Over the last few weeks, the dog hadn't really come out of her shell too much. She was skittish and slow to trust, but she fit in the crook of Tonka's arm perfectly. She usually sat in the dog bed he'd made for her in the barn and watched him work, never letting him out of her sight if she could help it.

Thinking about her made Tonka turn to look at the

bed, and when Beauty saw him glance in her direction, she got up and trotted over. As usual, Tonka picked her up. Spike made fun of him all the time, reminding him that the dog had legs and could walk, but Tonka didn't care about that either. He loved holding her and carrying her around.

Jasna strolled back to him with Wally at her heels. "Tell me you have a ring," she told him sternly.

Tonka grinned. "I have a ring."

"Good. Is it big?"

"Big enough." The truth was, the ring wasn't huge. But Tonka didn't want Henley wearing something too flashy that might make her the target of someone who wanted to steal it from her. He would spoil her in any way she wanted in the future to make up for it.

"Cool. Finn?"

"Yeah?"

"If Mom changes her name to Matlick...do you think... maybe...Icantoo?" Her last words were jumbled together, as if she was nervous to ask.

Tonka took a deep breath. It had been his plan to bring up adoption at some point, but he wanted both Jas and her mom to be completely comfortable with the idea before approaching the topic. "There's nothing I'd love more than for you to have my name," he told her.

Jasna's shoulders relaxed, and she beamed. "Awesome! I need to go find Alaska and see about that movie. Good luck, although you won't need it!" She raced away, with Wally at her heels, barking and jumping as if she was playing a game.

"What do you think, Beauty? Should we go ask Mom if she wants to get married?" Tonka asked the little dog in his arm, scratching her head as she moaned in content-ment. "I'll take that as a yes."

He headed for his cabin with a smile. Henley would be getting out of a group session in half an hour, and he wanted to be ready for her.

CHAPTER TWENTY-TWO

Henley was tired, but in a good way. The session this afternoon had been emotional and tougher than some. The men and women who were staying at The Refuge this week had all been in the same unit overseas when they'd been ambushed. They'd been pinned down by enemy fire for hours before backup arrived. It had affected them all differently, but she was glad to see they were all hanging in there together.

Sometimes it helped to hear other people's worries and fears, it made her own not seem so out of the norm. Henley had always worried about her daughter, wanting the best for her, but now that concern was ramped up even more because of what happened. She was working through her own feelings about what happened with Mike, twice a week, and she was feeling better. It helped that Jasna was the same little girl she'd always been. That she hadn't been traumatized by what happened.

Finn also helped immensely. He was always there, watching her with his intense gaze, as if he could see straight through to her soul. He'd taken her to the bunker Jasna had been brought to by her mysterious rescuer, and somehow just seeing it, knowing whoever had taken her from Christian's cabin had put her in the safest place they could find, made her relax a little bit more.

She'd decided to look at the mystery person as an angel, rather than someone scary who was out there watching and waiting.

When she walked out of the room into the lodge, Henley was surprised to see Jasna. "Hey, is everything okay?" she asked, her brow furrowing.

"Yup! It's fine. Great. Finn's at the cabin. He's waiting for you. I'm gonna eat up here at the lodge, and then Alaska and I are gonna watch a movie. So you and Finn can have some alone time. So...go on...have fun."

Jasna was being weird, but she was smiling, so Henley didn't think too much about it. She was all for having some alone time with Finn. She and Jasna were pretty much living with him now, hardly ever going back to their apartment in Los Alamos. She would've felt guilty about that, but she loved being with him too much to care. And since Finn told her more than once how happy he was that she and Jasna were with him, she decided to take him at his word.

"All right," she told her daughter. "But don't let Wally on the couch in the TV room. You can sit with him on the floor, but it's a pain in the butt for Ryan and the others to clean dog hair off the couches."

"I won't, Mom," Jasna said.

"I'm assuming Beauty is with Finn?" she asked.

Jasna rolled her eyes. "Of course."

"Right. Sorry, stupid question." Henley couldn't help

but smile thinking about Finn and his little shadow. It was amazing, watching the two of them together. They were definitely meant to find each other. "Okay, if you need anything, just let me know. Don't stay up here past eight-thirty."

"Mom...that's too early! Ten?" Jasna begged.

"Nine. You have school tomorrow. And if you continue to beg, it'll be eight."

"Nine it is then," Jasna said breezily. "Have fun. Bye!"

Then she turned and jogged toward the kitchen. Probably to bother Robert and Luna for a snack before dinner.

She waved at Alaska and mouthed "thank you" as she headed for the door. The other woman waved back.

The moment she left the lodge, Henley took a deep breath. The weather was still warm but it wouldn't be long before the cooler air moved in. She loved living in the mountains, even with the snow and cold they got in the winter.

Despite being exhausted, she perked up as she neared the cabin. It had been a while since she and Finn had time to themselves. Consequently, she wasn't nearly as tired as she'd been minutes ago. Looking at her watch, she saw they had three and a half hours before Jasna came home.

Her nipples hardened as she thought about all the fun they could have in that amount of time. A week had passed since she and Finn had made love, and she was more than ready.

She walked into the cabin—and let out a small screech as she almost ran into Finn. He'd either been standing at the door waiting for her to arrive, or he'd seen her approach and had come to welcome her home.

She opened her mouth to say hi, but he covered her

lips with his, and immediately Henley's libido roared to life. She dropped her purse as Finn slammed the door shut with his foot. He locked it, just in case Jasna came looking for them.

Memories of their first time together flooded Henley's brain as she scrambled to get her clothes off. At least this time, Finn was getting naked too. She grinned, remembering how he'd shuffled to his room after they'd had sex against the door, his pants around his ankles.

But then all she could think about was how good Finn felt. His hands roamed up and down her body, readying her for him. But she was more than ready as it was. It seemed that her body had been trained to be primed instantly whenever they were alone.

And Finn was just as aroused. His cock throbbed in her hand as she stroked him.

"I can't wait," Finn growled as he took her hips in his hands. "Jump up," he ordered.

Henley eagerly did as he requested. Legs going around his waist and her back resting against the door. "Put me in. Now," he demanded.

Just last week, they'd had a long talk about birth control and children...and had made the decision to forgo condoms. They were going to let nature take its course. If she got pregnant right away, they were both more than all right with that. If it took a while, that was okay too.

The first time Finn had made love to her bare had been unforgettable. They'd both actually been able to go slow, enjoy the moment, and while making love without a condom was a lot messier than either was used to, that certainly wasn't a turn-off.

Right now, slow and gentle was the furthest thought

from either of their minds. Henley lined up Finn's cock and he immediately pressed deep inside her. They both moaned as he bottomed out.

"I love you," Finn said as he pumped in and out of her.

"I love you too," Henley returned breathlessly. Her entire body was tingling, and she was panting with excitement and arousal. She tightened her legs around Finn's waist as he moved one hand under her ass and the other cradled the back of her head, his body weight pushing her harder against the door.

He stared into her eyes as he fucked her. It didn't take long before Henley felt her orgasm approaching. "Finn... Yes! God, please, more."

In response, his hips moved faster. Not able to stop herself, one of Henley's hands snaked between their sweaty bodies and flicked her clit.

"Yeah, that's it. Make yourself come around my cock," Finn ordered.

It didn't take long. She was too primed. Too in love with this man to hold back. She shuddered around him as she broke. A few thrusts later, Finn pushed deep inside and held still as he found his own pleasure.

As she was still attempting to catch her breath, Finn blurted, "Will you marry me?"

She stared at him in shock. "What?"

"Marry me," he said. "Be my wife. Give me babies. Live at The Refuge with me. You're my rock. My reason for living. Please say yes."

"Yes!" she said without any hesitation whatsoever. They'd talked about babies, but hadn't really talked about getting married.

Finn grinned, then put both hands under her butt and turned, carrying her toward their bedroom.

"But we need to come up with a better story than you asking me to marry you after fucking me against the front door," she scolded. "Because you know Jasna's going to want to hear every detail, and I'm not telling her what really happened."

Finn chuckled, and she could feel him moving inside her as he walked. She smiled.

"After I make you come three more times, we shower, you suck me off, and we finally emerge from our room to eat something, I'll ask you the way I'd planned. I'll get the chocolate éclair that I stole from Robert's kitchen and give it to you with a fork. I'll have a silly grin on my face, and will be all sweaty and nervous. You'll eat it, not noticing the ring I buried in the cream. I'll be worried you'll swallow the thing and we'll have to go to the hospital, but eventually, on the last bite, you'll notice there's something strange on the end of your fork. When you look up at me, I'll be on my knee next to your chair, begging you to marry me and make me the happiest man on earth. Will that work?"

Henley's heart melted. "You really have a ring in an éclair?"

"Yup. But as usual, when I get around you, I can't control myself and I jumped the gun."

"I think that's my line," she quipped when Finn lay her on her back on their bed. His cock slipped out of her as he straightened, and she gave him a little pout.

"I know, you'll get me back soon enough. But first...you need another orgasm."

Henley wasn't about to protest. She and Finn might

not make love every night, but when they did find the privacy to be together, they made the most of it. Something occurred to her then. "Jasna totally knew you were going to ask me tonight, didn't she?"

"I asked for her permission to ask you," Finn confirmed with a shrug.

Once again, Henley was reminded of how lucky she was.

"And you should know, once we're married and you take my name, she asked if she could as well."

Henley hadn't thought she could be any happier than she was a second ago. She was wrong.

"I mean, you might not even want to change your name, and that's cool. But I'd love to make Jas mine officially too. When you're both comfortable with that. I want to adopt her. Oh, and...she wants a brother or sister."

"I want to change my name. And it's a good thing we already decided we wanted more kids."

Finn stared down at her for a long moment, and Henley couldn't read his expression.

"What?"

"I'll never be the man I was before...but I'm beginning to think I'm now the man I was meant to be."

Tears sprang to Henley's eyes. She leaned up to kiss him and closed her eyes as their lips met. Then Finn broke the kiss and scooted down her body, smiling up at her as he went.

Henley inhaled sharply as he set about making the most of their alone time.

Later—much later...after Finn had proposed just like he'd planned to; after Jasna had returned home, admired her engagement ring and wanted to hear every detail; and

after Beauty, Wally, and Jasna had been tucked into bed—
Henley lay in Finn's arms in their bed and reflected on
everything that had happened in her life.

There had been some good, great, awful, and truly
horrific moments, but they'd all led to this moment right
here and now. And she was grateful. She had a happy and
healthy daughter, a roof over their heads, good friends, and
a man who loved her as much as she loved him.

She fell asleep with a smile on her face, and the knowl-
edge that whatever life threw at her next, she'd have Finn
at her side to weather the storm.

EPILOGUE

Spike was alone in his cabin. Sitting on his couch, staring into space. Things had been hectic since Jasna had been kidnapped and then rescued. He and the other owners of The Refuge had racked their brains to figure out how the girl could have gotten from the dilapidated cabin to the bunkers, but were no closer to figuring it out today than they were when it happened.

They'd also reviewed their safety protocols and had decided to add more security cameras around the lodge and the cabins, as well as game cameras throughout their property.

They'd done all they could under the circumstances. And even though he should be relaxing after a long day of work, he couldn't.

He was restless. He couldn't even say exactly why. He loved The Refuge. Was grateful to Brick for inviting him to be a part of it.

He'd also loved being a member of the famed Delta Force special forces teams in the Army, especially the camaraderie he'd had with his teammates. But he'd burned out. He'd been deployed more often than he'd been home his last two years in the military...had seen too much death and destruction.

He might not have the PTSD issues his friends and guests at The Refuge suffered, but that didn't mean he was unaffected by everything he'd seen and done.

And now that he'd been at The Refuge for years, he felt...itchy. Seeing both Brick and Tonka settling down with two of the most amazing women he'd had the privilege to meet, had him wondering if he'd ever be as lucky. Unlike a lot of men, Spike was more than ready. He was almost forty and didn't want to spend the rest of his life alone. But finding his match was proving to be extremely difficult, even more so in their sparsely populated corner of New Mexico.

His phone rang, startling Spike and making him frown. No one ever called him. Well, hardly anyone. He wasn't close with his parents or sister, and while he did his best to keep in touch with his former Army teammates, they usually emailed or texted.

Looking down, he was surprised to see Bubba's name on the screen.

"Yo! Bubba! What's up?" Spike said as he answered the call.

"Not much. You know, same ol' shit, different day," his former teammate quipped.

They made small talk for a few minutes, before Bubba got around to the reason for his call. "Hey, you heard from Woody lately?"

Spike frowned. "No, why?"

"It's probably nothing. But I got a call from his sister

Reese yesterday, and she wanted to know if *I'd* heard from him. It took some cajoling, but eventually I got her to tell me what was up."

"And?" Spike asked when his old friend didn't immediately continue.

Bubba sighed. "Apparently, he went down to Colombia a couple weeks ago. He told Reese he'd only be gone a week, tops. He's not back, and she hasn't heard from him."

"Shit. He went down there to find Isabella, didn't he?" Spike asked, sitting forward in his chair.

"Yeah. Things aren't good down there. Reese said Woody got an email from her, begging for his help in getting her and her brother out of the country."

"Fuck," Spike swore again. "And she hasn't heard from him? Reese, I mean?"

"No. But that's only part of why I'm calling."

Spike's stomach clenched.

"Reese is planning on heading down to Colombia to find him."

"What the hell?" Spike said, leaping up to pace.

He only vaguely remembered Woody's younger sister from when she'd visited her brother a time or two, when they were actually in the country between assignments. He remembered a tall, curvy woman with blonde hair and blue eyes. She'd always been impeccably dressed, and very shy and quiet. "She can't do that. Does she even speak Spanish? What the hell does she think she's gonna do?"

"I don't know, man. That's why I was hoping you'd heard from Woody, so we could get Reese to stand down," Bubba replied.

Rubbing his forehead, which was suddenly throbbing with a headache, Spike tried to recall everything he knew about Isabella Hernandez. She'd been their translator for a mission they'd been on not long before Spike had gotten out of the Army. She was in her early twenties at the time, and Woody had fallen fast and hard for the beautiful woman. She had a younger brother—he was in his teens when they'd been in the country—but that was all Spike remembered.

Woody had obviously kept in touch with Isabella, and Spike wasn't surprised that he'd rushed to her aid when she requested help. He was no longer in the Army, and had every right to go where he wanted, when he wanted. But for him not to keep in touch while gone—especially with Reese, who he was very protective of—meant something had gone wrong.

"I'll catch a flight to Kansas City tomorrow," Spike told his friend. "I'm sure Woody's fine. That asshole's only used up five of his nine lives."

"Awesome. I'd go down there myself, but my wife is going to have our baby any day now," Bubba said, the relief easy to hear in his tone.

"Congrats, man. And no worries, I'll talk some sense into Reese and do what I can to find out what's going on with Woody."

"Keep me in the loop?" Bubba asked.

"Of course. And tell Katie hello for me."

"I will. And...thanks, Spike."

"No need to thank me. I'll be in touch."

"Later."

"Later." Spike clicked off the connection and took a deep breath before turning to head to the laptop he'd left on the small table next to the kitchen. He never ate there —he hated eating alone—and he used the table more as a desk than anything else. He needed to buy a ticket to Kansas City. He'd meet with Reese Woodall, get all the information she had on Woody and where he'd been headed, and if necessary, he'd go down to Colombia and drag Woody's ass back to the States himself.

His friend knew better than to go into a situation alone. But if Isabella had told him she and her brother were in danger, there was no telling *what* Woody would do.

Spike just hoped the sister wasn't as impulsive as his friend. The last thing he needed to worry about was tracking *her* down, as well as his former teammate.

* * *

It looks like Spike is headed out of town to check on his former teammate...but you KNOW things aren't going to go as planned and he and Reese are going to get to know each other a LOT better real soon! HA! Pick up *Deserving Reese* today!

And before you ask...Raiden WILL get a story. He's a part of the Eagle Point Search & Rescue series. There's a bit of time before his book comes out (It will be called Searching for Khloe), but yes, you'll see Tonka again in that one! Raiden and Tonka are connected by what they experienced and there was no way I could write Raid's story and NOT include Tonka. Stay tuned!

Want to talk to other Susan Stoker fans? Join my reader group, Susan Stoker's Stalkers, on Facebook!

Scan the QR code below for signed books, swag, T-shirts and more!

Also by Susan Stoker

The Refuge Series
Deserving Alaska
Deserving Henley
Deserving Reese (May 2023)
Deserving Cora (TBA)
Deserving Lara (TBA)
Deserving Maisy (TBA)
Deserving Ryleigh (TBA)

SEAL Team Hawaii Series
Finding Elodie
Finding Lexie
Finding Kenna
Finding Monica
Finding Carly
Finding Ashlyn (Feb 2023)
Finding Jodelle (July 2023)

Eagle Point Search & Rescue
Searching for Lilly
Searching for Elsie
Searching for Bristol
Searching for Caryn (April 2023)
Searching for Finley (Sept 2023)
Searching for Heather (TBA)
Searching for Khloe (TBA)

Game of Chance Series
The Protector (Mar 2023)

The Royal (Aug 2023)
The Hero (TBA)
The Lumberjack (TBA)

SEAL of Protection: Legacy Series

Securing Caite
Securing Brenae (novella)
Securing Sidney
Securing Piper
Securing Zoey
Securing Avery
Securing Kalee
Securing Jane

Delta Force Heroes Series

Rescuing Rayne
Rescuing Aimee (novella)
Rescuing Emily
Rescuing Harley
Marrying Emily (novella)
Rescuing Kassie
Rescuing Bryn
Rescuing Casey
Rescuing Sadie (novella)
Rescuing Wendy
Rescuing Mary
Rescuing Macie (novella)
Rescuing Annie

SEAL of Protection Series

Protecting Caroline
Protecting Alabama

Protecting Fiona
Marrying Caroline (novella)
Protecting Summer
Protecting Cheyenne
Protecting Jessyka
Protecting Julie (novella)
Protecting Melody
Protecting the Future
Protecting Kiera (novella)
Protecting Alabama's Kids (novella)
Protecting Dakota

Delta Team Two Series

Shielding Gillian
Shielding Kinley
Shielding Aspen
Shielding Jayme (novella)
Shielding Riley
Shielding Devyn
Shielding Ember
Shielding Sierra

Badge of Honor: Texas Heroes Series

Justice for Mackenzie
Justice for Mickie
Justice for Corrie
Justice for Laine (novella)
Shelter for Elizabeth
Justice for Boone
Shelter for Adeline
Shelter for Sophie
Justice for Erin

ALSO BY SUSAN STOKER

Justice for Milena
Shelter for Blythe
Justice for Hope
Shelter for Quinn
Shelter for Koren
Shelter for Penelope

Ace Security Series

Claiming Grace
Claiming Alexis
Claiming Bailey
Claiming Felicity
Claiming Sarah

Mountain Mercenaries Series

Defending Allye
Defending Chloe
Defending Morgan
Defending Harlow
Defending Everly
Defending Zara
Defending Raven

Silverstone Series

Trusting Skylar
Trusting Taylor
Trusting Molly
Trusting Cassidy

Stand Alone

Falling for the Delta
The Guardian Mist

ABOUT THE AUTHOR

New York Times, *USA Today* and *Wall Street Journal* Bestselling Author Susan Stoker has a heart as big as the state of Tennessee where she lives, but this all American girl has also spent the last fourteen years living in Missouri, California, Colorado, Indiana, and Texas. She's married to a retired Army man who now gets to follow *her* around the country.

She debuted her first series in 2014 and quickly followed that up with the SEAL of Protection Series, which solidified her love of writing and creating stories readers can get lost in.

If you enjoyed this book, or any book, please consider leaving a review. It's appreciated by authors more than you'll know.

www.stokeraces.com
www.AcesPress.com
susan@stokeraces.com

Made in United States
Orlando, FL
11 April 2024

45703109R00192